A Sporting Chance

The Chances
Book 8

Emily E K Murdoch

ARE YOU SIGNED UP FOR DRAGONBLADE'S BLOG?

You'll get the latest news and information on exclusive giveaways, exclusive excerpts, coming releases, sales, free books, cover reveals and more.

Check out our complete list of authors, too!

No spam, no junk. That's a promise!

Sign Up Here

www.dragonbladepublishing.com

Dearest Reader;

Thank you for your support of a small press. At Dragonblade Publishing, we strive to bring you the highest quality Historical Romance from some of the best authors in the business. Without your support, there is no 'us', so we sincerely hope you adore these stories and find some new favorite authors along the way.

Happy Reading!

CEO, Dragonblade Publishing

Additional Dragonblade books by
Author Emily E K Murdoch

The Chances Series
A Fighting Chance (Book 1)
A Second Chance (Book 2)
An Outside Chance (Book 3)
Half a Chance (Book 4)
A Chance in a Million (Book 5)
Not a Chance in Hell (Book 6)
An Eye for the Chance (Book 7)
A Sporting Chance (Book 8)

Dukes in Danger Series
Don't Judge a Duke by His Cover (Book 1)
Strike While the Duke is Hot (Book 2)
The Duke is Mightier than the Sword (Book 3)
A Duke in Time Saves Nine (Book 4)
Every Duke Has His Price (Book 5)
Put Your Best Duke Forward (Book 6)
Where There's a Duke, There's a Way (Book 7)
Curiosity Killed the Duke (Book 8)
Play With Dukes, Get Burned (Book 9)
The Best Things in Life are Dukes (Book 10)
A Duke a Day Keeps the Doctor Away (Book 11)
All Good Dukes Come to an End (Book 12)

Twelve Days of Christmas
Twelve Drummers Drumming
Eleven Pipers Piping
Ten Lords a Leaping
Nine Ladies Dancing
Eight Maids a Milking
Seven Swans a Swimming

Six Geese a Laying
Five Gold Rings
Four Calling Birds
Three French Hens
Two Turtle Doves
A Partridge in a Pear Tree

The De Petras Saga
The Misplaced Husband (Book 1)
The Impoverished Dowry (Book 2)
The Contrary Debutante (Book 3)
The Determined Mistress (Book 4)
The Convenient Engagement (Book 5)

The Governess Bureau Series
A Governess of Great Talents (Book 1)
A Governess of Discretion (Book 2)
A Governess of Many Languages (Book 3)
A Governess of Prodigious Skill (Book 4)
A Governess of Unusual Experience (Book 5)
A Governess of Wise Years (Book 6)
A Governess of No Fear (Novella)

Never The Bride Series
Always the Bridesmaid (Book 1)
Always the Chaperone (Book 2)
Always the Courtesan (Book 3)
Always the Best Friend (Book 4)
Always the Wallflower (Book 5)
Always the Bluestocking (Book 6)
Always the Rival (Book 7)
Always the Matchmaker (Book 8)
Always the Widow (Book 9)
Always the Rebel (Book 10)
Always the Mistress (Book 11)
Always the Second Choice (Book 12)
Always the Mistletoe (Novella)
Always the Reverend (Novella)

The Lyon's Den Series
Always the Lyon Tamer

Pirates of Britannia Series
Always the High Seas

De Wolfe Pack: The Series
Whirlwind with a Wolfe

Noble titles throughout English history have, at times, been more fluid than one might think. Women have inherited, men have been gifted titles by family or gained them through marriage, and royals frequently lavished titles or withdrew them as reward and punishment.

The elder Chance brothers in this series agreed to split the four titles in their family line during the Regency era, rather than the eldest holding all four. It is a decision that defines their brotherhood, and their very different personalities.

Now with the next generation, one Chance father has allowed his son to inherit his title before his own demise, echoing kings and queens who have abdicated their titles throughout history. Perhaps his brothers, the uncles of this next generation, will follow suit...

Get ready to meet a family that is more than happy to scandalize Society...

Chapter One

July 3, 1840

"—BUT WE SHOULDN'T—"

"Oh, *shouldn't*," whispered Kathleen Andilet, peering around the tree and trying not to rustle the verdant leaves. "I know we shouldn't. You don't need to tell me a third time."

Her heart was racing and her eyes were wide, the vision before her something that had been hidden from her all her whole life.

Her sister twisted her fingers together, the movement of her white gloves catching the summer sunshine in the corner of Kathleen's vision. "But if we are seen—"

"Then don't be seen," murmured Kathleen, not looking around. "I didn't ask you to come."

Of course she hadn't. She had known Angela would have little interest in breaking the rules of Society like this and had therefore instructed her sister to remain home.

Well. *Home.* The rooms they had taken. Not quite the same thing.

But apparently, Kathleen could not be trusted on her own. Preposterous. She could most certainly be trusted.

Trusted to do whatever she wanted.

Gentle applause rose up in the scene before her and Kathleen's stomach lurched as she watched the gentlemen clap one of their number on the back enthusiastically.

"Can we go now?" hissed Angela, the glimmer of irritation in her blue eyes far too familiar.

Kathleen swallowed. "No."

She did not want to go. Despite the fact that it was absolutely outrageous that they had crept into the grounds of the place without anyone noticing, and that it was scandalous that they were staring at a group of gentlemen, almost all of them with their jackets off, their long, linen sleeves rolled up to reveal forearms of corded muscles and wiry hair, she did not want to look away.

It was…different. A different part of Society, and Kathleen had had quite enough of the dour, dutiful, appropriate Society to which they had been restricted their entire lives.

If Angela's scandal ever made it into the newspapers, they would be restricted even more.

"I don't even see why this is of any interest to you," hissed Angela, stepping toward her and whispering low. "It's only archery. How can you watch it over and over again?"

"Hush," Kathleen said fiercely. "They'll hear you."

But the gentlemen were too far away, thank goodness, to hear the two sisters bickering in whispers. Besides, Kathleen could not help but think, they had something far more interesting to occupy them.

The men were not restricted by Society's ridiculous expectations of dress. They could shed their obstructive coats, roll up their sleeves, and do whatever they wanted. It was women who were entrapped in long skirts and petticoats and corsets.

And that was before one started on the topic of pockets…

"But archery?" muttered her sister, evidently unwilling to give up the topic of conversation. "I do not understand you, Kathleen. It's just bows and arrows. A child's game."

Kathleen swallowed.

She had never seen anything less like a child's game in all her life.

It had been an accident, coming upon them. Yesterday evening, the glow of the sun had disappeared far swifter than she had predicted, and Kathleen had known it was unseemly for a woman on her own to be traversing across London. As she had hurried, she'd realized a shortcut could be gained by walking through what had appeared to be nothing more than a park, so she had ventured across as swiftly as she could.

And in the glowing embers of the daylight, she had seen them. Men. Men—and arrows whipping through the air faster than she thought possible. Focus, and accuracy, and power, an intoxicating mixture that had floated through the air and bewildered her.

When she had finally managed to slam the door of their rooms behind her, Kathleen had known precisely where she was going the following day.

"We shouldn't be here," murmured her sister.

Kathleen turned, dragging her eyes away from the men to look at Angela. There was a haunted look in her eyes, a look of panic and uncertainty.

Something painful twisted in Kathleen's stomach. Her sister was right, though she was loath to admit it. She would have been right regardless, for any pair of young ladies found in an unacceptable position, but given the situation they found themselves in...

"We'll go in a moment," Kathleen said quietly, regret filling her. "Just... I just want to wait a few more minutes."

Until he arrives.

The thought was not one she had consciously. It was therefore not one she could take captive, force down, and pretend had never occurred.

Because impressive though all the men were who were striding about were, pulling back bows with flexing arms and sending quivering arrows straight and true toward the targets many yards away, he was not there.

Kathleen swallowed. Not that she should be gawping over any gentlemen at all...but that one...

Her sister flinched and drew farther back into the small woodland within which they were hiding as a new figure stepped out of the building to their left to join his fellows.

And Kathleen's stomach lurched.

There he was.

She could not tell, precisely, why her attention had been drawn to him the previous evening. He was tall, yes, but not extravagantly so. She had been unable to hear his words so was unsure whether he was more articulate, more charming, perhaps, than the others.

Fine. She could be honest here, in the sanctity of her own mind.

He is the most handsome, the most delicious man I have ever—

"I don't know why you wanted to drag me here in the first place," hissed Angela, her words rapid and uncensored. "It was a foolish idea coming here. Ladies are not supposed to, and even if we were men, which we are not, we would have to be members and the membership here…"

Kathleen ignored her sister. It was not so difficult, with her pulse thumping so powerfully that it was all her ears could hear.

The gentleman had met with his friends now and he said something, something she could not catch from this distance. She could, however, catch the laughter and jollity that met his words.

A small smile crept across her lips. He was well-liked, then. He was amusing.

Kathleen swallowed as the gentleman removed his jacket and started to roll up his sleeves, revealing arms so flush with muscles, they appeared to be nothing but. Her stomach lurched, that darned pulse of hers still roaring, as her sister continued speaking words she could not hear and the gentleman picked up a bow and two arrows. And then he—

Air was forced from her lungs in a gasp.

It had been…almost fluid. As though he had not even had to think, but had just moved as another would walk.

The gentleman had lifted up the bow, fitted the arrow, pulled it back with an ease she had not witnessed in the other gentlemen, and let the arrow fly.

It thunked—right in the middle of the target.

Applause echoed around the lawn and Kathleen had to prevent herself from joining in. It was truly impressive, far more striking than any of the others' efforts, and she had been watching for a good while.

There was a tug on her sleeve. "*Now* can we go?"

Kathleen managed to drag her eyes away from the gentleman, whoever he was, and glared at her sister. "Is it not enough that you had your fun—are you to deprive me of all enjoyment merely because you were caught?"

It was badly said, and she regretted it the moment the words had left her lips. Angela's cheeks went pale and there was a pain in her eyes Kathleen had seen before but had never been the cause of.

She bit her lip. "I am sorry. Forgive me, I should not have spoken so."

"But you were thinking it. Even if you had not said it, you were thinking it," her sister said, swallowing hard and twisting her hands together again. "I knew you were."

Kathleen was much tempted to curse, but that would hardly help the situation. "Angela—"

"You should never have come with me to London," her sister muttered, expression downcast. "After the scandal. You should have stayed at home, untainted by my name, by my actions."

"I chose to come with you and I stand by that," Kathleen said fiercely, highly conscious that if they were not careful, their voices would carry over to the archers. "But...Angela, I cannot live a life entirely in the shadows. We have lost our good name, yes—"

"*I* have," interrupted Angela darkly.

"—but we are outside Society. We are not dead," continued Kathleen, trying to keep her voice level and low. "And yes, we are breaking the rules—"

"We will never be permitted back into Society's good graces if we are caught here," whispered Angela with wide eyes.

Kathleen bit down on her instinctive response: that after what had happened between her sister and a gentleman whom her parents had never identified to Kathleen, Society was unlikely to ever permit them back into its good graces at all. That ship, as it were, had sailed.

Not that much would be gained from pointing that out.

"Society makes rules to prevent people from having fun," Kathleen murmured instead. "The only Society we had at home was Mr. Keystone, and he was the dullest neighbor it was possible to be. As we are no longer a part of Society, I suggest we find fun elsewhere."

She turned back to the archers and her heart skipped a beat as her gaze beheld the one who had most recently joined them.

"And what fun can be gained by staring at gentlemen from a distance?" Angela's whispered question was one that made Kathleen smile.

"Oh, I can admire," she breathed, watching the way the gentleman pulled back that strong arm and let another arrow fly. "There is no harm in admiring."

And he was most striking. Kathleen had never seen anyone move so sinuously, with such grace, with such confidence in his limbs. Why, he occupied the world as a man who was absolutely confident that not only did he have the right to be there, but with the knowledge that he would be welcomed.

What was it like, to feel such certainty?

He would be a lord or the son of a lord of some kind, she was sure—far above their station even before Angela's disgrace.

"Who do you think he is?" Kathleen asked wistfully.

"Who? Which one?"

Which one, indeed. As though there were not clearly one of the gentlemen before them who was leagues beyond the others in both looks and talent.

"The tall one."

"The one in the green?"

"No!" Kathleen almost chuckled. Even after all these years,

her sister did not understand her taste in gentlemen at all. "Not the green, you know I have no interest in blonds. No, the darker-haired man, the one wearing that russet-red waistcoat."

Her attention followed him as he meandered back to the group while another of his number took up his own bow and stepped forward to throw back another arrow.

Whoever he was, he was clearly a valued member of the group. Why, there was laughter around him wherever he spoke. Perhaps he was a great wit. Perhaps he had done something of great amusement at an earlier time, and they were reminiscing about it.

Kathleen leaned against the tree and watched him. The easy manner of his frame… He stood there tall and confident, as though naught could assuage him.

"He looks like a very nice man." Angela's curt, low voice interrupted her thoughts.

"'Nice'?" Kathleen repeated in horror.

Nice. What a disgraceful description for a man who was almost Herculean in his archery prowess. *Nice?*

"Well, what else can we know of him?" her sister pointed out. "All we can see is that he wears red and likes archery."

"He does not *like* archery, he *excels* at archery," murmured Kathleen, her eyes unable to stop watching his movements. There he was, taking up his bow again. "He has won several competitions and has been feted for his talent."

"He has?"

All too late, Kathleen remembered her sister did not have quite her imagination.

"I mean, he might have done," she said with a smile, dragging her gaze momentarily away from the man to smile at her sister. "You never know."

Her sister's face, on the other hand, was far too knowing, her lips pursed and her brow furrowed. "You get yourself too tangled in dreams, Kathleen."

"We have little else," Kathleen said before she could stop herself.

She had spoken too loudly. Freezing, then darting behind the tree, which was not quite wide enough to hide her skirts, Kathleen felt her pulse pounding as she gestured wildly at her sister. "Hide!"

Cheeks flushed, Angela stepped behind another tree.

Kathleen's heart was relentless now, her lungs tight. *If we were seen...*

It was bad enough that they had suffered a scandal as a family because of Angela's rash actions. Her father had said Kathleen should stay with them at home, but she had been insistent on accompanying her older sister. She would look after her, she had said.

Had she now done nothing more than drag her sister into even more trouble? Worse, because it wasn't at the dance at the village inn, but here in London?

Pulse hammering, Kathleen peered around the tree trunk.

"Kathleen!"

Despite her sister's hissed admonishment, she risked a glance. She needed to see how bad it was, did she not?

It was bad. The gentlemen were peering into the woodland curiously, as though hunting for a stag. Perhaps that was it. Perhaps they thought the disturbance was the work of an animal.

Kathleen's throat tightened. The men were holding bows and arrows! Would they shoot into the woodland, see if they could catch the mysterious creature that had made such a noise?

She darted back behind the tree. What was she supposed to do? How were they supposed to leave unseen?

"This is all your fault," hissed Angela from the other tree. "I wanted to walk in Hyde Park, but oh, no, we had to—"

"Be quiet!" Kathleen hissed.

We will not be found here. That thought was impenetrable in her mind; the Andilet family had suffered enough. She would not be the additional cause of more disaster. And that meant if she had to march out there and explain she was merely lost, and goodness, could one of the gentlemen point her in the direction of the nearest park fountain?

No, that would not work. The place was private ground. She had most carefully ignored the signs last night and this morning.

Kathleen bit her lip. She would have to do something, if they were coming this way. But were they, or had the gentlemen merely returned to their arrows, thinking no more of the strange sound they had heard?

There was nothing for it.

"Kathleen!"

Once again ignoring her sister, Kathleen peered out from behind the tree…and was relieved to see the gentlemen were laughing and chattering away. One of them, *her* gentleman, as she now considered him, loosed an arrow that flew true through the air, hitting the target almost exactly in the center.

"They didn't see us," Kathleen breathed, stepping out from the tree and gazing at them. Gazing at *him*.

"It was close. Too close," murmured Angela.

Perhaps it had been. Perhaps the whole idea was ridiculous, and they should depart this moment.

But Kathleen could not bring herself to go. Not when her gentleman was still here, his tall frame clear even from this distance. Was he as amusing as he appeared? Perhaps he was quieter, as a general rule, but enjoyed moments like this with friends. Perhaps some of them were his brothers. Perhaps they knew each other from childhood days or had met as adults in one of the gentlemen's clubs that appeared to be everywhere in this city.

Perhaps, perhaps. She would never know. The image of the man she had created in her own mind would be the only one she would ever know.

No gentleman wished to make the acquaintance of a Miss Andilet.

No, there would be no introduction, no matter how wistfully she leaned against this tree and looked at him. All she could hope for was the opportunity to gaze upon him. And imagine. And wonder.

"Well, *I* think we should be returning home!" Angela's voice was sharp, louder than it had been before, and as she spoke, she took a step back.

And stepped on a twig. It cracked.

Kathleen froze as every single gentleman before them turned their heads—straight toward the woodland where they were standing.

"Do not move a muscle," she hissed at her sister.

It was too late. In a panic that Kathleen should have expected and could never have halted, Angela gave a slight scream, turned, and ran. Her footsteps cracked more twigs, her blundering through the leafy branches made a dreadful noise, and her scream—

Well. It echoed around the lawned area where the gentlemen were standing.

Not standing. One of them was approaching.

"Angela—Angela, come back!" hissed Kathleen after her.

She could not help the irritation in her voice, and it only increased as her sister clearly refused to return. That, or she could no longer hear Kathleen over the ruckus she was making as she ran.

Oh, what a disaster.

Perhaps it was her own fault, for forcing Angela to come. Perhaps Kathleen should have ventured across London here on her own. It would have raised some eyebrows, a young lady walking out alone, unaccompanied and unchaperoned, but her solitude was not so shocking.

Or no more shocking than ought to be expected, if they had heard the scandal from the country…

"Angela!" Kathleen called after her sister in as low a voice as possible, but the trouble was, she could no longer see her sister at all.

Well, there was nothing for it. She would have to depart too, which was a crying shame. She still hadn't had her fill of staring at the gentleman who—

"So," said a voice that was melodious and yet clearly amused.

Kathleen whirled around. It was the handsome gentleman—the one who had arrived late, who had been so extraordinary with his archery by the targets.

He wasn't standing by the targets now. He was standing right before her, mischievous grin on his face, strong arms crossed over his broad chest, mere feet from her. Now that he was so much closer, she could see his russet waistcoat was exquisitely embroidered, his shirt of the highest quality, and there was a pin in his cravat that could have been a crest.

Kathleen swallowed, her feet unconsciously retreating. Her back hit the tree trunk and her lips parted as she stared up at him.

Goodness, but he was all the more impressive this close.

"You're the Peeping Tom," the gentleman said with a laugh. "How intriguing to make your acquaintance."

Chapter Two

L ORD LEOPOLD CHANCE took a deep breath. Then he stepped forward.

"Graycott! I did not think you would be here this early—it's before midday. How are you awake?"

He had expected there to be laughter. There was always laughter when he walked into a room these days, and today was no exception.

Viscount Graycott smirked, deepening the dimples in his elongated face, as Leopold approached him and a few of his friends. "Your surprise at my being awake is nothing to my surprise of you being here at all, Chance."

Leopold maintained the smile, but it was an effort. "Now why would you think that?"

"The news is all about Town," said Graycott, nudging one of his friends, a bloated gentleman Leopold did not recognize. "You cannot pretend not to have heard the rumors. You started them, after all."

"*Caused* them," sneered his bulbous-nosed friend.

The worst had already happened, so it was not too difficult for Leopold to maintain his smile, despite the great provocation. "I cannot think what you mean."

There was laughter rippling through the group now, all save one. Leopold caught his cousin's eye, but Samuel looked away, the Chance intelligence in his expression, even if it was marred with discomfort.

So, clearly just being related to him was something to which to avoid calling attention. Excellent. As though his father's disappointment had not been enough.

"I did not think you would be coming," said another man with bushy, dark eyebrows and a laugh that echoed around the carefully mown lawn area just outside the club. "If I had known—"

"Don't tell me, you would have stayed at home," Leopold said as pleasantly as he could manage, pulling off his jacket and throwing it down with the rest of them.

For a moment, just a moment, he saw the flicker of discomfort among his friends.

His former friends, it appeared. A little whiff of scandal, and the whole pack of them seemed to wish to be rid of him.

Which was most unfair when the scandal itself wasn't even true.

But were they really going to kick up a fuss about his jacket being in a pile with their own? He was a Chance, the son of what Society was calling "the dowager duke," now the brother of the current Duke of Cothrom. Would a card game really put an end to his reputation?

"Perhaps I should have stayed at home," Graycott said with a laugh that was far too cold to hold actual merriment. He brushed at an imagined piece of lint on his shirt, his hollow cheeks twitching as he strained to keep from smiling once more. "Perhaps the company would have been more refined."

Leopold doubted it. The last he heard, Graycott's mother had another head cold and his sister had caught it too. Red noses all round.

Still, that was hardly something to speak of in public, so he comforted himself with the prospect of some archery. That was what he had come here for, after all. The tug on the arm, the slowing of his breathing, the satisfaction of the *thunk* as the arrow kissed the target.

Not Society, and politics, and rumors, and gossip. If he'd wanted that, he could have stayed at home and talked to his sister, Maude.

"How is everyone doing?" Leopold asked lightly, picking up a bow and a couple of arrows. Not that he would need more than one to hit his mark. "I see *someone* has been improving."

The butt before him, fifty yards away, held a number of arrows. From what he could see, the person who had shot before him had either gained in skill, the arrows growing closer to the center, or had had a blinder of a first shot and then panicked and gotten progressively worst.

Graycott's thin lip curled. "I don't need improving. I was demonstrating."

Leopold's smile did not waver, but it took a great deal of effort. "Well done that, man."

It had been a mistake to come here. A mistake to think he could just step back into Society, as though the card game had never happened. What was it that his father had said?

"We do not tolerate scandal in this family, Leopold. You will go out there, and you will clear up this misunderstanding. You will."

There had not been a choice in the matter, though perhaps coming here rather than White's had been a poor choice. At least there he could have explained himself, explained the whole misunderstanding. Here, with Graycott—

"Are you going to shoot or not?" Graycott said in a bored tone.

More laughter—laughter at his own expense, Leopold knew. Graycott may only have been a viscount, but he had a title of his own. Leopold was a second son. His father had once held a multitude of titles in his estate, but he'd made the rather peculiar choice of sharing the titles with his brothers long before any of their sons had been born. And now, his father had acted against Society's expectations once more, bequeathing his last remaining title to his eldest son well before his own demise. Still, with all of his father's generosity to others, Leopold had naught but his name, though even that was a burden sometimes.

Everyone knew the Chance family.

And then Leopold raised the bow to his chest and all the laughter, the cruelty of it and the crassness of it, fell away. So too did the sky, the lawn. Nothing remained but his breathing and the arrow.

Leopold welcomed it. Welcomed the quiet, the softness, the opportunity for his mind to stop and just think about the arrow. The point. The desire within it to fly straight and true.

His attention shifted to the butt. The target. The target that desired the arrow.

He breathed out, long and calm.

He let the arrow fly.

There was muffled applause. The applause grew in volume as Leopold blinked and the sky and the lawn rushed back and he saw his friends and acquaintances clapping—some of them grudgingly, it was true, but still. They could not ignore his talent.

"Yes, well, very clever, doing it once." Graycott jut out his chin. "But I don't suppose you could do it again."

Leopold's smile did not crack. Not an inch. "I would never dream of monopolizing the butts in that way. Whose turn is next?"

A small squabble arose between two gentlemen as Leopold stepped aside and returned the bow to its hook, and in that small movement, his focus was pulled away from the circle of friends and away, past the rack of bows, beyond it. To the woodland that encircled the righthand side of the archery butts.

Where a woman was standing.

Leopold blinked. It was definitely a woman. No gentleman would wear something that vibrantly pink that fell all the way to the ground.

A woman—here? Standing there? Doing what?

"—suppose you are permitted at White's still, Chance? I say, Chance, are you listening?"

Leopold whirled around. Graycott was glaring with barely concealed dislike, along with a few others who had clearly not enjoyed being shown up at the butts.

Samuel, Leopold's own cousin, was inspecting the ground. Evidently, it was uncomfortable, being a Chance around him.

His stomach lurched. He had not thought it would be this bad. It had only been a card game, after all. Did not many people have card games that went awry? He surely could not be the only one.

"If you don't wish to continue, Chance, do not let us detain you," said Graycott with a laugh that was most unfriendly. "It was my assumption that one came here to practice one's archery, not gaze off into the distance."

Leopold glanced over his shoulder. The woman in pink was still there. Had no one else seen her? Were they oblivious, as well as arrogant and unpleasant?

"Right. Archery." He picked up a bow, a different one this time, one with a harsher draw, and stepped forward.

This time, it did not take Leopold long to move into the almost trancelike state he enjoyed whenever he had a bow in his hand. It was easier, more pleasant to leave behind the world and concentrate on nothing but the soaring path of the arrow. A second, a third, a fourth—each arrow pulled back with ease, each arrow craving to be in the center of the target, and Leopold gave them what they wanted.

When he blinked, it was to see Graycott's disgruntled brow.

"I don't know why you come to practice, if you are just going to show off," he muttered.

Leopold continued to smile, but his jaw tightened painfully. It was just one of those situations, he supposed. If he had been poor at the butts, Graycott would have ridiculed him as a bad archer. But because he was good, he was criticized for showing off.

There was no winning with some people.

Inclining his head as graciously as he could manage, Leopold stepped aside and placed the bow into the rack. As he did so, he glanced over at the woodland.

She was still there.

Curiosity swelled within him. Ladies were not permitted to

be members of the London Archery Club. Precisely why, he had never considered. She certainly wouldn't be able to pull a bow at his level. She had probably never touched an arrow in her life. It was unfair. His cousins Frank and Teddy would certainly think so, but that was the rule.

Still. The fact remained that she should not have been here. Yet there she remained, clearly watching them.

A prickle of something Leopold did not quite understand rippled down his spine. It was strange, being watched and knowing you were being watched.

Truly, how had none of the others seen her?

Leopold glanced about the laughing gentlemen, chuckling at a joke he had missed and was clearly not a part of. No, they did not appear to have spotted her—which was strange because the pink of her gown was quite brilliant against the vibrant green of the leaves.

Something stirred within him as he watched his cousin attempt to pull back a bow that was far too heavy for him. Why was being watched so…so odd? So distracting?

"Not strong enough, Chance." Graycott sneered. "I thought you were all supposed to fine specimens?"

Leopold fought down the impulse to crack his knuckles across Graycott's nose and instead picked a second bow from the rack by his side. He did not look at the unpleasant man, but strode forward to offer the bow to his flushing cousin.

"Pay them no heed," he murmured, taking the other bow from Samuel's hands.

There was a hint of thanks in his cousin's eyes. "Easy for you to say."

It was *not* easy for him to say, but Leopold knew this was not the place to argue about it. What he had done—or in truth, what Society *thought* he had done—was hardly worthy of such displeasure, but there it was. That did not appear to matter.

When Leopold returned the unwanted and far-too-heavy bow to the rack, there was a noise. A voice—two voices.

There are two of them?

"What was that?" Graycott's voice was sharp, as though Leopold had done something wrong.

Leopold turned hastily. Precisely why he wished to hide the presence of the ladies, he was not sure. "Nothing—I almost dropped the bow and muttered an oath. My apologies for disturbing the shooting."

Graycott rolled his eyes. "And I thought you being a card sharp was bad enough."

It was within him to bristle, Leopold knew. He had inherited his father's sense of right and wrong, but sadly not his father's ability to always be on the right side of an argument. Or a debate.

Or a hand of cards.

Still, he could hardly let that go without challenge. "I am not a—"

"That's not what I've heard," said Graycott's friend, a burly gentleman whose name Leopold would remember at any moment. "You lost a fortune, I heard. Your family's fortune—your brother the new duke's, apparently, though why your father would give up his title before death, I do not know."

"The Chance family." Graycott snorted. "They are…unusual."

Leopold met his cousin's eyes but said nothing.

"Well," said Samuel briskly, "I am for St. James's Park, I have a meeting there with a gentleman about a pair of pointers I may wish to purchase. Leopold, will you—"

A screech, the sound of someone running, someone shouting. Leopold could not prevent them from turning around this time.

"Dear God, is that a woman?"

"I'll deal with it," said Leopold before he could consider why he was saying such a thing.

It was a foolish thing to do. Now the raised eyebrows and muttered whispers were surely going to blow this, too, out of proportion, he could not help but think as he stepped toward the figure in pink who had attempted, poorly, to hide behind a tree.

The trouble was, she was…distracting. Before Leopold had another go at the butts, he had to know who this woman was, what her purpose was. She was infiltrating his mind, burgeoning curiosity that simply could not coexist with the calm required for a ruddy good shot.

So he would walk over, remind her that this place was for gentlemen only, and send her on her way. Easy.

It was only when he was a few feet away that he realized a few things.

Firstly, that she was facing away from him, hissing after someone who had clearly departed.

Secondly, that she was far more elegant than he had expected. This wasn't a woman who had crept out of her place of employment to gawp at her betters. No, from the refinement of her poise and the quality of her clothes, this was a lady well-bred, and therefore, it was all the more astonishing that she was here, and unaccompanied, at that. Well, unless the other person had been her chaperone. Though he doubted a quality chaperone would encourage creeping about amidst the trees.

And thirdly, Leopold felt a warmth flooding through him that was most unaccountable.

"So," he said, with no idea what he was going to say next.

The woman whirled around and stared boldly—with such a boldness that Leopold found his lips parting.

Then the shock of how she had been discovered seemed to reach her mind. The lady took some hurried steps away, careering into the tree, which halted her movements.

And Leopold smiled, and said the first words that came into his mind. "You're the Peeping Tom. How intriguing to make your acquaintance."

Precisely what he had expected her to say in return, he did not know. His sister was hardly the shy, retiring type, but she knew her place in Society and what was expected of her.

This woman, however… "Surely, I am a Peeping Thomasina?" she shot back with an arched eyebrow.

Leopold gave a laugh, hardly able to believe what he had heard. "I suppose so."

She was bold—bold to be here in the first place, bold not to run after her companion, and bold to speak to a stranger like himself with such confidence.

It was…alluring.

Her companion.

Leopold's stomach lurched. A gentleman, perhaps? Had he in fact interrupted what had been a… liaison?

The thought was most unpleasant. Not that he had a particularly strong view on liaisons in general—he'd had a few of his own—but he'd found the lack of connection rather trying. He hadn't had a woman in his bed for over a year now.

No, it was unpleasant to think that this woman, this particular woman before him, had been engaged in such a thing.

Jealousy? Hell, where had that come from?

"What is your name?" Leopold asked quietly.

A genteel flush pinked her cheeks, as well it should have. It was not proper to ask such a direct question. They ought to be introduced, really, though precisely how he would orchestrate such a thing in a woodland on the edge of the London Archery Club, Leopold did not know.

He should walk away. He had enough problems at the moment with his reputation; he did not need Graycott or anyone else whispering that Leopold met ladies in woodland in broad daylight for activities far too outrageous to speak of.

But he could not.

She was…beautiful.

Not in the way most ladies in Society were. She was not dressed in a day gown, but a blouse tucked into a high-waisted skirt. The two were precisely of the same color, a brilliant pink. The color would have swamped most women, but somehow, her personality shone through it and seemed, somehow, rather *enhanced* by it.

Her eyes were brilliant, a blue he had never seen before. Her hair, a soft brown, blonde in the sunlight but nearing chestnut at the nape of her nape.

And her lips…

"I do not see why I should tell you my name."

Leopold started. The woman was looking defiantly up at him.

Right, right, of course. Propriety. "My name is Leopold. Leopold Chance. Lord Leopold, actually," he said without thinking.

The lady's eyes widened. "I see."

"And you are?" Leopold persisted.

Precisely why, he did not know. The woman was nothing to him, to be sure. He could walk away at any moment, return to… Well, not his friends, but his companions. Perhaps he could accompany his cousin Samuel to St. James's Park. Perhaps he should call in on his club, attempt to combat the rumors that were growing apace. Perhaps he should go home and try to explain it all to his father again.

Yet here he was, bound to the spot by a woman whose presence was so intoxicating, he could not move.

The lady thrust her chest out for a moment, but then her expression softened. "I…I am Kathleen. Kathleen Andilet."

She spoke as though she were admitting some terrible crime. It was not a name Leopold recognized, not a common one.

"And are you new in Town?"

Miss Andilet's mouth gaping softly suggested he should have known. "I—my sister and I… Yes. Yes, we are new in Town."

The delight that had soared through Leopold at the word 'sister' was almost criminal.

He should not feel such delight at hearing that she had a sister, that perhaps the other figure had been her sister, he told himself, despite everything else in his body singing to the contrary. *Why, she still could have been here with a man! You don't know anything about—*

"In fact, you just missed my sister," said Miss Andilet, waving a hand behind her and solidifying all of Leopold's delight. "She will be saddened not to have made your acquaintance, my lord."

"And I hers," Leopold said politely—before the question he really wished to be answered spilled from his lips. "Miss Andilet, what on earth are you doing here?"

Ah. I have been too forward. That was the trouble with having a sister like Maude; she was so direct, preferring bluntness to beating about the bush. And she was older, five years. She had taught him about Society and the world, and Leopold had always looked up to her, always been encouraged to ask questions.

Which was all very well, when you were asking your sister at age seven precisely why gentlemen had to bow and ladies had to curtsey.

This was not the same, accosting a strange woman with such a direct question when she was entirely alone.

Alone except for him, naturally.

"Here?" Miss Andilet did not back down. "Talking to you, naturally."

Leopold clamped his lips together. "Yes, I know, but I mean, why are you here in the first place? You and your sister, why did you come here? You must know this place is private."

He did not expect her retort.

"You mean this place is closed to ladies," Miss Andilet said sharply.

"Yes. Well." Leopold was not sure what to say to that. "So you did know?"

"It is not permitted for a woman to archer here," she said, tilting her head. "But as I was not archering, I am not sure why you are so concerned."

Leopold opened his mouth. Then he closed it again.

She has a point. It was a point well made, one he had not considered. Why, if a woman wished to come here with a husband or a brother, to watch the archery…why should she not be permitted to do just that?

It was a thought that had never occurred to him, and now it was only in his mind because this Miss Andilet had put it there.

"And if it comes to that," she continued, "why should a lady not be permitted to shoot? I would imagine archery is not that difficult, all told."

Leopold laughed but immediately stopped as he saw her serious expression. "You cannot be serious."

"Is it so preposterous that a woman would wish to learn archery?" Miss Andilet spoke confidently, without a single concern, apparently, in her mind that she was speaking so directly not only to a man, but a gentleman—the son of a titled gentleman.

He hardly knew what to say, save to scoff. "A woman simply could not—"

"Why?"

Leopold's mouth was open again, and once again, he did not know what words to put within it.

Because, he wanted to say. *Because a woman simply could not do it. Because a woman is incapable—she would not have the strength, nor the serenity of mind, to accomplish it.*

Because that is not the way it is done.

"I don't think you could teach me, anyway," added Miss Andilet, a hint of challenge in her tone. "I am not certain you are sufficiently talented."

And that was when Leopold quite lost his head.

"You think so?" he said quietly, stepping forward.

Miss Andilet clearly wished to retreat, but there was a small matter of a tree behind her, and that made it most difficult—near impossible. "Y-Yes, I think."

"So you believe I could not teach you?" Leopold said, raising a hand to lean against the tree. He placed it just to the right of her face, leaning toward her.

He did not miss the way Miss Andilet swallowed, nor the way that she looked immediately at his broad chest before returning her gaze to his eyes.

She desired him, then—or at least, her body did. He could not exactly tell whether she was conscious of the way she leaned toward him, looking hungrily up at him as though she wished him to lower his head and—

Leopold managed to stop himself, just about. *That is going too far.*

"I do not believe you could teach me archery," Miss Andilet said softly.

"I bet I could."

"And I will take that bet," she said smoothly.

Leopold's eyes widened as panic flooded through him. "No, I did not mean—"

"I bet you could not teach me archery, and I will bet a...a florin."

"'A florin'?" he repeated.

A florin was almost nothing. It was an old-fashioned coin, to be sure, but it was an old-fashioned-style bet. A foolish one. One that could not be measured.

Aha, that is my escape.

"One simply cannot measure such a thing," Leopold said smoothly, relief pouring through him. "As such, we cannot—"

"I am sure there is some sort of standard I should reach after a month of tuition," Miss Andilet said airily, as though she frequently accosted men and challenged them to impossible tasks. "Let's say that if you can teach me well enough to do an archery—"

"Shoot a bow."

"Yes, to bow an arrow—"

"Shoot an arrow." Leopold had not intended to interrupt again but had been forced to.

"—to shoot an arrow," continued Miss Andilet blithely, "from a thousand feet—"

He had also not intended to laugh, but really—*what nonsense!*

"Fine," Miss Andilet said, raising an eyebrow. "What do you consider a reasonable distance?"

He should not have fallen for it. Leopold knew better, except that he didn't, not when he was standing this close to a woman who looked like that. "A novice, within a month? Fifty yards would be the *most* one could achieve, and that's only if—"

"Excellent! So if I can shoot an arrow to hit one of those things from fifty yards within a month, you've won," Miss Andilet said triumphantly. "If not, then I have won."

Leopold could not do anything but stare. She was in earnest. She was truly in earnest! "But this bet is ridiculous. You could simply refuse to learn."

"Oh, I promise to do my best. I always do," said Miss Andilet blithely. "I am a quick learner, in the main, and it will be your teaching that is lacking."

This was entirely out of hand. "But—"

"A bet is a bet, is it not?" Miss Andilet had somehow stepped out of his frame, away from the tree, and now looked remarkably happy with herself. "I would have thought a gentleman would keep to his word."

His word? But he hadn't—and he couldn't, his reputation was already precarious as it was.

"You will teach me archery," Miss Andilet said cheerfully, "or I will teach you the error of your ways. What do you say?"

What do I say?

Leopold knew precisely what he should say. That it was ridiculous. That he was not foolish enough to be drawn into such nonsense. That it was a tease and he was flattered, but he had his family to think of. His name. His own reputation, should it come to that.

And yet…

And yet, she was so alluring. Not just her beauty, but the fact that she was here. What was a woman dressed so elegantly doing, spying on gentlemen like that? Was her sister her chaperone, and what kind of chaperone abandoned their charge in the middle of the woodland? Who was Miss Kathleen Andilet, and how could he know her better?

Why, by teaching her archery, naturally.

Knowing within every inch of his body that this was a mistake, Leopold nodded. "It is a bet. When shall we begin our lessons?"

Chapter Three

July 5, 1840

THIS WAS ABSOLUTELY the most foolish thing she had ever considered.

Kathleen knew that. She knew it when she carefully dressed that morning, selecting her favorite chiffon high-necked blouse and pairing it with the blue skirt that had such an exquisite waistband.

She knew it as she ate breakfast with Angela, allowing her sister to chatter on over buttered toast.

She knew it as she stepped outside with a parasol on her arm, telling her sister she wished to visit the lending library and see if they'd had any half-decent novels come through. It was unseemly to go alone, she knew, but she'd managed to convince Angela no one would take note of her. It was true few in London knew her at a glance. Perhaps only by name. Besides, it was her sister who had taken off—screaming—all by herself to head home the other day.

She knew it as she walked through the streets of London, every step taking her closer to a place that she knew she should not have been.

And she most definitely knew it when she stood outside the London Archery Club, gazing up at its front door flanked with columns, a footman standing beside it.

Oh, Kathleen, she thought wretchedly. *What do you think you're doing? This is not a place for you.*

"I do not believe you could teach me archery."

"I bet I could."

"And I will take that bet."

The memory of Lord Leopold's words flickered in her mind like a flame.

Lord Leopold. Of course a gentleman like that was a lord—there was no possibility that he was a mere mister.

A man who walked like that, held himself like that, looked like that… No, he was always going to be a lord.

Kathleen swallowed. Every inch of the London Archery Club was designed to make it absolutely clear she was not wanted. The intensity of the formality, the severe knocker on the oaken door, the fact there was a footman there deigning whether or not to open the door…

It was a gentleman's club. For archery, yes, but for gentlemen most of all. It was the sort of place Kathleen would never be permitted to go, even if she had been with her family. Now that Angela had fallen into disgrace, it was most definitely not the sort of place Kathleen should go. Particularly not so brazenly unchaperoned. Not that a chaperone would have *allowed* her to go in the first place.

And yet she was here. She was here because of a foolish infatuation with a gentleman she did not know. She was here because she could not get Lord Leopold out of her mind.

Which was foolish to the extreme.

"Are you meeting your…your brother out here, miss?" asked the footman suddenly.

Heat flushed across Kathleen's cheeks, despite her best of intentions. "No."

It was not the most circumspect answer. What she should have said, Kathleen knew, was *yes*. Or that she was not meeting a brother, but a husband—she was wearing her summer gloves, after all. The footman would not be able to see she was not wearing a ring.

As it was, her instinctive answer had made the man raise an eyebrow. "In that case, move along."

Move—move along?

The sense of injustice of it all rose up within Kathleen before she could hold herself back. "How—"

How dare you. That was what she wanted to say, but the memory of her father's kindly meant instruction reverberated in her mind.

"Ladies are to be admired, not attended to. I know you don't like it, Kitty, but that is the way of the world."

That was the way of the world, indeed. Kathleen kept her head high as curious pedestrians passed her by on the pavement, and she rose up one of the steps leading to the London Archery Club door.

The footman, a slender man with upright posture, moved to block her path. "I am afraid you cannot enter, miss."

"Well, then," Kathleen said, speaking far more sharply than she knew she should have, "I will find it most difficult to accept my *invitation* to meet with a member of the Chance family, then."

She had believed that the mention of such an illustrious family would sway the man. After all, who had not heard of the Chances? A few scandals, yes, but not proper scandals. It was not a true scandal if everything was hushed up, or fixed with a marriage.

If only Angela's difficulties could be so easily solved…

But apparently, the footman was not as impressed by the Chance surname as she had been. "A Chance? Which one?"

Which…which one? How many *were* there?

Kathleen recalled vaguely reading about the Chance family in a newspaper a few months ago—a wedding, wasn't it? Three brothers, or four, she could not remember, who had all had children.

Well, if they'd all had at least one son, there would be many Chance gentlemen. Blast.

She did not really wish to give Leopold's first name; he had taken a risk, she knew, by agreeing to meet with her in the first place. His reputation would be hardier than her own, him being a gentleman, but there was being responsible and then there was asking for the rumor mill to ramp up.

The pinched look on the footman's face was unpleasant. "You aren't really going to meet a member of the Chance family here, are you?"

It was his disbelief in her story—admittedly unusual—that prompted Kathleen's ire. "I only wish to learn how to be an archer, sir. He has agreed to instruct me."

The footman scoffed. "A woman? Learn archery?"

And that was when Kathleen decided enough was enough.

"Show me," she demanded, striding up the final three steps and jabbing a finger at the footman's chest. He practically stumbled to step back out of her reach, but there was nowhere for him to retreat. "Show me where it is written that a woman cannot learn archery."

"B-But I—really, miss, I cannot—our club rules say—"

"Oh, I am sure your silly little club decided to write a rule that women were not allowed in, remarkably backward of you, but there we go," Kathleen said darkly, rage fueling the words that she knew she should not speak. "But where is it written that women cannot learn archery? Tell me, man, or retract your words!"

"Miss Andilet?"

Kathleen dropped her finger and turned with flushed cheeks to see—

Lord Leopold.

He was standing on the pavement with his jaw dropped.

Oh, damnation. Which was another thing her father had attempted to stop her from saying.

That was the trouble with her temper—it always flared up just when it would be most inconvenient. In public. With strangers. Over nonsense.

Why was she attacking this man about an expectation in Society that he'd had no part in establishing? Could every gentleman, every man be blamed for the lack of freedoms for women?

And did she *have* to lose control just when the dashing and devastatingly handsome Lord Leopold had arrived?

"I am having a disagreement," Kathleen said weakly. "With this man."

"Woe betide any man to have a disagreement with you, it seems," Lord Leopold said jovially, advancing up the steps and halting beside her. "What appears to be the problem, Cooper?"

"It's—you know the rules, Lord Leopold," said the footman, pulling himself upright and glaring at Kathleen, who glared back. "I cannot break those rules for anyone."

It was all Kathleen could do not to snap back that rules were made and therefore could be unmade. Really, she should have been presented with a prize for her restraint.

"The lady wishes to learn archery," Lord Leopold said calmly. "It is not a crime, Cooper."

Cooper's eyes narrowed. "It is against club rules."

"It is against the rules for women to become members. Miss Andilet is not requesting membership," Lord Leopold pointed out.

Kathleen swallowed. He was so…so *impressive*. Not overbearing, never that, but with a presence that certainly made her wish to agree. To give him anything he wanted.

The footman looked torn. "It has never been done, my lord."

Lord Leopold tilted his head. "And that means it never *can* be done?"

Exactly why Lord Leopold Chance was doing this, and for her, she could not tell. Perhaps, Kathleen thought wildly, he was a rebellious young man. Perhaps he enjoyed pushing the boundaries of Society. Perhaps she was merely a good excuse for him to raise a fuss.

The footman shook his head, and Kathleen's heart sank as Lord Leopold seemed to lose his verve, likely growing weary of the debate.

"It simply cannot be allowed, my lord."

She had been foolish to even attempt this. Her desperate

attempt at flirtation with Lord Leopold the other day had been bad enough, but to follow through, to turn up and expect the place to acquiesce to her wishes…

"I should return home," she said quietly, half to Lord Leopold, half to herself.

Kathleen expected him to agree—perhaps even to smile, to point out that she should have thought of this when she had suggested the bet.

Instead, Lord Leopold sighed. "I hope your archery skills are innate, Miss Andilet, for I cannot afford many lessons of this nature."

Leaning forward toward the footman as Kathleen stared, a significant amount of whispering took place between the two men. She could not catch the wording exactly, but there appeared to be a negotiation of some sort.

When Lord Leopold leaned back, the footman smiled broadly.

"I shall add it to your tab, my lord," Cooper said with a bow, stepping out of the way of them both.

"I am sure you will," Lord Leopold said dryly. "Well then, Miss Andilet. Shall we continue?"

He… He bribed the man?

Kathleen could hardly breathe. Maybe her instinct to return home was the right one. This man was surely a rake, if he believed a small amount of money could get him whatever he wanted. He was a man who did not care for the rules of Society!

And neither do I, she reminded herself. Except… Except that for her, that meant wearing one less petticoat when it was hot and hoping no one would notice, or helping herself to a third cake in company, even if it was frowned upon. At its most extreme, it meant pretending she was of the working class and brazenly walking about without a chaperone, as she was doing right now.

As if her parents had even thought their reputations were worth salvaging enough to send a chaperone along with the sisters when they'd fled the scandal.

But she did not gad about paying men to permit women where women were not permitted!

"Are you not coming?"

Kathleen blinked. Lord Leopold had stepped through the door, which she had not noticed had now been opened, and was waiting for her to follow.

Follow, into a place she was not permitted to learn a skill ladies were not encouraged to practice.

Just as she was about to make her excuses and hurry home, ready to share the whole adventure with her sister, Kathleen caught Lord Leopold's eye.

And saw the challenge.

"Of course," Kathleen said airily, stepping forward as though she had been merely detained by her appreciation of the external architecture.

Her lips parted as the door closed behind her. The external architecture was nothing to the internal architecture.

There were columns, yes, but these were wider and taller, reaching the top of a double-height ceiling. A great chandelier hung between two of them, illuminating, in the evenings, she was certain, the great expanse. She could barely see the ceiling, but what she could make out was elegantly painted with Greek and Roman gods, all in their splendor. There was red velvet carpet placed upon the marble floor, and even that was impeccably clean and extravagantly impressive.

"Now, let's get outside and find some butts."

Kathleen almost fell over. "I beg your pardon?"

"Butts, Miss Andilet, butts," Lord Leopold said calmly as he strode forward toward a door. "We must have butts."

Had she truly heard him say—no, she could not have…

"Butts, Miss Andilet!" he called over his shoulder, not bothering to glance behind him, perhaps presuming that she was following him.

Kathleen knew she should not. This man was a rake, that much was certain. Shouting such a word about the place, where anyone could hear him, anyone could see them together…

Her feet darted forward, her body lunging toward the man who was most evidently not suitable for her company. He had stepped through the door and she followed him onto the green lawn and blazing sunshine.

They were where he had been before. Kathleen looked to her right and yes, there was the woodland where she and Angela had hidden.

It looked remarkably close, from here. Bother—no wonder they had seen her.

"Excellent, there is no one here," said Lord Leopold brusquely, pulling off his jacket.

"I…" Kathleen had intended to say something, and it would have been a very intelligent, clever something, she was certain.

If she had not been momentarily distracted by the fact that Lord Leopold was taking all his clothes off.

Not all of them. Kathleen realized in an instant that he was merely repeating the change of attire that he and all the other men had performed when she had been watching before. The jacket off, the cuffs of his shirt unbuttoned, and the slow roll of his sleeves up his arms. His very strong arms. His arms that looked strong yet soft. Why, if she reached out—

Kathleen managed to stop herself. Thank goodness Lord Leopold had been looking in the other direction.

"I hoped we would be alone," Lord Leopold said as he glanced her way, his cheeks going a little red.

Her own cheeks could have boiled a kettle.

Now what, precisely, did he mean by that? Did he mean that he'd hoped to get her alone—for what purpose? Or was he embarrassed by her, mortified by her presence and desperate not to be seen by her?

"So. Archery."

Kathleen blinked. *Archery.* Yes, that was the reason they were here. That was the pretense, that was the bet. The bet she had made merely so that she could spend time in this man's presence.

Her father was right. She *was* just as bad as her sister.

"Have you any experience with archery before? Any at all?" asked Lord Leopold, as though they were seated at a dining table and he was merely asking her a question.

The sun was too bright. That, or Kathleen was being dazzled by the man, which arguably was just as likely.

"Miss Andilet?"

Kathleen, she wanted to say. *Call me 'Kathleen.'*

She was not that daft. "No. No," she said firmly, attempting to get a hold of herself. "No, I have no experience with archery whatsoever."

"In that case, we will start with the basics," Lord Leopold said with a brief smile. "Please look at my butt."

Kathleen almost fell over her own skirt.

"I…I do not believe you wish me to do that, my lord," she whispered, hardly able to speak as her attention was inexorably drawn to the impressive form of the man's behind.

She really shouldn't have looked at it, and she really should not have *enjoyed* looking at it—but then, the man had instructed her to do so. After all, it was perfectly natural. A lady could enjoy and appreciate the fine form of a gentleman, as long as he did not notice. After being invited to do so directly…

"Now, we aim toward the butt in the hope of hitting the center," came Lord Leopold's most intrusive words.

Kathleen blinked. Her gaze had settled on the man's delicious derriere in his trousers, but now that she looked up, she could see that Lord Leopold was pointing at the target several yards away.

At… At the target.

"The—the target is called a 'butt'?" she asked in horror.

Lord Leopold turned to her, his slackened face a picture of amazement. "Why of course. What did you think I was speaking of?"

And this, Kathleen thought, *is the moment for the ground to open up and swallow me whole, and for my existence to be written out of the history books.*

Not that she would ever make it into the history books. That was for gentlemen. And queens.

"Butts," she said decisively, begging the flush that was flowing up her stomach not to reach her décolletage. "We aim arrows at…at butts."

"Just so. The crucial thing to remember…"

Whatever it was, Kathleen would never remember. One could not remember what one had never heard.

Because as she looked at Lord Leopold, she was a tad taken with the curve of his mouth, the way his tongue flicked over his lips as he spoke, the confidence of his voice… Not the words themselves.

Kathleen swallowed hard. She should not have been getting so easily distracted by such a gentleman. She should not have been getting so easily distracted by *any* gentleman.

Here he was, risking his… Well, not his reputation, exactly, but certainly risking gossip by abiding by his side of the bet to teach her archery, and all she could do was think about his behind!

She glanced at it one final, she told herself, time. It really was a most delicious—

"Are you paying attention?"

"Butt," Kathleen said instinctively, her eyes flickering to his face.

Lord Leopold was smiling. Why he was smiling, when she was busy making a complete ass of herself, she did not know.

Wondering whether the ground truly would swallow her up if she continued to make such an idiot of herself, Kathleen tried to laugh. "I mean—butts are a part of archery! Yes, I am paying attention. Most certainly, I was not distracted in the least."

His raised eyebrow suggested her witty repartee had not exactly worked. "Indeed. In that case, can you tell me anything about archery?"

Kathleen swallowed, but she stepped to the side and airily waved a hand. "That is a butt."

Do not look at his—

"Yes, well done," said Lord Leopold with a laugh. "Anything else?"

If only her mind had been a tad more focused. If only she had tried harder to listen to his words.

If only Lord Leopold Chance did not have such a delightful—

"No," Kathleen admitted, a wry smile creasing her lips but swiftly disappearing. "I was not paying attention."

"I thought as much. You know, it's not very fair to bet me that I cannot teach you," Lord Leopold pointed out quietly, "when you are the one not attending."

Words rushed through her mind. Words like, *I was attending to you, but not a part of you I should be staring at.* Words like *you are intoxicating and I want to stand closer to you.* Words like *I don't know why you agreed to this foolish bet. We didn't even agree terms and that makes me wonder why you are here.*

And how I can keep you here.

Words like that. Words Kathleen would never say.

"Let's start again," said Lord Leopold brightly. "So. Your bow is constructed of two primary elements: the bow and the string. The bow has an upper limb and a lower belly, either side of the grip. The strings…"

And she truly did try to pay attention. Kathleen had rather enjoyed lessons with the governess she had shared with Angela and their brother, while he had remained at home, and her mind was curious. If anyone else had been giving the lecture—old Miss Clarke, for example, the governess who had taught her years ago—she would most definitely have paid attention.

As it was…

"…and that is why yew is the best wood for bows, because of its strength and flexibility," finished Lord Leopold. "Any questions?"

Questions. A thousand questions, most of them inappropriate.

Kathleen tried to smile. "You know a great deal about archery."

Flattery was one of the keenest ways to entertain a gentleman. Her mother had been very clear on that; to pretend ignorance and flatter a man's intelligence, that was the surest way to his affections.

Both Angela and Kathleen had once attempted to argue with their mother on this, but their mother had just smiled. *"Well, it worked with your father."*

Apparently, it was not going to work with Lord Leopold. He frowned. "It is not 'a great deal.' It is the basics. Do you seek to flatter me, Miss Andilet?"

"No!" *Heaven forbid.* "No, I just—"

"Because this is naught but a lesson. An archery lesson, to be clear," he continued, and there was a strange sort of stiffness in his back now, his hands clasped behind it. "I would not wish—I mean, you and I both have reputations to maintain. We are out in the open, I am not hiding what we are doing, for I do not believe it needs to be hidden. I have nothing to hide. But still, you know there are others who would not approve of you being here with me without a chaperone present."

Kathleen blinked. It was a relatively long speech to defend himself from an accusation she had not made. And the comment about the chaperone? She would not address it. If she did, she might have to explain what she and her sister were doing in London to begin with, and she had not the heart for that at present. "I just… You know more than I do. About archery, I mean."

Lord Leopold appeared to be battling something internally. Precisely what, Kathleen did not know. Maybe he regretted rising to her bait. Maybe he realized just what a foolish thing he had done, to agree to teach her archery.

"Let us talk of the history of archery," he said quietly, his eyes flickering with interest.

Not an interest in me, Kathleen reminded herself. *In archery.*

"Yes, let's," she said weakly. "That feels like a safe topic."

"I beg your pardon?"

"Nothing," Kathleen said hastily, trying to smile at the handsome man who surely had no business being so strong. "Tell me… Tell me why butts are called 'butts.'"

Chapter Four

July 8, 1840

"Remind me again, why am I here?"

The crush was unbearable. No, if Leopold were honest with himself, it was not the crush of people that was unbearable, but the crush of their gazes, all following him around Mrs. Burton's drawing room.

His brother grinned. "Because we are Chances, and we received an invitation, and it would look pretty poor on us if we only accepted invitations from dukes and marquesses, wouldn't it?"

His brother Thomas, the new Duke of Cothrom, could be as kind and dutiful as he wanted, Leopold wanted to say, but why did that mean he had to accompany him?

As though his brother could read his mind, Thomas added, "And besides, Victoria can't join me. She's...indisposed. And I wanted company. I know hardly anyone here."

Leopold repressed a smile as the two of them halted at the fireplace—mercifully unlit—and managed to find a small moment of quiet as the pianoforte started up in the other room. As the droves of guests Mrs. Burton had thought fit to invite rushed over to see who was playing, they were afforded a moment together.

"She is...indisposed, is she?"

Thomas, his tall figure softened by his kind nature, which was always glimmering in his expression, glanced at him, cheeks slightly red. "Yes. Yes, indisposed. Why?"

Leopold was no fool. He knew precisely what 'indisposed'

meant. He was about to have a niece or nephew. "No reason. I just—well. I had hoped to have a quiet evening, rather than be dragged out here to be paraded around."

"Is that Lord Leopold—*the* Lord Leopold Chance?"

He groaned. At least, he allowed a groan to part his lips, but he managed to clamp it down almost immediately.

"Father would be proud," his brother teased under his breath as the room started to fill up again, the crowds evidently unimpressed with the pianoforte playing.

Leopold snorted. "Father would not wish for the Chance name to be bandied about in the mouths of gossips, as well you know."

Father. William Chance, the head of the Chance family, and a formidable man.

Not that he was frightening, not in any way. If anything, Leopold would say his papa had softened the last few years. He'd heard tales that in his youth, the young Dowager Duke of Cothrom had been truly formidable, keeping his three brothers in line by sheer force of will, which would have been a remarkable feat, indeed.

William Chance liked order, and respect, and respectability. He hated gossip and slander and any behavior that was likely to engender either.

It made being his son a tad difficult.

"I don't want to be here," Leopold muttered out of the corner of his mouth. "My shoulders ache and my back is stiff."

"That is your own fault for spending all day with a bow in your hands," his brother shot back, accepting a glass of wine from a harried-looking footman and sipping it. "A gentleman would have better things to do."

Like make heirs, Leopold thought but did not say with a wry grin as he helped himself to his own glass of wine.

Well, his brother had a point. Gentlemen of their standing did not generally go about practicing their draw or flinging back their shoulder in an attempt to let an arrow fly an additional fifty yards.

It wasn't that it wasn't done—there was naught scandalous about it.

It was just… Well, it wasn't done. No one wanted to do it.

No one except him.

"Besides, Mrs. Burton has been a splendid addition to Society," Thomas added, his genial nature showing through even as the room continued to be filled. "I suppose I can keep you away from the card tables, if I need to?"

The question was delicately put, and Leopold could not fault his brother for asking it in the way he had.

He *could* certainly fault him for asking the question in the first place, however.

Leopold's scowl was hopefully not too noticeable. "Thomas, I told you before, when I lost that money, I never intended to lose so much."

"The problem is, Leopold, is that everyone in Town is talking about it," his brother said unnecessarily.

"Yes, that's the one, the card sharp—"

"—heard he swindled many a person out of—"

"—someone finally put him in his place—"

Leopold wished he could close his ears to the whispered gossip that surrounded them just as easily as he could shut his eyes, but it was impossible. It felt like every single person in Mrs. Burton's drawing room—and there was a great number—was looking at him, pointing at him, talking about him.

"You take these things too much to heart," murmured Thomas.

Leopold snorted. "You try telling that to Father."

If only he could close his sensitivities to the memories of that conversation. Much of it had been scrubbed from his mind, the thought of it too difficult to bear, but snippets still forced their way through into his memory.

"*—utter disgrace, destroying our good name… spent years to maintain our reputation and you destroy it in—*"

"Look, all I ask is that you stay away from the card tables

tonight." Thomas had stepped close to him, so close that he could whisper in Leopold's ear. The awkwardness with which he murmured spoke volumes.

Leopold did all he could to ensure his shoulders did not sag.

His brother did not trust him. He had known it, deep down, but to have it so clearly stated—albeit not with words—was disheartening.

He was Lord Leopold Chance. He had gained a great deal of money through playing cards—through skill, mark you!—and because he had lost a significant amount a month ago, the whole of Society wondered whether he had been cheating in the past.

Cheating. Him!

"I am not going to promise you any such thing," he said aloud, keeping his voice level even as his anger rose. "And if you ask me again, I shall leave."

Thomas swallowed. "Look, Father asked me to keep an eye on you."

And that was when Leopold decided to leave.

Not because Mrs. Burton was of a much lower class than themselves, as were most of her guests. Some of Leopold's closest friends from families without titles, and judging by the quality of the wine he had sipped, their hostess had spared no expense.

Not because he particularly had a desire to play cards in public, after all the gossip and murmurings about him.

But because his brother and father, two of the people in the world who should most trust him, who should believe him, did not.

"I'm leaving," Leopold said quietly, placing his almost-untouched glass of wine on the mantelpiece.

His brother's face fell. "No. Leopold, I didn't mean—"

"If I cannot be trusted to attend a card party, I may as well be at home with Maude," Leopold snapped, trying to bite down his ire and not doing a particularly good job. "I'll see you later."

His mind was reeling and his anger burning through him as Leopold pushed through the crowd, across the drawing room toward the hall, trying to ignore all the stares, the whispers, the way one gentleman even had the gall to point.

"Ooof!"

"Ouch—ow!"

Leopold reeled back from the person he had just barged into. "My apologies, I…I…"

Words did not appear to be forthcoming. This was most disconcerting, for two reasons.

Firstly, because he appeared to have completely winded the poor person who had accidentally stepped between himself and the door to the hall.

Secondly, because the person in question was none other than Miss Kathleen Andilet.

"You," he whispered, unconsciously stepping closer to her and staring into her eyes.

"'You'?" Miss Andilet whispered in turn, a hand clasped to her chest, her breaths shallow.

Leopold could do nothing but stare.

She was…

Well, he had known she was remarkably striking when he had first accosted her, accusing her of being a Peeping Tom.

"You're the Peeping Tom. How intriguing to make your acquaintance."

"Surely, I am a Peeping Thomasina?"

His stomach lurched.

He had not quite noticed…but here, in the low sunlight of the late afternoon, the crush of Mrs. Burton's many guests, and the attire one expected a lady to wear at such an event…

Leopold swallowed. She was magnificent.

Not in a showy way. The more he looked at her, the more he realized that Miss Andilet could not be a showy young woman, as his mother would put it. Her gown was simple, and the single gold necklace with a small pendant was neither fabulously jeweled nor probably that expensive. Her hair was piled up upon her head with no feathers or adornments, but the curve of her neck and the swell of her heaving breasts as she caught her breath...

"Lord—Lord Leopold?" Miss Andilet whispered.

"Miss Andilet," Leopold murmured, stepping toward her.

And then he halted.

Dear God, he was in the middle of someone else's drawing room, stepping closer—far too close—to a woman he was not supposed to know. *Damn, but I am thinking with my loins, not my head.*

He didn't know her. Not officially—they had never been introduced.

And surely, in a public venue such as this, at least, she had come with a chaperone. A chaperone who might be searching the crowds for their charge, spying this interaction this very moment.

Leopold turned wildly, his eyes searching for his brother. Perhaps Thomas had once met her. Perhaps he could come to their rescue.

"Ah, I see that you wish to make the acquaintance of our dear Miss Andilet!"

Never before had Leopold been more delighted to be borne down on by a hostess. He smiled weakly at the approaching apple-shaped Mrs. Burton and wondered whether he would ever escape this card party without creating a further scene of gossip.

"I do?" he said vaguely, before sharpness returned to his mind and voice. "I do, yes, thank you. If you would do the honors, Mrs. Burton."

Mrs. Burton, a widow of notable stature whose husband had made a small fortune running tea from China, beamed as a curl of her gray hair danced across her dimpled cheek. She was clearly delighted to be doing the honors—a duke's son, under her roof, requesting her assistance in a social situation!

"My dear Lord Leopold, may I present Miss Kathleen Andilet, newly arrived from the country," simpered Mrs. Burton. "Miss Angela Andilet, the elder of the two sisters, is sadly indisposed for tonight's revelry, and I was charged with keeping an eye on our young lady here since she came alone. I spent time with her father in the country, you see. Good… Good family. Good man, really."

Leopold bowed low, as was befitting his own station more than her own. Miss Andilet's sparkling eyes did not leave his own and when he straightened up, Mrs. Burton continued.

"Miss Andilet, may I introduce you to Lord Leopold Chance, son of the Duke of Cothrom. Although now I suppose I should say brother of the Duke of Cothrom! It is all very strange, Miss Andilet. We were all quite astonished when we heard."

Miss Andilet's brow had furrowed. *Her exquisite brow*, Leopold could not help but think. There was an elegance in it that he had not expected. Not realized was possible in the mere inch of movement.

"Your brother," she repeated. "I suppose I should offer you my condolences on the loss of your father."

"Oh, no, the Chance family do things differently," twittered Mrs. Burton, making Leopold wince. "Yes, I was quite surprised when I heard—not over there, you silly girl, over here!"

Their hostess stormed off in a flurry of lace and irritation. Leopold glanced over to see a maid attempting to find a place to put down a tray of delicious-looking cakes, taking shallow breaths and appearing just as harassed as the footman had been.

"The Chance family do things differently," said an amused, quiet voice. "Why am I not surprised?"

Leopold turned back to Miss Andilet and realized there was a most inexplicable heat within him. Dear Lord, it was rising.

Am I…flushing?

"Yes, I suppose in a way, we do," he said aloud, stepping to the side of the room and feeling a strange sense of gratification when Miss Andilet mirrored him. "My father decided to relinquish the title to my brother about six months ago. As the father of the current duke, Society has come to refer to him as 'the Dowager Duke of Cothrom.'"

Miss Andilet's eyes widened. "That is unheard of."

"That's the Chance way," Leopold said, trying to smile through the awkwardness. "We never were ones for obeying all the laws of Society. Even my father—he is the most stringent stickler for the rules I ever met, until they disagree with him. Then he completely disregards them."

She smiled at that, and the smile warmed Leopold in a way he had not expected. Not just desire, though he could not ignore the desire that was burgeoning inside him. No, it was more than that. She made him feel…

Comfortable.

Comfortable? It was hardly the heady lust he had known before.

"I like the sound of your father," Miss Andilet said quietly. "It sounds as though you have inherited the best of him."

Leopold had not intended his chest to swell at that compliment, but he could not help it. "You say that and you have not even met him," he could not help but point out.

"No, but even from the short description of him, I can see he has a strong moral compass yet also a desire to follow his own sense, rather than the tired rules of Society," Miss Andilet said quietly as she looked out at the other guests of Mrs. Burton's. "Something I wish I could do more often myself."

It had also not been his intention to step closer to Miss Andilet. There was certainly no need for it—he could hear her perfectly well from where he was standing. Yet something drew him closer.

Perhaps it was lust. There was certainly something magnetic about this woman. Slight and inconsequential as her clothes marked her, there was something…something alluring about this woman.

And she was here, at Mrs. Burton's.

That simple fact jolted something through Leopold's body he had not expected. Well, meeting her in the woodland of the London Archery Club, then meeting her once by appointment…she could have been anyone. He certainly had no clear idea of her standing in Society.

But here she was, a guest of Mrs. Burton, the widow even asked to be her chaperone for the evening. To be sure, neither of them had titles...but then, his own mother had been a mere "Miss" before she had become a duchess.

Leopold's lungs constricted, just for a moment.

And that meant Miss Andilet was an actual prospect.

The thought roared through his mind as his whole body responded in delight. Where had this need come from? Why were his interests so instantly aligned to this woman he barely knew?

Barely knew—and yet wanted to know?

"You must be stiff."

Leopold almost fell over. "I-I beg your pardon?"

"From all the archery that you did the other day," Miss Andilet continued blithely, as though she had not just said something which could have been taken as wildly inappropriate. "All that talk of butts—you must be exhausted. And your shoulder, does it not ache?"

Trying to collect himself and reminding himself that his mind may have been in the gutter, but Miss Andilet's certainly wasn't, Leopold tried to smile. It was his fault, really. It had been amusing, all his mention of butts...until he'd found his gaze meandering into a quite disreputable direction. "Ah, yes. Yes, it does ache a little. I apologize that our lesson was cut short—the place was getting rather crowded. You have not yet had the opportunity to draw a bow yourself."

"Perhaps in our next lesson," said Miss Andilet, her eyelids fluttering almost coquettishly. "Our bet is still on, is it not?"

Their bet? Leopold needed no bet to wish to see this woman again.

"Mrs. Burton certainly draws an interesting crowd, does she not?"

Leopold blinked. "I-I beg your pardon?"

Miss Andilet smiled as someone began to play the pianoforte again and a footman whose wig was now on backward offered them glasses of wine. She took one and then turned back to Leopold. "I said, Mrs. Burton draws an interesting crowd. I had no idea that she had such lofty connections as yourself. I have even heard that the great card sharp, one of the Chances, is in attendance tonight. A relation, I presume?"

And that was when all the warm, delightful feelings started to sour.

The great card sharp, one of the Chances.

Oh, hell. Was it possible his maligned reputation had truly traveled that far? Was it not enough that he had merely been good at cards—now people he did not even know were actually calling him a card sharp?

"I do not think the nickname is warranted," was all he could manage to say through a tight jaw.

Perhaps wine would help. Yes, wine would always help.

Leopold threw back the glass and a wash of the wine hit his throat. It was indeed a very good vintage. The trouble was, one wasn't supposed to inhale it.

Coughing profusely and attracting the stares of those around them, Leopold wondered whether it was worth staying.

A hand landed gently on his arm. A warm hand, one that reassured yet tempted. That was when he knew he could never leave this place while Miss Andilet was still within it.

"Are you quite well?" Miss Andilet's face was a picture of concern. "I do apologize. I should not have brought up your relative. I... I suppose it is a great family embarrassment, such a reputation for one of your own."

Blinking through the tears his coughing fit had created, Leopold wondered whether he could escape this conversation without having to admit to the truth: that he was the one everyone was gossiping about.

He tried to smile. "Oh, I don't know. As a family we are mostly inured to such—"

"There he is—Lord Leopold, old chap!" Mr. Lister, a short man with sunken eyes, smirked as he paused by them in his walk toward the door. "I do hope you aren't going to cheat us all at the card tables later, Lord Leopold."

Leopold's jaw stiffened. Mr. Lister was a person hardly worthy of the label 'gentleman' and had been a most unpleasant and persistent suitor of not one, but three of the Chances of his generation. His father before him had been similarly unpleasant, Leopold's mama had said. The Dowager Duchess of Cothrom had him barred from her soirees. Leopold would have given the man a fresh opportunity to prove himself, had not the man attempted to kiss his sister, Maude.

She had not precisely broken the man's nose, but it had been seriously bruised for several weeks.

He had to say something. Leopold knew he had to respond. That dratted Mr. Lister was waiting for a response.

Damn my mouth. Why isn't it working?

"Such a shame you lost all that money." Mr. Lister sneered. "But I suppose it was on purpose, to prevent people from guessing that you were cheating. Such a desperate attempt."

The man moved away just as Leopold realized his tongue was, indeed, able to move.

But there was no point. The man had gone, the unpleasant and entirely false words spoken for all to hear, and—

Oh, blast. For Miss Andilet to hear.

When she spoke, her cheeks were pink. "It's you. You are the member of the Chance family whom everyone is saying is a card sharp. You are the one who lost all that money. You are the one people are saying is...is a cheat."

Leopold did his best to remain calm. Really, he thought he should be congratulated for just how calm he managed to stay. When he spoke, there was only a hint of pain and loathing in his words. "That is my current reputation, yes. It is not the truth."

He wanted to say more. He wanted to say that he had always been good at cards, and it was other people's jealousy that had led to these rumors.

That he had lost, yes, but he had not cheated before, during, or since that card game.

That a man's reputation could be lost so quickly and so unfairly, and he did not know how to restore it.

Say something, man! "It was a misunderstanding, that was all— I believed the bet to be one thing, my opponent another."

"A bet is a very serious business," came her gentle reply.

Leopold's stomach lurched. This was not the sort of conversation one should be having with young ladies, and this was most certainly not the correct location to have it. The conversation one should not have, that was.

Oh, blast it all.

"I paid the man, but there was a great deal of misunderstanding and irritation," Leopold said stiffly, desperate to finish the story off and move on. "The rumors exaggerate all. The money, the disagreement, and the fact was that *I did not cheat.*"

The last few words were spoken with such emphasis that the people around them paused in their conversations for a moment. Leopold's cheeks burned. They burned all the hotter when people continued their conversations, this time with additional glances in his direction.

Miss Andilet's expression softened. "Well, then. I… I am sorry I listened to the rumors."

"Gossips will always seek to tear down another," Leopold said, keeping his voice to a low murmur as he felt more eyes glancing over. *I should never have come.* "They no doubt live in fear that it could happen to themselves, for they believe there is nothing worse than a ruin. Miss—Miss Andilet, are you quite well?"

Her face had suddenly changed. Oh, the beauty remained— there was a delicacy and a beauty in her face that Leopold was almost certain could not be altered.

But she had gone pale, her eyes unfocused, as though she were thinking of something most terrible. Leopold glanced over to where she was staring but could see naught that could accost her in such a terrible manner.

"Miss Andilet?"

She blinked. When she blinked for a second time, her eyes focused, and she turned to look at him with her lips slightly pressed together, a little shake of her head.

Is she disappointed? In me?

"I am afraid I need to depart," she said vaguely. "Good evening, Lord Leopold."

"Good evening, Miss Andilet, but should you be leaving without—"

Without her chaperone?

That was what he had intended to say. Mrs. Burton did not notice her charge disappearing. Indeed, she had been distracted by half a dozen guests since she had left their sides. It did not matter; Miss Andilet had slipped from the drawing room at a pace Leopold had not thought possible, disappearing from view and taking her delightful company with her.

What had he said?

"You do not seem to have made much of an impression."

Leopold groaned as his brother nudged him in the shoulder. "Yes, thank you, Thomas."

"I'm just saying, if you need any guidance, with the ladies, I'm your man."

"The day that I come to you for help with the ladies is the day that hell freezes over," Leopold said, attempting to force some levity in his voice as his gaze remained fixed on the door that Miss Andilet had just departed through.

His brother snorted. "Yes, I suppose that's true. Now, we cannot play cards—at least, *you* cannot play cards. With whom do you wish to converse next?"

Leopold tried to smile. *No one*, he wanted to say. *I wish to go home and think about Miss Andilet, and all I wished I could say to her.*

Chapter Five

July 11, 1840

“**A**ND YOU ARE quite certain this Lord Leopold isn’t planning on ravishing you?”

Kathleen almost dropped her parasol. *“Angela!”* She looked to either side of them, but no one seemed to have heard her sister’s scandalous words.

“Well, I’m just saying—it is not typically for a gentleman of any standing to wish to teach random young ladies how to play around with a bow and arrow,” said her sister calmly, as though she accused gentlemen of such things on a daily basis. “I mean, what does he want with you?”

It was a very good question, and not one Kathleen wished to consider on a Saturday afternoon as they walked genially down a London street.

Mostly because the thought was unlikely to lead to a positive outcome.

Either Lord Leopold did wish to ravish her, which was most objectionable and utterly scandalous…or he didn’t. Somehow, the latter option was far worse.

“I do not believe Lord Leopold is using the archery lessons as a pretense to ravish me,” Kathleen said firmly—or at least, as firmly as she could while attempting to keep her words quiet.

The last thing the Andilet sisters needed was more gossip…

“I still do not understand why he is offering to teach you in the first place,” fretted her sister as they turned a corner. “Really, Kathleen, I am most suspicious.”

Of course she was. Kathleen knew her sister was only speaking from the pain of her own scandal, but it was most irritating to be denied any sort of excitement merely because her sister had not managed to escape the gossipmongers.

Besides, Lord Leopold was not that kind of gentleman. Kathleen did not know how she knew, but she knew. She'd believed him when he'd said he was not a cheat, whatever rumors said.

"I just don't know if I should permit you to go alone," Angela said, chewing her lip. "It's bad enough Mother and Father sent us to London without a proper chaperone, but it's not too late for you. I am the elder sister. I may be ruined, but I am still supposed to keep you safe."

"Nothing is going to happen to me," Kathleen said decidedly, as though she did not wish it to. "All Lord Leopold wishes to do is…is teach me to shoot with a bow and arrow."

Because I mentioned a bet, she thought wistfully, *and I wish I had been circumspect. I wish I had created some sort of penalty, something delicious. If one's reputation was already ruined, why not enjoy it?*

She swallowed hard as they turned another corner and the London Archery Club came into view.

The two sisters halted and Angela glanced at her. "You are determined?"

Determined. It was one of the words their father had used for both of them as children—first as an encouragement, and then as a reprimand.

A shiver of uncertainty flowed up Kathleen's spine, but the mere promise of Lord Leopold's company was enough to decide her.

"We will be out in the open, where anyone can see us," she said with a brief smile. "Nothing untoward will happen, I can assure you."

"You can assure me of naught but that you have no *intentions* for anything untoward," said Angela darkly. "And what does even that matter, if people notice you are unaccompanied by a chaperone? Perhaps I should have attended Mrs. Burton's card party. Perhaps I would rest easier if I had been introduced to the gentleman."

The unsaid words between them—that Mrs. Burton's invitation had clearly not included the elder Miss Andilet, and though Kathleen had declared she would not go due to the slight, Angela had encouraged her to go regardless—hung in the air, heavy with discomfort.

Kathleen cleared her throat. "I shall not be long. You... You may accompany me, if you wish."

She certainly did *not* wish. Not that she had any indecorous intentions toward Lord Leopold, definitely not...but still. There was something delightful about being in his presence. Encountering him at Mrs. Burton's had been a shock, and her mouth had run away from her, and she had sorely embarrassed herself.

"I have even heard that the great card sharp, one of the Chance family, is in attendance tonight."

"Sadly, I have an appointment."

Kathleen blinked. "You do?"

"Do not sound so surprised," said her older sister with what she evidently thought was a smile. "Yes, I need to see a solicitor."

"A solicitor?" Kathleen tilted her head. "Did Father ask you to see his man in Town? Is he still making the payments to our landlady?"

"Yes, yes, that's all fine. Don't you worry about it. But I must go, I must meet... I would not leave you alone otherwise, but as you say, you will be in company."

She had not said that. In fact, Kathleen had been very clear to be vague on such a matter—but she was hardly going to correct Angela on that score.

"Keep your hem out of mud and yourself out of mischief. If you can," added her sister with a wry smile. "And do not have too much fun."

Kathleen swallowed the retort that Angela had not followed such sage advice. It was not kind, and she could hardly blame her sister for what had happened. It was not Angela's fault that the man had not married her.

Then her mind caught up with her. "Solicitor? Why do you need to speak to a solicitor?"

"Nothing for you to worry about," her sister said breezily. "You go and enjoy yourself."

Kathleen frowned. It was just like being at home again, in the country. *Never you mind, Kathleen. Just grown-ups sorting something out. Go and play.*

But she was a woman now, an adult, one and twenty years of age. Should she not be worried, if there was something to worry about?

Angela squeezed her hand. "I mean it. You did not have to come here due to your own disgrace; you should enjoy some merriment. Perhaps conversation with a gentleman, the son of a lord, no less, and fresh air will do you the world of good. I will see you at home later."

Before Kathleen could say a word, or remark on the fact that Angela herself was scandalously navigating around Town unaccompanied, her sister had bustled off in a completely different direction.

So. That left her…late, for her archery lesson.

"You are late," said Lord Leopold brightly as Kathleen stepped out of the back of the London Archery Club and toward the butts.

Easy as it would have been to blame the footman, she resigned herself to the truth. "I am, and I have no excuse for it."

Lord Leopold raised an eyebrow just as he lifted the bow and pulled back the string. "No excuse whatsoever?"

Kathleen thought back to the five and twenty minutes she had spent sitting before the small square of a looking glass, turning her head this way and that as she attempted to do something more interesting with her hair. She thought about the three gowns currently strewn on her bed after being tried on and discounted. She thought of the earbobs she had put on, taken off, put on again, taken off…and now could not remember whether she was wearing them or not.

"No excuse whatsoever," she said aloud, attempting to surreptitiously lift a hand to her ears. *Ah, right, I am wearing them. Good.* "You… You have started without me."

His jacket was shed, his shirt sleeves were once again most agreeably visible. Better, Kathleen watched as his muscles knotted, strained, as the bow pulled taut against him. The arrow did not shudder, remaining unbelievably still as it was held in the balance.

Kathleen found she was not breathing. It was even more difficult to take a breath when Lord Leopold suddenly let loose the bow, the arrow soaring through the air straight and true. The satisfying *thunk* of it hitting the target—the butt, as Kathleen reminded herself—was the only sound.

Lord Leopold gave out a laugh and turned back to her. "I was not sure if you would come."

"Come?" For some reason, the innocent word sounded most unruly in her mouth.

Perhaps Lord Leopold heard it too, for he colored. Or perhaps his flush was more to do with his next speech. "After the card party at Mrs. Burton's. Discovering that I am the one Society is talking about, and none too complimentarily."

Ah. Well. He did not seem to know that she had her fair share of scandal in her family and had weathered that storm relatively well.

"I… I am sorry I was the one to bring it up in our conversation," Kathleen said awkwardly.

He had not approached her, but he hardly forbidden her to come close—and she wanted to step forward, wanted to feel the warmth of his presence.

Kathleen's feet held her to the lawn. They were alone, yes, but anyone could come across them at any time. She had to remember decorum. She had to remember what happened to ladies who were found in awkward situations.

"It was only natural of you to wonder," Lord Leopold said

quietly, pulling another arrow into the bow and pulling it back, facing the butts once again.

The movement afforded Kathleen another opportunity to look at him, which was always welcome, but this time, she saw something she had never seen before.

Discomfort. True discomfort, a twitch of his jaw, a pulse in his neck—his very fine neck. A tension in his shoulders.

Lord Leopold let the arrow fly. It did not even reach the butt.

"It is not up to me to decide whether or not the gossip about you is true," Kathleen said quietly. "I know what it is to hear gossip and know it not to be true, so I would not wish to believe anything and everything I hear."

He turned to her, his eyes aglow. "You have? Known things not to be true, I mean?"

If he'd had any idea what she had overheard in the village about her own sister, he would not have asked such a thing. As, however, he clearly had not heard the scandal that had thankfully not followed them from the country to Town, Kathleen was hardly going to be the one to illuminate him.

Angela would not thank her if she were.

"I... I am afraid I panicked. At Mrs. Burton's card party," she found herself confessing instead, twisting her hands together before her. "I was... I was so embarrassed."

"You? Embarrassed?" Finally, Lord Leopold lowered the bow and stepped toward her, closing the distance between them, and Kathleen could feel her temperature rise a whole degree with every step. "But why? It was an innocent enough remark."

"But I know better than to listen to rumor and...and spite," Kathleen said, gazing into his eyes.

For it had to be spite, did it not? This was not a man who could cheat. He barely looked as though he had it in him to consider that another gentleman would cheat.

No, there was an honor in this man that went down to his very bones. He was an honorable man.

More's the pity.

"I... I thank you."

Kathleen blinked. "You thank me?"

Lord Leopold inclined his head, his smile nervous but most certainly there. "There are few in Society who would afford me such grace, or believe in my innocence so readily."

Burning heat shot through her. "I-I didn't—I mean, I would never—I-I merely meant—"

"But you came here today for an archery lesson, not one on manners or my history," Lord Leopold said brusquely, stepping from her and toward a rack of bows she had barely noticed. "Let us make a start. I'll ask you, forgive my indecorum, to remove your things."

"My-My 'things'?" Kathleen swallowed and wondered how her knees were still holding her. It was astonishing, truly, how he managed to have such an effect on her. Did he know? Had he any idea he was so intoxicating, so breathtaking in his ability to unsettle her?

He smirked. "Yes, your hat. Your gloves. It will allow you better movement and control."

"I-I see." She did as bidden, placing the items on the bench behind her.

"So," said Lord Leopold. "Here."

He thrust a bow into her hands and Kathleen gasped at the sudden weight.

"Too heavy?"

"I—I—"

"Here, let us try with this one," Lord Leopold suggested, taking the bow from her hands and immediately replacing it with another one. "Better?"

Kathleen stared at the bow in her hands.

What she wanted to say was that it was a work of art. Merely seeing one held by another, you could not fully appreciate the carved flow of the wood, the impressive balance. Why, it almost felt as though she could balance it on the end of her finger.

And the bowstring—intricate and complex, carefully woven

and remarkably crafted. It looked merely like a piece of string from a distance. This close, Kathleen could see the cleverness required to create such a thing.

"Miss Andilet?"

Kathleen looked up and said the first thing that came to her mind as she caught the gentleman's eyes. "Beautiful."

Lord Leopold blinked. "I beg your pardon?"

"It's—the bow, it's beautiful," stammered Kathleen, trying not to look at the curve of his forearm. "It's... It's art."

His eyes somehow darkened. "Now what makes you say that?"

It was not censorious, his tone, but it was curious. It made Kathleen's mouth dry and all her decisiveness not to stare at Lord Leopold's chest entirely superfluous.

"It... You can see, feel the care and attention that has been lathered on it," she found herself saying, moving the bow about in her hands, wondering at the beauty of it. "It's art, yes, but it's also a tool. Perhaps the bringing together of both art and tool is what makes it so...so beautiful."

Kathleen looked up, her words now failing her, and saw something flicker across Lord Leopold's face. *Pleasure? Confusion?*

"I have never heard anyone speak of it like that, Miss Andilet," he said quietly.

The formality of the address somehow rankled. "Please. 'Kathleen.'"

It was most definitely not the sort of invitation to intimacy that her sister would have approved of, but it was too late to recant. Besides, Kathleen did not want to.

Here, on the impressive lawn of the London Archery Club, with no one around them and the struggles and difficulties of retaining their social standing, Kathleen could just be Kathleen. She had always been Miss Kathleen. Her sister was Miss Andilet.

Not that the formality had protected *her*...

"In that case, I suppose you should call me 'Leopold,'" said Lord Leopold quietly.

How had he managed to get so close to her? Kathleen's breath caught in her throat as she realized that Lord Leopold—Leopold, a name which she could absolutely not speak without its prefix—was standing so close to her.

He reached out, a hand caressing the bow just as her own hand moved up it. Their fingers touched and heat and power and crackle sparked between them.

Kathleen rocked back on her heels but managed to stay upright.

Did he feel it too?

As she lifted her eyes to meet his, she could not tell. Lord Leopold—Leopold—was closed to her, his expression void.

"So," he said, and perhaps there was a winded quality to it, "let us work on your stance. It would be so much easier, I suppose, if I could see your legs."

Heat blossomed up within Kathleen.

"Not that I would ask—I mean, obviously I can't ask you to… Never mind," Leopold said hastily, cheeks pinking.

To see him so easily overcome by awkwardness… It was most attractive.

And confusing, Kathleen could not help but think. Here was a man who was completely content in himself, a powerful man, a man with a presence that made her weak at the knees and wish to goodness she had lost her reputation already so she did not mind ruining it a little more…

Yet there was a humility to him. Lord Leopold Chance sometimes got his tongue in a tangle, and it was most endearing.

Perhaps *too* endearing.

"My stance," Kathleen said quietly, trying not to smile.

Leopold's cheeks were still pink. "Yes. So, you'll want to have your left foot forward, like so."

He demonstrated, giving her the perfect excuse to stare at his legs. And mighty fine legs they were. His trousers were of the fashionable cut, tighter than they were being worn in the country, and as Kathleen's gaze traveled upward…

"Yes, you'll see that my hips are twisted like so," Leopold continued.

Kathleen swallowed—hard. "Yes. Yes, I see."

There was something buzzing in the air, a sort of lightning but without the thunder. An electricity, a sharpness, a metallic taste in her mouth and a tingling between her thighs.

"Now, you'll want to raise your bow like this."

Kathleen suddenly recalled she was holding a bow. Yes, because she was having an archery lesson. Because of a bet. No other reason.

"Like—like this?" she said quickly, mimicking him as she lifted the bow up to her chest.

Leopold straightened up, stepping out of his archer's stance, and examined her critically. Then his eyes widened, his lips parted as unrestrained desire flickered over his face.

Ah. Yes.

"I… I suppose it gets more complicated," he said, his voice hoarse to Kathleen's ears. "When there is… Ahem. Something in the way."

The *something* in the way was her bosom. Kathleen had never particularly enjoyed her very full bust, a characteristic she shared with her mother. Gowns and blouses never quite covered it up sufficiently, always threatening to burst through buttons and erupt through stays.

It appeared that a large bust was also rather inconvenient in the practice of archery.

"Ah," said Leopold in a strangled voice, his focus fixed powerfully on Kathleen's hand on the bowstring. Her hand on the bowstring that was pressed against her right breast.

Kathleen immediately let the bow fall to her side. "If you do not think it possible—"

"No, no, I just… Please, forgive me."

And he truly looked as though he wished to be forgiven. Indeed, he was walking forward, standing to her left, and looking most…

Well. *Eager* was not quite the right word, but it was not far off.

"If… If you will permit me to assist you?" Leopold said quietly.

Kathleen looked up into his eyes and saw nothing but innocence mingled with wickedness. How that was possible, she did not know, but she could see in that moment that Lord Leopold Chance was fighting two equally strong desires: to assist her with archery, and to touch her.

And if the two desires could be combined…

"Yes, please," said Kathleen, her mouth dry and her pulse thumping in her ears. "I would be grateful for your assistance."

She had to prevent herself from whimpering as Leopold wrapped his arms around her, placing his hands over her own on the bow. When he—when *they* lifted up the bow, it was almost like being embraced by a stranger.

No, not a stranger. There was something so familiar, so deliciously comfortable about being held like this by Leopold.

Kathleen breathed in, breathed him in, a mingling of bergamot and cedar and something that was uniquely Leopold, and wondered once again how her legs were holding up.

His pulse—she could feel his pulse in her hand, and it was thundering just like her own. His mouth was close to her ear, and when he—when *they* pulled the bowstring back, his thumb grazed her breast.

An accident, of course, Kathleen told herself, mind spinning, head giddy.

An accident, that Leopold brushed his lips against her ear. Her neck.

An accident, that his thumb once again grazed her breast. It was certainly not his fault that Kathleen uttered a low moan, the sensation of his touch sparking a need within her she had never felt before.

An accident, that she lowered the bow and twisted in his arms and his lips were ready, pressing against hers, pressing decadence onto her very soul as Leopold kissed her.

Kissed her passionately—his arms were still around her and were now drawing her closer, the bow forgotten by them both. Kathleen whimpered with pleasure as his mouth worked her own, parting her lips, silently requesting entrance. Entrance she gave him.

The instant his tongue swirled bliss through her mouth, she clung to him, the bow dropping to the ground, but Kathleen did not care.

She was being kissed. Thoroughly kissed, passionately kissed, by a man from a noble family with his own scandalous reputation, in the middle of the day—in broad daylight!—where anyone could come across them.

Where anyone could come across them.

Kathleen broke the kiss, broke free of Leopold's embrace, and broke the moment. "I am so sorry, I did not mean to—"

"'Sorry'?" repeated Leopold. He looked a little dazed, truth be told. "'Sorry'?"

"Yes, I—I should have been listening to your most interesting instruction, and not getting lost in—I mean, carried away by… this."

Did he have to look at her like that? As though she were the most delicious thing he had ever tasted? As though he wanted her back in his arms?

Fighting off the impulse, Kathleen tried to laugh. "Not very sporting of me, distracting you like that so that I can win our bet!"

It was a foolish thing to say. She did not believe it, did not mean it—but what was even more foolish was that Leopold, his back stiffening, the lump at this throat bobbing, appeared to accept it.

"Ah. Right, I see," he said ruefully, leaning down to pick up the discarded bow. "I should have guessed, Miss Andilet."

Miss Andilet.

Yes, that is the price of playing with a man, Kathleen thought with a sinking heart. And she was not—she had never—

He had been her first kiss.

And now she had ruined it by pretending that it had all been an act. A trick.

"Let us practice your draw," Leopold said quietly. He handed her the bow and stepped back, clearly unwilling to tempt himself again.

Kathleen swallowed, the absence of him unsettling. "Right. Yes. My draw."

Chapter Six

July 15, 1840

L EOPOLD INHALED SLOWLY, deeply, feeling his chest rise and expand and fill with the calming, hot summer air. The bow in his hands moved slightly, but as he blew out the breath, slow and steady, his arms stilled.

The perfect moment.

That was what his old archery tutor had spoken to him about. The perfect moment, the perfect balance between inhaling and exhaling, when you realized there was a stillness within you that went beyond just not moving.

A stillness that told you that you were precisely where you needed to be, when you needed to be there.

Leopold searched for it, straining for the balance, seeking the perfect moment.

It did not come. He loosed the arrow.

"I knew I'd find you here," came a cheerful voice.

Leopold did not need to turn around to recognize it. "What are you doing here?"

"Cannot a man go searching for his little brother?" said Thomas, grinning as he stepped between Leopold and the butt, which had been hit squarely in the center.

It was a challenge not to roll his eyes. *"Little brother*—I am six and twenty years old!"

"You're fifteen months younger than me, so I am afraid you will always be my little brother," rejoined Thomas with a laugh. "And don't get too irritated, because I've brought with me… a surprise."

"It's been years since I've been here," came the quiet voice of the Dowager Duke of Cothrom. "It hasn't changed a bit."

Leopold straightened up, tension immediately coursing through his shoulders. "Father. What an honor."

And it was, in a way. Oh, William Chance was hardly a recluse; he liked his routines, that was all, and archery had never factored into his routines, as far as Leopold could remember.

Wait—the archery club hasn't changed a bit?

"I suppose old Cooper is still here," said Leopold's father with a dry laugh, his salt-and-pepper hair no hindrance to his good looks. "He once had to reprimand your Uncle John for shooting at him in the dark. Uncle John thought he was a fox."

"Surely, Cooper cannot have been here all those years later," Leopold pointed out.

"I believe it is the grandson of the former Cooper who now serves as footman," Thomas explained. "Is that not right, Father?"

It was all Leopold could do to quell his smile.

He liked his brother—he really did, which he knew made them unusual in the noble families of England. Thomas was a good man; a trifle irritating at times, and altogether far too eager to please their parents, but there it was. Yes, he'd risked then spent the family fortune; yes, he'd then married a fortune and somehow managed to make the woman fall in love with him; and yes, it had turned out that Thomas' spendthrift ways had actually been to support an orphanage, which had only endeared him further to the family.

That was how it was with Chances, Leopold thought ruefully. There was always more to the story.

"Hmm. I dare say you are correct," replied their father with a nonchalant shrug. "Is this where you have been spending all your time, Leopold? We hardly see you anymore, your mother and I. You would be a useful chaperone for Maude."

It was not a rebuke, not as such. As the sun poured down and sweat threatened at his temples, Leopold knew that if it were a rebuke, he would be in absolutely no doubt.

But it was not far shy of a rebuke. He had responsibilities—they all did. They were Chances. They had to appear in Society, had to make good names for themselves and uphold the family name…

It was all so trying—especially when he could be here, practicing his archery.

"I've been mostly here, Father," he said aloud. "I recently assisted Cousin Evelyn in a painting too. But I hope I have not neglected Mama and Maude overly much."

"Hmm," said his father.

It was worse than affirmation. At least then, Leopold could have debated the point with him.

"I am afraid I have commitments here," Leopold said quickly, as though that could explain his absence from the family home. "I… I am teaching someone archery."

It was immediate, the stiffening, the discomfort, the look of mortification on the dowager duke's face. "Leopold Chance, you are *working?*"

"No! No, not at all, no money changes hands. It is a pastime, not a profession," Leopold said hastily.

God forbid one of the Chances work for their bread.

They were nobility. Beyond gentry, most definitely beyond those who had to work for a living or had the ignominy of working in trade.

His father's features softened, but only slightly. "Oh. A favor, then, for a gentleman who never had an archery tutor of his own?"

Precisely what made him stay silent, Leopold did not know. He certainly could have corrected his father. It would not have been difficult.

"I don't believe it," said Thomas.

Leopold turned to his brother with wide eyes. "You do not believe I would make a suitable teacher?"

Thomas had picked up a bow and was waving it about in a

most uncouth manner. "Oh, it's not that—I just don't think you have the patience for it, that's all. Teaching. I feel sorry for the poor man who is receiving your instruction."

"We do not know how inexperienced the gentleman is," pointed out their father—fairly, Leopold thought, though the guilt of not correcting them weighed heavily on him. "It could be that Leopold is actually quite patient with someone outside the family."

"No, I don't believe it, and there is naught you can do to persuade me." Thomas grinned, whirling the bow around in his hands in a most distracting way.

Leopold glanced down at his pocket watch before returning it to his waistcoat. It was ten past the hour. That meant that any moment now—

"Leopold, I am sorry I am late, I—oh."

He smiled, his expression surely tighter than was polite, as Miss Kathleen Andilet approached the trio of gentlemen almost at a run. Skirts flying, cheeks pink, a curl of hair that had escaped from her hat and was descending down her elegant shoulders…

Leopold cleared his throat. "Father, may I present to you Miss Kathleen Andilet…my pupil. Miss Andilet, His Grace the Dowager Duke of Cothrom."

"Your father?" Kathleen said in horror.

"Your pupil?" his father said with just as much horror.

The two looked at each other, evidently astounded at the other person's existence.

Thomas walked over to Leopold and nudged him in the arm with a grin. "What have you done, Leopold?"

Leopold wasn't sure. This was either the worst idea in the world, or the cleverest. His father may take offense at the entire situation, offering a taut politeness that would quell any potential for—

Potential for what?

"I haven't done anyone. Anything," he added hastily under his breath, trying to ignore his brother's chuckle.

"Your Grace," murmured Kathleen as she lowered herself into a deep curtsey.

"Miss Andilet," said Leopold's father, inclining his head. He did not bow.

Leopold's throat knotted as he watched Kathleen straighten and look up, pink in the face, at the strained response from his father.

What was I thinking? This was a disaster. Not that he had any reason for introducing Kathleen to his family. Not that the kiss they had shared had meant anything—she had said herself, it had been naught but a tease.

Not that he had spent the last few days thinking about it, unable to stop, unable to remove from his mind the softness and the eagerness and the—

"Well, I must depart," said his father curtly. "My brothers require a great deal of management, and I must see them about a certain scandal. Miss Andilet. Come, Thomas."

"Duty calls," Leopold's brother said with a grin as he began to stride away. "Delighted to make your acquaintance, Miss Andilet."

"Oh, yes, acquaintance—hello. Your Grace." She curtsied again hastily. "The duke?" She looked to Leopold, who nodded, his tongue too tied to make the proper introduction.

Thomas looked about the place, though there was no one else in sight. "I suppose you could tell me your chaperone is somewhere around a corner here, is she?" He directed an arched brow at Leopold specifically. Feeling all the more like the *little* brother, despite what he'd said earlier, Leopold couldn't help but swallow.

"Oh, uh... I *could* tell you that," she said helplessly as the two most senior Chance gentlemen strode away from them, Thomas a distance behind the dowager duke and snickering all the while. "But it wouldn't be true," she whispered, the truth spilling out to herself and Leopold only.

Leopold wondered whether it would be possible to merely

sink into the ground and become a part of the lawn. It would certainly be better than remaining here to look at the woman he had thoroughly kissed, and who had then been almost entirely snubbed by his father.

Perhaps she had not noticed. Perhaps she was more gentry than nobility. Or more country than Town.

Kathleen turned to him with pink cheeks. "Your father is very…very commanding."

Leopold threw out his chest and attempted to be nothing but nonchalant. It did not work. "Yes. Yes. He is."

"I am sorry."

He blinked. *Sorry.* "I beg your pardon?"

Kathleen was smiling but there was pain in the smile, not joy. "I embarrass you—my name. I mean, your father clearly knew… And your brother, he was hinting…"

"My father is like that with most people," Leopold said honestly. "And my brother is just as you saw him, too." And then, "Your name, what do you mean by that?"

"Nothing," Kathleen said hastily, her smile broadening as she laughed. "Nothing, I am speaking nonsense, do not mind me. Still, I am sorry that I put you in that position."

"I am the one who is sorry. My father is a bit cold to strangers. Especially in unexpected situations. And my brother is a tease."

They both fell into silence, the tension between them achingly sharp.

Leopold knew there were words, words he could say, perhaps even *should* say, but he could not comprehend what they could be. All he could think of was that kiss. It was hard to believe it had only been days ago—days filled with longing and repressed anger over the fact that she had so easily swayed him.

That she had played him, in truth, like the fool of a man he was.

How had a woman had such an impact on him? How was it possible that he should be so affected by her?

And why had she looked so discomforted when introduced to her father? They... They did not know each other, did they?

"I... I feel myself a mite fatigued from our last lesson," Kathleen said awkwardly, struggling to remove her gloves before placing them on the bench beside her. There was something about her, something unnerved. "In fact, I think it would be best if we—"

"Yes, we cannot have you overstretching yourself," Leopold said, grasping at the possibility to spend time in Kathleen's presence without risking a repeat of that kiss. Precisely why he wanted, why he *needed* to be in her presence, he was not going to investigate. "Shall we take a walk?"

Her eyelids fluttered. "A... A walk?"

He had not believed it to be such a ridiculous suggestion, but clearly, it was a surprising one.

Kathleen's face was a picture. A picture rather like one Evelyn could paint, Leopold could not help but think. His cousin was a talented artist, indeed, but the longer he looked at Miss Kathleen Andilet, the more he realized there was something about her that simply could not be replicated on canvas.

It was the intelligence—no, it was more than that. Something about the eyes. Something that seemed to suggest she was about to laugh at any moment, but not at someone's expense.

Here was a woman who saw the joy in the world, even if it was hard to find. Even if it was sometimes out of reach.

Even if she had to make the joy herself.

"Yes, a walk. I think—I mean, I can continue to teach you about archery, while you rest your arms," Leopold said, suddenly realizing he had been staring at the young woman some moments in silence. "If... If you want to, that is. I am sure you have many calls on your time. Many suitors."

What had possessed him to say the latter phrase, Leopold did not know.

It was senseless. Foolish, really—a desperate attempt to gain an answer to a question he could not bring himself to ask.

Kathleen appeared to know. Her half smile was too knowing, truth be told, as she started to walk slowly to the left so that they encircled the butts. "Yes, indeed. Many suitors. Far too many."

The jolt of jealousy and anger was one Leopold had not expected, but it felt wholly natural. The thought of another man courting Miss Andilet—of kissing her, of perhaps more… Did she meet other men without a chaperone present, so brazenly, so boldly?

"You are quiet," she said softly.

"I am often quiet," said Leopold without thinking. He laughed, his nerves forcing their way out. "I am sorry, Miss Andilet."

"I thought we agreed that I was to be Kathleen, and you were to be Leopold?" She did not look at him as she spoke the words, preferring, it seemed, to look directly ahead of her.

Leopold swallowed. "Yes. Yes, we did."

It was an intimacy far beyond that of a kiss. For a gentleman, the son of a former duke, to be addressed by his first name…

"You said you are often quiet," she said. "You spoke to me boldly enough, when we first met."

The memory softened the tension within him, and Leopold's smile was genuine now. "Whenever I have a bow in my hand or I have recently been shooting, I feel…more myself. As though I am solely myself. Does that make sense?"

"It makes sense, though I have little experience of it," Kathleen said quietly.

A few other gentlemen had stepped out of the club and were approaching the rack of bows. Leopold thanked her silently for agreeing to his walk. He would not have enjoyed the gentle or not-so-gentle teasing they would undoubtedly have received had they stayed. As it was, he hoped the men didn't look their way— or if they did, that they confused Kathleen for his cousin or sister.

He was well aware he should not be alone with her—his brother had picked up on the fact that this wasn't the first time, either. But he couldn't help himself. He had a feeling that if he pushed the issue, Kathleen would simply slip away.

"Archery, then, is your passion."

Passion. Such a word, spoken so innocently by an innocent young lady, should not have enflamed a man. But it had.

"Argh," said Leopold inarticulately. Clearing his throat, he tried again as they turned a corner, meandering away from the butts and more toward the woodland. "I mean, yes. All sport is, really. It sounds terrible, but I can think of no better way to put it. I have always preferred sport to people."

"To people?"

Leopold shrugged. "My parents and siblings excluded, I suppose. I mean, when you are focused on your sport—hunting, or billiards, or boxing, but I prefer archery over all else—then all one's problems fade away. One cannot concentrate on them, you see. One cannot even acknowledge they exist. They melt away for you are focused on something different. Better. Higher."

When he realized that nothing followed his remark but silence, he glanced to his side. Kathleen was smiling, but it was not a mocking smile, or a teasing one.

"You speak as though you refer to God."

He could not help but laugh at that. "I suppose in a way, it is not a dissimilar feeling to that of being in church. Connecting to something larger than you, I mean, higher than you, more than you could simply be on your own."

"You feel that while you shoot?"

"When I have a bow in my hand," Leopold said, the words flowing from him now, easily, without thought, "and an arrow in the other, it is as if I stand atop a precipice with no concerns of falling. I know I can fly at any moment, and indeed, the sensation when I knock an arrow into place..."

It was like flying. Like ecstasy, and passion, and complete calm. Like he had never felt with anything else before.

Only then did he realize that the last few words had not been spoken aloud.

"It is like...like searching for meaning in your life and then finding it, and it was in your hands all along," Leopold finished, a tad lamely. "I am sure that sounds preposterous."

"No, not in the slightest." Kathleen's words were warm, and she slipped her hand into Leopold's arm without hesitation.

The weight of her was…comforting. More than comforting. It filled an emptiness Leopold had not known was there.

"All my life, I have sought meaning," he found himself saying as they continued to walk, the woodland giving them shade from the oppressive heat of the day. "I am a second son, and if my brother and his wife continue on like they are doing, I shall soon be several sons away from the title—a title I do not particularly want."

"You are unusual in that, I presume," Kathleen said with a grin. "My impression of the nobility is that most brothers hope their eldest never has an heir."

Leopold made a face, attempting to show through it his distaste for such a thought. "A title… It brings nothing but duty and responsibility, and I have seen the weight with which that has burdened by father. My brother, being made duke while our father still lives, I can already see the change in him, though slight. But in a way, I envy him."

"The title?"

It was difficult to put into words and Leopold had never attempted it before. Never found himself in a conversation like this, where it would feel natural to say it.

"No, I mean…the purpose."

Kathleen squeezed his arm, a silent encouragement to continue, and Leopold wished to thank her for it but found he could not.

Instead, he said, "My brother Thomas, he has a purpose. A direction, a meaning for his life. He will live and work for it all his days, I know he will, and he will do well. And when he dies and his son takes up the mantle, my brother will go down in family history, English history, even, perhaps, as a man who served his country. Served his family. Served the title."

What was he doing, spouting all this nonsense?

Kathleen did not appear to think it was nonsense. She was smiling, nodding her head elegantly in a way that made him remember just what it was to brush a kiss against that neck.

"You seek determination."

"Being a second son has its advantages. Do not mistake me," Leopold said with a chuckle. "But knowing there is no path for me, that there never can be one… Archery fills that gap within me, that ache I have for a sense of direction. I cannot explain it any better."

"I think you have explained it well." Kathleen's voice was low, as though they shared secrets. And did they not?

As they turned a corner around the woodland, the London Archery Club disappearing momentarily out of sight, Leopold exhaled. "I have never felt the entire weight of my father's expectations, and he is…not a harsh man, but a direct one. He is clear in his prospects."

"My father is much the same," said Kathleen, her smile faltering. "But you should try being a daughter of any birth order, not just a second son. It would not matter if I did find something like archery, something that sparked my pulse and gave me a sense of purpose. I could not pursue it."

She spoke quietly, calmly, as though she were merely remarking on the weather. Already, Leopold knew her better than that. He could see the tension momentarily tightening her jaw. Hear the forced lightness.

Sense the sadness.

"You are restricted by being a woman," he said quietly.

"I am restricted by Society," Kathleen countered with a rueful smile. "But as I cannot change Society, I have learned, in the main, to embrace what I can do. Come to London. Walk without a chaperone with relative ease. Learn archery."

There was a teasing smile in her voice and Leopold could not help but squeeze her arm—something he knew immediately was far too forward.

"Archery is not a bad passion to discover," he said quietly. "It is an ancient skill, one practiced by all peoples across all history, as far as I can make out. We have stories about archers who have lasted generations, do we not? Robin Hood, who stole from the rich to give to the poor."

"William Tell and his apple," said Kathleen with a laugh. "Palnatoke."

The recognition of the unusual name spurred Leopold to smile in turn. "Fancy *you* knowing about Palnatoke!"

"I read," Kathleen said, her cheeks pinking. "Especially now I am making such impressive progress with a bow."

Their laughter mingled through the hot summer air and Leopold felt a tug in his loins that had nothing to do with lust and everything to do with…with more than lust.

"Diana," added Kathleen, brushing a curl from her eyes. "And her hunts."

"Cupid," said Leopold without thinking.

Their laughter halted.

At least, his did. There was still laughter dancing in Kathleen's eyes, eyes he could not tear his own gaze away from, but Leopold did not know if she was laughing with him or at him.

At him, surely. He was being a fool, a capital fool, and if he was not careful, he was going to do something ridiculous.

Like kiss her again.

Not that she wanted him to. She had only accepted his kisses as a jest, he tried to remember.

"Your passion…"

Leopold swallowed, his mouth dry. "I beg your pardon?"

"For archery. Your passion for archery, it is remarkable," Kathleen said, looking away as they started to walk back to the club. "Inspiring, even. I admit I begin to feel a flutter at the subject now myself."

"Well, do not let it go to your head," he tried to joke. "Not that I have ever gone to anyone's head in the past."

"Haven't you?" Her perfect, round mouth fell open.

It was an innocent enough question, except Leopold had never felt less innocent in his thoughts in all his life.

There she was, looking up at him, asking him such a question, and she was touching him, no gloves, her hand on his bare forearm, and for a moment, just a moment—

Leopold could not breathe. The balance: it was here. It was her. The world was stilled, stilled in a way he had never known before. There she was, and there he was, standing together, not walking—precisely when they had stopped walking, he had no idea—and he did not need to breathe in or not, there was just this moment, this perfect moment.

Kathleen laughed awkwardly and pulled her hand from his arm. "I have taken up your precious time, my lord. You undoubtedly wished to accompany your brother and father on their errands. I should not have kept you."

Keep me, Leopold wanted to murmur. *Keep me, I could be yours if you wanted me.*

"And look at me, out here without my gloves!" She laughed delicately. "I suppose there's no going back for them now. Not with all those people there." So she had noticed them, too.

"Of course," he said aloud, mouth dry, hating himself for saying nothing. "It's probably best you don't. Good day, Miss Andilet. Miss Kathleen."

Chapter Seven

July 17, 1840

"**Y**OU'RE READY."

"I am not ready."

"What have all these preparations been for, if not to prepare you for such a moment?"

Easy for him to say. Kathleen's arm quivered as she maintained the bow draw, the arrow balanced upon her fingers shaking as she struggled to maintain her steadiness.

She was standing about twenty feet from the butt. It was a shameful distance, all told. She had seen Leopold draw at least four times farther back than this—but as he rightly had pointed out, she had no strength in her arms.

Kathleen could still recall the shock of heat that had flowed through her at the sudden realization that Leopold had been looking at her arms.

She glanced at them again now. She had never given her arms much thought, not until a nobleman had. A nobleman with a terrible reputation who would surely be pushed beyond the brink of ruin once it was widely known that he was spending copious time with her.

"You have to trust yourself, Kathleen."

Kathleen swallowed as waves of heat poured over her. Thank goodness she could blame the weather—the sun had been blazing all morning.

But she could not lie to herself. She knew the burning, twist-ing feeling inside her was due only to Lord Leopold Chance's close proximity. The way he was looking at her. The intensity of his attention, which was not to admire, no matter how much she may have wished it.

No, Leopold always examined her with the careful eye of a tutor, nothing more. It was somewhat disheartening, but then, Kathleen was hardly an expert in the wooing of gentlemen.

And yes, she'd kissed him. Or he'd kissed her. She could hardly recall, her memories swirling not with thoughts, but with sensations.

"I'll miss," she said quietly.

Leopold's gentle chuckle was far closer behind her than she had expected. "Yes, you'll always miss."

Kathleen almost let the arrow down at that remark. "Then why teach me?"

"You'll always miss, if you never let free the arrow," came his quiet reply.

It was difficult to argue with that.

Kathleen inhaled deeply and tried to remember everything Leopold had taught her. It had been a great deal, which was why it was only now that he was allowing her to let loose her first arrow.

Careful of your stance. Do not twist your ankle overly. Knees nice and supple. Reduce the tension in your shoulders—it could be done by willpower alone, apparently, not that Kathleen had much luck with that.

Breathe deeply, but slowly. Allow your hands to be rigid, but not so rigid as to prevent the bow from its natural movements. Lean into what the bow wants. The bow wants to clasp the arrow, then it wants to release it.

Kathleen blew out, slowly. Leopold stepped to the side, mere inches from her, his gaze trained on her lips.

Which was more than a little distracting.

Far before she had intended to, Kathleen let go. The arrow, unprepared as it was, soared—

About seven feet. And not in the direction of the butt.

Leopold's chuckle was both warming and infuriating. "Well, for a first try, not bad."

"Do not speak to me," Kathleen warned as she lowered the bow and rolled her aching shoulder.

"But for a novice—"

"I *said*, do not speak to me," repeated Kathleen, trying to keep her tone light as her pulse quickened.

Leopold's smile was far too enticing, damn him. "You should have seen my first attempt."

Try as she might, she could not glare at that. "Was it as terrible as mine?"

He was laughing now as he took the bow from her and examined the bowstring. "Let us just say, I did not manage to let the arrow fly."

"You did not?"

Leopold shook his head wryly. "I dropped both arrow and bow in my frustration. I could not draw back, as you do. I had not the strength."

Now that was more like it. Kathleen was not one to demand compliments; she had not led a life of a lady in fashionable Society in London or Bath or Brighton. But she was human. It was most pleasant to be positively compared to a young Leopold.

Wait a moment. A young Leopold.

"Precisely how old were you," Kathleen asked tentatively, "when you first attempted this?"

It was the twinkle in his eyes that told her before Leopold even opened his mouth. "Oh, I don't know. Four. Perhaps five years old."

Kathleen did not even think—she did not have to. The numerous archery lessons had developed between them a comfort she had never experienced with another.

Nudging him hard with her shoulder, she said, "How can you compare myself, a full one and twenty, with yourself at four years old!"

He was laughing now, and she was laughing too, and for a

moment, Kathleen could forget the scandal of her sister, the distance from her family, the pittance she lived on and the frustration of her own prospects.

It was merely herself and Leopold laughing and teasing each other on a splendid lawn with the summer sun beating down on them.

That was surely the reason that when they ceased laughing, Leopold was remarkably close. Standing very close, truth be told. Far closer than was necessary.

Not as close as she would want.

Kathleen swallowed the memories of that kiss, a kiss she regretted not for the sake of the kiss itself, but for its aftermath, and took a hesitant step away. He did not follow her.

It's all in your mind, Kathleen Andilet, she told herself sternly as Leopold carefully replaced the bow she had been using on the rack. *The man kissed you, to be sure, which probably happened to lots of people, and he clearly has no wish to repeat it. He was a lord—surely a rake! Do not daydream. Do not allow yourself to believe nonsense.*

"Well, I believe we can make it official," said Leopold casually.

Kathleen dropped the arrow she had just pulled out of the ground. "We can?"

"I think it's been a sufficient amount of time," he said, turning and examining her critically. "Don't you?"

All she could do was gape. What the…? He could not mean what she thought he meant. Could he?

They had not spoken of matrimony. They had not spoken of the future much at all, choosing to shy away from such topics, she knew not why.

Perhaps because Kathleen knew she could not tell him of the misfortune her sister had found herself in. Perhaps because having heard the story of his own particular scandal—not that it was much, as far as she could see—he did not wish to tempt fate.

But now he was suggesting... Was he not?

"I...I do not know what to say," Kathleen said helplessly,

leaning down to pick up the arrow again and twisting it in her fingers.

There was more than a hint of mischief in Leopold's eyes. "You do not think so?"

She was entirely lost, and in truth, it was not very sporting of him to tease her this way. The fact that she enjoyed it so much was neither here nor there.

"As I said, I believe we can make it official," he said, leaning against the rack and crossing his arms over his chest. His strong, shapely forearms over his broad chest.

Kathleen swallowed. Her mouth was inexplicably dry, and she found herself taking a few steps toward him. The need to be close to him...she did not wish to examine it too closely, but it was most certainly there.

"You... You do?"

Leopold nodded, his lopsided, teasing smile broadening. "I think you are officially the worst archer in the history of the London Archery Club."

Kathleen's face collapsed into laughter as relief—and disappointment—flooded through her.

She hadn't actually thought he'd been about to... No, he would never have. They were not even officially courting. Yes, they had spent a great deal of time together, and alone. Without a chaperone. There had been a possibility that someone would have demanded he marry her. Her sister? Her father?

Oh, it had been a foolish thought, indeed, and not one she should have entertained for one single minute.

"I protest," she said aloud, hoping her smile did not indicate the myriad thoughts that had flown through her mind. "Considering that I have only been learning a couple of weeks, I believe I am doing quite well!"

"You think?" asked Leopold as he picked up a few stray arrows they had discarded as part of their lesson.

"I do," Kathleen said firmly, knowing that this was flirtation on her side, and surely his own, and deciding not to care. "I know which way around to hold a bow. I would suppose that it took four-year-old Leopold much longer to ascertain that."

His laughter was like a reward for a hard-won battle, and she luxuriated in it. There was something…something so freeing, so relaxed about Leopold when he was laughing. She had noticed it last week; when he laughed, all the cares of the world seemed to melt away from his shoulders, his forehead smoothing, the lilting smile he treated her with somehow broader.

And then the laughter faded, and all the cares appeared to rush back, and he returned to being someone who had burdens he could not carry.

"Yes, well, you are improving. The first shot you take is always the worst, I find," Leopold said, replacing the arrows in the rack. "It's onward and upward from here on out."

"You think?" Kathleen had not meant to echo him, nor to sound so wistful.

This bet of theirs—it was foolish, now she came to think on it. She liked this man, liked him far beyond what was acceptable, but she would certainly never expect anything from him.

And she was lonely. Hard though it was to admit, Angela was not able to be her sole companionship. Not for the rest of their lives.

Oh, heaven forbid.

It was pleasant, to find a friend. To make one.

Whether Leopold considered her a friend… No, almost certainly not. A gentleman always had more friends than a lady; he could go more places, speak to more people, and besides, he was the son of a duke! Kathleen was no expert, but she presumed it was far easier for sons of dukes to befriend people than daughters of country gentlemen who were accompanying their disgraced sisters to London.

"Well, that brings today's lesson to an end," said Leopold quietly, his voice breaking into her thoughts.

"It is a shame," Kathleen said honestly. "I was enjoying it— though I agree, to save my poor shoulder."

"Is it truly that bad?"

Before she could say anything, before she could think, Leopold had stepped over to her.

It was all Kathleen could do not to moan. That would hardly do, and besides, it may draw out spectators from the club.

And that was the last thing she wanted. Not while Leopold's fingers were pressing deep into her shoulder and arm, a pressure that from anyone else would have been most unwelcome, but somehow, from him…

"Oh, dear God," she murmured, unable to help herself.

Leopold's low chuckle was far too close and far too familiar. "I discovered a method of massaging some of the life back into the shoulder after a long session at the butts."

Kathleen tried not to think about one particular butt as his fingers stroked and caressed and pressed into her shoulder. "H-How interesting."

Her eyes had closed unconsciously, and all she could think about was the movement of his thumb slowly down her shoulder blade, the way his ungloved fingers were brushing along her arm before digging mercilessly into her flesh.

This should not be happening. A gentleman should absolutely not be touching a lady like this—and where anyone could see us!

She would weep when it was over.

"How does that feel?"

Heavenly. Blissful. As though I want you to touch me like this all over. "Fine," managed Kathleen.

"I know my technique is a mite inexpert," said Leopold with a wry chuckle. "But I hope that you will feel the benefit of it tomorrow."

She was certainly feeling the benefit of it now. Dear Lord, she could remain like this forever.

The door to the club opened, its hinges creaking. Kathleen's eyes snapped open at the precise moment that Leopold's fingers left her. He stepped back, creating a distance between them of mere feet.

It was enough.

"We should depart," said Leopold in a low voice.

Kathleen nodded, trying not to show her disappointment at their lack of contact in her eyes, nor the disappointment in the fact that he clearly did not wish to be seen with her.

Which was all to the good, she tried to tell herself as she adjusted her hat and gloves and they walked in silence back to the club, the gentlemen now stepping up to the butts staring at them curiously. It was good that no gossip nor slander could be created about them. It was good that Leopold would never be put in the awkward position of being forced to marry her. Yes. Yes, that was good.

It felt terrible, but it was good.

Stepping past the footman Cooper and onto the bustling street was a most disconcerting sensation. For almost an hour, Kathleen could have believed she'd been back in the countryside again, the place she loved. But now she was standing with carriages and horses racing past her, copious noise, people rushing past along the pavement. It was all too much.

"May I walk you home?"

Kathleen almost tripped over her skirts. A hand lunged forward, clasping her waist, and she was righted. Her skin burned under numerous petticoats.

Leopold was standing right beside her, his arm around her waist steadying her. He was looking into her eyes, a blazing look that she could not describe.

He let go. "Careful."

She had never wished to be less careful in her life. "Y-Yes. Yes, thank you."

"Let me walk you home," Leopold said cheerfully, as though he frequently offered this to a number of ladies without chaperones in sight.

With a sinking feeling, Kathleen realized that he may well have done just that. At least the escorting part, if not the lack of chaperone. "Oh, no, it's not necessary."

"I know it's not necessary. I am offering to," he said simply. "Left or right?"

That was one of the things about Leopold, she thought as she wordlessly pointed to their left and started to walk sedately. It was not that he could not take *no* for an answer. He just did not understand the answer, and therefore he ignored it. From any other gentleman, it would have been a most off-putting trait. Somehow, because it was Leopold, Kathleen found she did not mind.

"You said you had not been in London long," Leopold said conversationally as they waited for a few carriages to pass before they crossed a street. "Did you come with your whole family?"

A knot twisted in her stomach and Kathleen tried to smile. "No."

This was a mistake. Only too late did she recall that this man was a duke's son. She could not expect him to walk her home when home was most definitely in the wrong part of London.

"No? Did you come with parents, or siblings?" Leopold's chatter was aimless, he was not seeking to entrap her. Was he? "I myself have three siblings, and I cannot tell you how pleasant it has been since Thomas married and brought Victoria into our household."

Kathleen tried to smile, though the tension building within her made that difficult. She used the excuse of a busy pavement where they could not walk side by side as a reason to cease speaking, but the moment they could walk together again, he picked up the conversation.

"So, why did you come to London in the first place?" It was barefaced curiosity in his expression, a soft, openness to his features, nothing more. "For the Season? But you did mention you were only lately in Town."

Well, it was only a matter of time before he heard the truth, anyway. Kathleen was astonished he had not heard of the scandal before now—Andilet was hardly a common surname.

Perhaps London was just large enough for a provincial scandal to be forgotten in a place like this.

She took a deep breath. "I... I came to London with my sister, Angela. You almost met her, the first time we met."

"Yes, the absconding Peeping Thomasina." Leopold laughed as they turned a corner. "I would like to properly meet her, at some point."

Why? Kathleen wanted to ask. Perhaps the better statement would be, *Not after what I'm about to tell you...*

"Lord Leopold, I have to tell you something."

He raised an eyebrow at that. "I thought we had left such formalities behind."

The crowds were thinning now as they departed from the fashionable streets and continued in quite the wrong direction for someone like him. Kathleen bit her lip. It was all going to come out soon, anyway. It was best, surely, if it came from herself.

"Lord Leopold, you may wish to end our archery lessons when I tell you that...that my sister experienced a scandal in the country."

Leopold's footsteps did not halt, not exactly, but he did slow his pace. "A scandal?"

And that's that, Kathleen thought wearily. It was too much to hope that he would look past such a thing. His father was too great an influence on him, to be sure, but she could not truly blame him.

No family would wish to be aligned with such a family as hers.

"Yes, a scandal," she said quietly. "My sister was involved with a...a gentleman."

"Ah," Leopold said slowly. "A scandal."

Kathleen wished she had the bravery to look up at his face and see just what his expression was, but she could not bring herself to. This would be the last time she saw him, after all, and it would pain her to the extreme to see his revulsion.

"Yes, so I suppose you will wish to end our friendship or acquaintance or whatever this is," she said in a rush, "and I do not blame you. Goodbye, Lord—"

"Kathleen, wait."

She had only moved a few inches away and yet it was not only his words pinning her to the spot.

Leopold had reached out and taken her wrist.

Kathleen swallowed, trying not to think of the searing heat flowing from his hands to her wrist. What did he think he was doing?

"You wish to protect me," Leopold said slowly, his brows furrowed as he closely examined her. "Protect my reputation."

Her shoulders sagged. "Yes. Leopold, you—Lord Leopold, I do apologize. You have already received pain at the whim of the gossips. The last thing you want is me—"

"Let me be the judge of whether I want you or not," he said fiercely. His eyes widened as air caught in her lungs and he added, "I mean, it is only fair for me to hear the whole story before I pass judgment, do you not think?"

It was more than almost anyone else, including their father, had offered.

Yet Kathleen hesitated. "I don't know it all. Besides, it… It is not truly my story to tell."

Leopold released her wrist and she fought the instinct to bring it to her mouth and kiss it. "I can respect that. Your loyalty to your sister, it is utmost."

"I cannot pretend I have no frustration with her at times," Kathleen said with a rueful smile. "After our father disowned her, I made the decision to come to London with her. Our lodgings are inadequate; we are here without a chaperone, as our father thinks his fallen daughter and her steadfast supporter no longer worthy of one; and our pittance from him is just as inadequate as our lodgings, but…but I could not abandon her. Not when I believe her guilt is not so heinous as our father may think."

It was challenging, to be so circumspect—but how could she be anything else, when speaking of a story that was not her own, and a past that she did not truly understand?

A few people passed them on the pavement, but Leopold made no move to continue on. "I admire you greatly, you know."

Kathleen's cheeks burned. "You do not have to say—"

"I would not say it if I did not mean it," he countered with a smile before she could even get her words out. "You have sacrificed much for a sibling. That is honorable. Your loyalty prevents you from defending her entirely, which frustrates you, yet still, you hold do it. That is even more impressive."

Do not allow yourself to be flattered, Kathleen told herself carefully. *He is the son of a lord. He is treating you as no more than another nobleman who treats a person well might.*

That is all.

"Well, sadly, my honor does not repair that lost by my sister," she said aloud with a remorseful smile.

"I suppose not," Leopold said quietly. He stepped toward her, lowering his voice. "But that is better than just abandoning her. People like your sister, people like that, they deserve a sporting chance to make a new life for themselves."

And all of a sudden, the warmth disappeared from the day. Kathleen looked up at him, this handsome, charming, utterly kind man, and did not understand how he could say such a thing.

"'People…' 'People like that'?" she repeated quietly.

There was a flash of uncertainty, of discomfort, of sudden realization in his stormy eyes. "I—I did not mean… I apologize."

Kathleen said nothing, the twisting pain in her gut overwhelming her ability to speak.

"I… My father considers scandal as the most dreadful, the most despicable—my father is quite unlike my uncles, of course, who see scandal as a mere distraction or momentary hindrance… I did not mean to speak so disparagingly," Leopold continued, his face one of genuine contrition. "I am sorry."

It was all she could do not to stare. The disparaging way he had spoken, that was to be expected of a nobleman…but the apology?

"I… Thank you. I did not expect you to apologize," Kathleen

admitted.

Leopold's laugh was dry. "I was raised to apologize. Now, let me escort you to your *inadequate lodgings*, and you can tell me all about the part of the country where you grew up. No butts there, I take it?"

Chapter Eight

July 21, 1840

L EOPOLD SMILED AT the servant Marston as he entered the London Archery Club. "No Cooper today?"

"My uncle is taking a well-earned rest," said the broad-shouldered footman with a smile as he bowed low. "It is my honor to serve."

Yes, that was precisely the sort of thing Marston often said. Not that Leopold could hold it against him—the position of a servant was, after all, designed to be servile.

He had left the house that morning with a skip in his step. There was something about the days when he had made a promise to see Kathleen. The sun shone brighter. The birds sang louder. Breakfast always tasted better—so much better this morning, he had gone downstairs to compliment Cook, who had promised him that there had been nothing different about the way she'd made things.

The only answer could be that it was Kathleen herself who made the day better, and Leopold was hardly going to argue with that.

Not even when his conscience reminded him that associating with such a woman, such a family…

"Yes, a scandal. My sister was involved with a…a gentleman."

Leopold pushed the thought determinedly from his mind as he entered the club. Although the realization had come from a quarter he had not expected, he had finally discovered something he enjoyed more than archery.

Seeing Kathleen.

He was early—he liked to be early, to make sure he was ready by the rack of bows and arrows to watch her step out of the club and over toward him.

There was something very…very alluring, about the way Kathleen walked. The sway of her hips. The curve of her breasts. Try as he might, Leopold could not deny it: she was a very attractive woman, and absolutely not the person he had found himself daydreaming about last evening when he'd been charged with be chaperoning his sister, Maude, at a ball.

A ball Kathleen would never be invited to.

The thought dimmed his pleasure for a moment. *Remember,* Leopold told himself resolutely as he signed in at the front desk, *she is not for you.*

Not that you could even be thinking of matrimony or anything of the sort, not while your own scandal whirls about you…

"You look happy, if I may say so, my lord," murmured the servant at the front desk of the club.

Leopold started. It was not typical for anyone to comment on his mood—but then, he had been smiling inanely.

He removed his top hat, placed it under his arm, and grinned. "I *am* happy."

It was a happiness built on dreams that could never be realized, yes, but it was happiness.

Leopold was no fool. His older brother, Thomas, had married a woman who had seen straight through the Chance heir, something that all his siblings had thought was rather good for him. Their father had accepted Victoria because she was so charming, and she came from a good family, and she had been willing to forgive Thomas all his faults—not something Leopold had ever been tempted to do.

But he knew, deep down, that his own situation was different. He was a Chance, yes, and from the senior Cothrom estate branch, but he would never be permitted to marry anyone he wished, especially not a woman entangled in a familial scandal.

Miss Kathleen Andilet was a woman he would never be allowed to have. And he would have to learn to accept it.

"Ah, Chance, I thought I heard your dulcet tones."

In the mouth of anyone else, it would have been a compliment. As it was…

"Lord Graycott," said Leopold, turning and trying to smile. There was such a thing as manners, after all. "How unexpected to see you here."

"Yes," drawled Graycott, lounging on a sofa with a few other gentlemen on surrounding armchairs, glasses in hand. "We're enjoying a tipple after a reasonably impressive competition. A competition that I won, of course."

Leopold's smile did not waver. He would not let it. "Of course."

No matter that he had not been invited to join. No matter that he would have won, almost certainly, if he had been included—and his very exclusion was, Leopold knew, due to the rumors about his propensity to cheat.

The injustice of it all swept through his torso like lightning, leaving nothing in its wake but destruction and bright clarity.

"Oh, don't worry, I can see your disappointment," said Graycott with a laugh that was echoed by his companions. "If you wish for a competition, we have a small betting pool going on. It is a touch unorthodox to let you in, as you are so close to the situation, but I am sure we can make allowances for you. Everyone else seems to."

More laughter, more smirks, and all at his expense. Leopold tried not to permit his smile to falter. "Oh? I was not aware there was another archery competition scheduled."

"There is one in a few weeks, but that is not what we are discussing." Lord Graycott rose and smirked before continuing. "No, it's about that protégé of yours. Your Miss Andilet."

Every muscle in Leopold's body stiffened. "I beg your pardon?"

"Yes, we're wondering how long it will be before she throws

herself on you and demands matrimony. I hear tell she has good reason to. All that time spent in a *gentleman's* club and without a chaperone." Graycott sneered. "It's surely all an act, obviously. What woman actually wants to learn archery?"

"Miss Andilet is coming on leaps and bounds in her skill," Leopold snapped, heat rising. He should have been silent. He should not have defended her. "And I think it bad manners, and badly done, to place bets on a young lady!"

"You speak as though it's never been done before." Graycott's voice was as unpleasant as ever, but he appeared to be gaining some significant enjoyment from the taunting. "You speak as though you defend her honor. Do you, Chance? Have you feelings for her—is she already under your protection?"

"End the betting pool," Leopold ground out through gritted teeth.

Oh, this was beyond the pale. How could they think of doing such a thing—and with an innocent woman's reputation!

Well. Mostly innocent. That kiss they had shared, that had not been utterly innocent, and Leopold knew full well he should never have spent time with her unchaperoned, but that wasn't the point!

"It's only a joke, Chance. You should learn to smile more," said Graycott with a wide grin. "I ask again: is she under your protection? Have you succumbed already to the minx's tricks?"

"I have succumbed to nothing—she is naught but an acquaintance, a pupil," lied Leopold fiercely. "She is not the sort of woman to attract me."

The ferocity was half-aimed at the idiotic Graycott, half-aimed at himself. This was most unpleasant; the betting pool itself was an outrage, but the fact that he was therefore forced to defend her, defend himself, lie about how he felt for her…

Because it *was* a lie. It was only in this moment that he realized it, but it was a startling revelation, and it was simple.

He had feelings for Kathleen Andilet.

Precisely what they were, Leopold did not know. He had

never felt this way about a woman before, never encountered this painful, aching need to be with her. It was confusing. It was maddening.

It was dashed inconvenient.

"It's just a bet," muttered one of Lord Graycott's friends behind him. "I don't understand why he's getting so upset about it all."

Just a bet.

"Excellent! So if I can shoot an arrow to hit one of those things from fifty yards within a month, you've won. If not, then I have won."

Just a bet. Leopold could not help but think of the bet he and Kathleen had entered into, a bet that had been ill-advised at the time yet was scorchingly attractive now that he knew her.

Little had he known then precisely where such a bet could lead.

"I said to drop it," Leopold said sharply.

There was absolutely going to be a moment when there was not pain in his lungs and sharpness prickling in his heart, but this was not it. He glared, maintaining eye contact with Lord Graycott until he absolutely could not bear it, and even then he continued.

He would not, could not permit Kathleen to be the butt of their jokes. She was not just some harlot who was entertaining his time to trick him into matrimony. She was—she could be—

"Oh, you are not fun at all, Chance." Graycott sighed, throwing himself back down onto the sofa and rolling his eyes. "Fine. The betting pool shall be put aside, though Lord knows how we will manage to entertain ourselves without it."

"I do not care," Leopold said roughly. "Miss Andilet does not exist for your entertainment."

"No," agreed Graycott with a pointed arch of his brow. "She exists for yours, doesn't she?"

It was fortuitous, perhaps, that at that precise moment when Leopold lunged toward the man with his fist upheld, there was a ruckus to his right that drew all his attention.

"Unhand me!"

He knew that voice. "Kathleen—Miss Andilet?"

Desperately attempting to ignore the snorts and knowing looks surrounding him, Leopold let go of Lord Graycott's lapels—precisely how he had come to grab them, he was not sure—and marched over to the door, where Marston was arguing with the lady in question.

"I tell you, I have been permitted entrance by both Mr. Cooper and Lord Leopold, Lord Leopold Chance," Kathleen was saying to the irate footman. "Ah, there you are. Please tell this man I am allowed here."

"Release Miss Andilet," Leopold said sharply, drawing on all his reserves, all the occasions he had heard his father speak in such a refined and yet dismissive matter.

It worked. The footman let go of Kathleen's sleeve and glared up at the lord.

"She cannot come in," he said gruffly.

"I will say again," said Kathleen tartly, "I have come in before and I will do so again, and no one will stop me. Is that not right, Lord Leopold?"

And Leopold hesitated.

It was not that he did not wish for her to enter. It was all he could think about at the moment. His days appeared to move from one archery lesson with Kathleen Andilet to the next. All other days were mere time wasted.

She was starting to mean more to him than… Well, than any lady had a right to.

But…

"Have you feelings for her—is she already under your protection?"

Leopold bit his lip. Usually, when they met for their lessons, the place was empty—he always arranged it so, as best he could, based on the rota at the front desk. It was easier that way. He did not wish for spectators and he had been certain Miss Andilet would feel the same way. And now she was not Miss Andilet, but Kathleen, and he had kissed her, and he was starting to feel far more than was appropriate for a young woman from a scandal-embroiled family that his own family could never accept.

"Yes, that's her, there," Lord Graycott muttered from behind him somewhere. "Look at them."

Leopold swallowed. It was not the decision he wanted to make, but it was the right one. He would not subject Kathleen to the sneers, jeers, and stares of Lord Graycott and his idiotic friends. He would explain it all to her on another occasion, but on this occasion, he had to do what he knew to be right.

Even if she would not appreciate it.

"I am sorry, Miss Andilet," he said quietly. "But you should not come in."

Kathleen's jaw dropped, and her breath hitched. Her face was an absolute picture of betrayal and shock, and it tore at Leopold's heart so deeply, he wondered how it was still beating.

"There," said the footman smugly, which was certainly no great help. "Now, if you'll just step back down to the street, Miss Annerly—"

"Andilet," Kathleen snapped, making absolutely no move to leave the club. "Leopold—Lord Leopold, I do not understand. Why would you do this?"

"As I said, Miss Andilet, you *should not* come in *today*," Leopold said, attempting to tell her without words precisely that it was a bad idea on this occasion, not a censure of her ever returning to the place.

Dear God, the idea of her never returning to this place...

"Are you having me thrown out, is that it?" Kathleen hissed under the laughter from the gentlemen behind Leopold. "You have tired of me and now seek to end our friendship? Or is it that you have rethought our...our discussion from the other day and have decided I am no longer worthy of your family's reputation?"

That was a low blow, and the worst of it all was that Leopold could not deny it had crossed his mind.

Her sister's scandal, the details of which he did not even need to know, was a stain on her reputation, and anyone associated with her would suffer the same fate. It was unpleasant to think so, but Leopold was no fool. He had been raised to know precisely how one single member of the family could destroy everything that generations had built.

One wrong connection, and it would all come tumbling down.

His silence was evidently read as agreement. Kathleen's lips trembled, her features becoming discomposed, all her pained thoughts written across her face.

"I cannot believe you, and yet I suppose I should not be surprised," she said curtly, glaring at the footman as he approached her so fiercely that he took a hasty step back. "There was a reason I kept the truth from you. Thank God I did not actually confide all in you. Good day."

Kathleen whirled around, skirts flying, only resulting in Leopold's gaze drawn to her wonderful waist, the curve of her hips. Damn it, it was impossible to think when in this woman's presence!

She had stormed out before he could think to say another word.

"Thank you, my lord," said Marston with a bow. "It is always wonderful to have the support of—"

"That woman is never to be denied entrance again, do you hear me?" snapped Leopold, jamming his top hat on his head and racing after her.

He did not hear Marston's reply, if he made one. He was far too occupied with chasing after Kathleen down the street, her pace remarkable and surely due to ire more than natural speed.

"Kathleen," Leopold panted when he caught up with her, grabbing her arm to whirl her around.

She shook him off easily. "Are you not afraid to be seen with me?"

Yes, he wanted to say, *but I don't care. Somehow, you matter more, and I don't understand it, and I cannot explain it, and I would deny it if anyone but you asked me.*

Ask me, Kathleen. Ask me if I care more about you or my reputation.
"I need to explain myself."

"I think you made yourself perfectly clear at the club!" Kathleen shot back, her pace undaunted. "To think that I trusted you! That I thought—for a moment, that friendship could—but I was mistaken, dreadfully mistaken!"

She is also speaking at the top of her lungs, Leopold thought desperately, and he could not permit her to gain even more notice when he wished to explain precisely why he had acted in such a way.

If only there was—ah.

"And the next time I am so foolish as to believe a gentleman could—aargh!"

Leopold wished she had not yelped so loudly. It was all he could do to stop himself from placing a hand over her mouth, which surely would not assist matters.

As Kathleen righted herself after he had pulled her suddenly to the left, she glared. "Where are we?"

"Kensington Gardens," Leopold said in a low voice, grabbing her arm and pulling her farther into the silver birch grove. "Few know of it. I thought we could have a conversation here."

"I have no wish to hear your paltry explanations for rudeness and betrayal," said Kathleen harshly, pain glimmering in her eyes. "You think you deserve the stage to declaim your rights?"

"I think you deserve to know that had you walked into that club, on this day, at that hour, you would have found yourself the center of gossip and mockery!"

Leopold had not intended to speak so bluntly. The words resounded in the small grove of trees where they were utterly alone, and Kathleen's mouth opened, but no sound came out as he watched her register what he had just said.

It was poorly done, perhaps, but it was done, and that was the most important thing. Now she could forgive him and—

"I heard how you spoke about me," she said quietly. "I was there far longer than you realized. I am naught but an acquaintance, a pupil, I think you said. I think you even specified that I was not the sort of woman to attract you, which was interesting to hear."

Leopold groaned, pulling a hand through his hair. He would never have said such a thing if he had known—but of course, he should never have said such a thing at all.

Blast it all to hell.

"I was in a tight spot," he said, his jaw constricted. "I-I felt put upon. There was no right response to their remarks. I did not wish you to be embroiled in another scandal—"

"Oh, I am sure absolutely no one is talking about what just occurred at the London Archery Club," Kathleen said, a devastating air in her words.

Leopold cursed under his breath.

"And there is no need for foul language."

"There is every need!" He did not precisely explode, but he certainly spoke far louder than he had intended to. "Damn it, Kathleen, you are an intelligent woman. You must understand the impossibility of what we have started! This—this friendship, this tutoring of archery, it is not within the bounds of propriety!"

She was staring now with wide and uncomprehending eyes. "I do not understand."

"I am not your brother, nor father, to be spending so much time with you, and unchaperoned!" Leopold said, desperation pouring through him as the fears he had battled since the moment he had encountered this beautiful, inexplicable woman spilled out of him. "Spending time with you is a risk, to both of us, and we both have humiliations in our pasts that have not entirely cleared. I am put upon from all sides, pressure from my family to be more than I can be, pressure from Society to entertain and to be interesting, yet never to step beyond the boundaries that appear to move all the time! To be associated with each other in such a way, for our—our friendship to be misconstrued—"

"Then why do it?" Kathleen shot back, her cheeks pink. "Why continue to teach me archery, why—"

"Because I cannot stay away from you!"

Leopold was breathing heavily. His pulse throbbed in his throat, his fingers tingled, and there was a ringing in his ears he could not quite comprehend.

And then he realized why.

"Because I cannot stay away from you!"

Kathleen was staring up at him, utterly astonished. Her lips, her painfully kissable lips, were parted. She was closer, closer than he remembered, and Leopold wished for nothing more than to pull her to him and show her, rather than tell her, why it was impossible for him to stop teaching her archery.

Oh, there was so much more that he wanted to teach her.

"I cannot stay away from you," Leopold repeated, his voice ragged. "If I could do it, then I would, but you draw me to you in a way that is inexplicable, Kathleen, and you should know—you should know that I can offer you nothing, and I do not even understand my own feelings, but they are there and they are burning, Kathleen. Time spent apart from you is nothing to the time spent with you and that…that is why I could not permit you entrance today. Because if I did, and you became the subject of ridicule from men who are not worthy of you, then my position in Society would force me to step aside. Step away. And I would die, Kathleen."

He should not have been saying this. He knew he should not. All his upbringing and education and his father's precepts cried out that this was wrong.

Nothing had ever felt more right.

"So… So that is why I continue to teach you archery," said Leopold, voice cracking. "Don't ever think I do not have your best interests at heart. Even if they are at war with my own."

"Leopold—"

He spun on his heels and marched away before he could hear any more. He could permit himself to—not when he was mere inches away from kissing that woman senseless until she did not know her own name.

Until she wondered whether it was Chance.

Chapter Nine

July 23, 1840

"**Y**OU LOOK AWFULLY morose, Kathleen."

It was not the sort of compliment one wished to hear as the evening settled in, but Kathleen could hardly argue with her sister. She had already caught a glimpse of herself in the windowpanes before she had drawn the curtains against the dark skies.

She *was* morose.

"Naught but a little tired, Angela," she said aloud, trying to smile as she turned to her sister.

Her sister did not look particularly convinced. "You are bored."

"I am nothing of the sort," Kathleen said inflexibly. "I have my book."

"A book you have not opened in the last half an hour," Angela pointed out. "What is wrong with it?"

Kathleen glanced down at the book and tried not to say the words which instinctively came to mind. The answer was not one her sister would like to hear, even though it was the truth.

It was perfectly simple. It was an excellent book—an old fashioned one, she had to admit, but there was little Ann Radcliffe could have done wrong.

The trouble was…Kathleen had read it seven times these last three months.

"Nothing is wrong with it," she said quietly.

"Yet you do not read it," said her sister quietly. "Why?"

Kathleen swallowed. She was hardly going to be the one to point out that with their limited funds, there was almost nothing they could do in the evenings to entertain themselves. Invitations were few and far between, and when they did arrive, they were usually addressed only to Kathleen, and so she felt obliged to decline, especially after she had accepted the one time and Mrs. Burton had been so rude about her sister. They had eight books, and no funds to buy more, not even enough to join the circulating library; no pianoforte to play; no games save for a pack of cards, and there were only so many times one could play Patience.

And so they spent almost every evening here, in the drawing room. What *Angela* called "the drawing room." It was their only living quarters, the three rooms they had taken split between them as far as bedchambers were required, leaving them with this easterly-facing room as the only place where they could eat, sit, and converse.

And converse they did, for there was little else to do.

"It does not appeal to me this evening," was the only response Kathleen felt she was capable of making.

What she should absolutely not do was think about all the entertainments that could be found at home.

Home. It felt so far away. The pianoforte was undoubtedly being played by mother, or the violin by their brother. Perhaps there was a game of cards occurring, a game that required four people. Perhaps someone had reached up to the bookcase in the drawing room that was packed with novels and interesting travelogues, so many that one simply could not grow tired of them. Maybe a few of their neighbors had come for dinner, bringing bright conversation and a few duets on the pianoforte. Maybe there were sufficient guests for charades or dancing. Maybe right at this moment, her parents and remaining siblings were preparing to attend a dinner, or go to a ball, or—

"Kathleen?"

Kathleen jumped. "No."

"No…what?" asked her sister, a suspicious frown on her face.

It was all Kathleen could do not to sigh. This was not what she had expected. Truth be told, she had half-thought their father would relent and send for them, accepting the mistake Angela had made and forgiving them, bringing them back into the family. Her sister would never marry, to be sure, but they would be together. They would be a family again.

That desire had faded the longer she had known Lord Leopold Chance.

"Because I cannot stay away from you!"

Shifting in her seat by the empty fireplace, Kathleen tried not to think about it. Tried not to think about him. About the confusing words he had spoken, the muddle in which he had left her mind. The way he had looked at her when he had said… And yet he had not said enough, had he? No promises, no inkling of his feelings, save that he enjoyed her company greatly. That he would die if they stopped meeting. But what did that mean? What could it become?

"You are unsettled. You have been unsettled since you started archery," remarked her sister quietly.

Kathleen dropped her book. "No, I haven't."

"You are unsettled merely by the mention of the topic." Angela sighed, putting down her own book and fixing her younger sibling with a look painfully reminiscent of the type their mother preferred. "Kathleen, do you not think—"

A knock at the door interrupted whatever speech Angela was going to give, much to Kathleen's relief. It was never pleasant, being lectured by an older sibling, but it was all the more exasperating when said speech came from a sibling who was technically living in disgrace.

"Who is it?" asked Angela, moving to the door.

Who, indeed? Kathleen was not aware of a single acquaintance in the whole of London who would have been willing to be seen attending on the Andilet sisters in their own lodgings. And at this time of night! And without an invitation!

The answer to that question was swiftly given. "Lord Leopold. Lord Leopold Chance."

Kathleen rose hurriedly, almost tripped over her own skirts rushing to the door, and grabbed her sister by the shoulders. "Leopold Chance!"

"There is no need to repeat the name. I caught it quite well!" hissed Angela in response. "But what is he doing *here*?"

"He cannot be here. There is absolutely no way."

"You must have told him where we lived. How could you?"

"I never thought he would come here!"

"Erm…this door is remarkably thin," came Leopold's helpful voice. "Apologies, but I can hear everything you are saying."

Heat burned Kathleen's cheeks as she stepped hurriedly away from the door and looked piteously at her sister.

"No," Angela said flatly.

"Oh, come on, he is a gentleman. He would not—"

"You think we, of all people, can risk our reputations by welcoming in strange men in the middle of the night?" hissed her sister.

Kathleen's pulse was thundering painfully in her ribcage and she did not know whether she was irritated and startled at Leopold's sudden appearance on the other side of their door, flattered that he had somehow discovered her precise whereabouts, for she had parted with him a block away before, or mortified that he was about to rescind all the pleasant things he had so recently told her.

Besides, she was still more than a spot aggrieved at the pivotal role he had played in denying her entrance to the London Archery Club. She was sure she would not care about the gossip he'd warned her about half as much as he did.

"What on earth is he thinking?" whispered Angela.

"Sorry, I can still hear you," came Leopold's apologetic voice through the door.

Trying not to laugh and still utterly torn about whether she wanted to see him at all, Kathleen marched forward, pushed aside her sister's frantic fingers, and opened the door.

Leopold looked…

Well. Like Leopold. Perhaps she had imagined him to be wearing some sort of dashing highwayman's outfit, or some sort of other dramatic wear to signal he was about to whisk her away from Town on horseback, but it was just Leopold. He was smiling, though the smile was a tad awkward, and he came bearing…

Cake?

"I was passing my favorite patisserie and thought you might like to—I mean, I don't know if you like…and having not had the pleasure of making Miss Andilet's acquaintance, I…" Leopold's throat bobbed. "Cake."

He thrust out the box into Kathleen's arms.

She turned and looked beseechingly at her sister, who rolled her eyes.

"Come on in, Lord Leopold, do." Angela turned and strode back to her seat, dropping onto it in rather bad grace, but Kathleen was not fooled. Her sister would do almost anything for her younger sibling's happiness, and when there was cake involved, it was even more of a challenge to deny it.

Kathleen managed a small smile as she placed the box on the only console table in the room. "Please, Lord Leopold. May I introduce Miss Angela Andilet, my sister? Angela, Lord Leopold Chance."

Leopold, having removed his hat and gloves and placed them beside the box, stepped across the room and bowed low—far lower than Kathleen's or her sister's station required. "Miss Andilet. I am honored to meet you."

Trying not to notice her sister's flush at the surprising courtesy which Leopold had paid her—a courtesy no one had paid her in quite some time—Kathleen opened up the box.

And gasped.

"Oh my goodness," she could not help but whisper.

"I hope you like them."

It was fortunate, indeed, that Kathleen had not still been holding the box, for she surely would have dropped it. Leopold had somehow moved to her side, his breath blossoming on her shoulder, his presence intoxicating and befuddling.

"What is it?" Angela's voice was not sharp, precisely, more concerned.

Kathleen hastily picked up the box of cakes, stepped around the hulk of a man, and moved to the sofa where her sister was sitting. "See what Lord Leopold has brought us."

She was not surprised to see Angela's eyes widen. "That... That is most generous of him."

It was. Kathleen was hardly an expert in French desserts, but even she could see that the creations brought to them by Leopold were elegant, refined, and truly expensive.

They were also the first desserts that she and her sister had partaken in since coming to London.

A few minutes of busyness—her sister retrieving plates and napkins, Kathleen busily attempting not to meet Leopold's eye—and the three of them were seated in an awkward silence as they ate cakes.

Kathleen looked up and met her sister's eye, giving her a pleading look she knew Angela would understand.

And she did. She rolled her eyes first, but she understood.

Angela cleared her throat. "I hope you do not mind excusing me for one moment, Lord Leopold."

Leopold had been staring at Kathleen, something which she had also been attempting not to notice. His head whirled around. "I beg your pardon?"

Her sister gave Kathleen a look, one which read 'if you make the same mistake as me, I will kill you,' and rose with a swish of her skirts. "I have a letter I must finish, and my writing desk is in the other room. Do excuse me."

Kathleen mouthed her thanks as Angela left the room—halting, naturally, to select another tasty treat for her plate. And then the door closed, and she and Leopold were alone.

Alone.

"I wanted to apologize," Leopold said swiftly. "Again."

It was all she could do not to smile. He did not know Angela, naturally, so he could not be certain just how much time they would have, just the two of them. Little did he know that if Angela was anything like as agreeable as she normally was, she would not return from her bedchamber until Kathleen herself called her.

"There is nothing to apologize for. At least, not anything for which you have not apologized already," Kathleen said awkwardly.

The way she had flung such harsh words at him mere days ago… It felt astonishingly rude now.

Besides, they were seated together on the same sofa, eating cake. Kathleen could not explain why it felt so special, but it was a type of intimacy they had never shared before. Kissing, yes, but was there anything more sensual, more arousing, than watching a man lick at a cake before pressing it between his lips and moaning at the sweetness of the center?

Kathleen shifted as an ache settled between her thighs. Most unaccountable.

"I think there is a great deal to apologize for," Leopold said quietly, his words still rushed. "I have thought about this a great deal, and I think what staggers me the most is that for all of my life before then, I have never considered the fact that my sister would never have been permitted entrance to the London Archery Club."

Now *that* was not something she had expected. "It had never occurred to you?"

Leopold winced as he put down his cake on the plate and put it on the floor beside the sofa upon which they were seated. "I know it sounds monstrous, but my sister and I were raised so very differently. Not differently from others of our means, of course."

Now it was Kathleen's turn to wince. "I fully understand the differences, Leopold. You and I are not that different in terms of social class. My family is—*was* on familiar terms with a baronet, though poor Mr. Keystone will have to fill his father's shoes now."

"Was" on familiar terms. Why had she made it so obvious that her sister's disgrace had brought them so low?

The tension that filled the air could not be dissipated by mere cake. Leopold swallowed. "Yes, yes, I know that. Not about the baronet, to be sure, but that your family is of a similar class. I merely meant…whereas my sister was taught at home by governesses, my tutor was dismissed when I turned seven and I went to school. School, then university. By the time I returned home, my sister had grown and I was little involved in her social circles. The idea that she could not go where I went freely…it did not factor into my thinking."

Kathleen could well believe it. There were few opportunities to feel such a frustrating injustice in the country, where the fields and the streams and the village were open to one and all. Where chaperones were expected, if one discussed such matters, but really, no one cared if a young lady went on a walk with only her unmarried sister for company—or even entirely on her own.

No, it was only here in Town that she fully realized the limitations of her sex.

"But I understand now. At least, I am sure I cannot understand, but I understand my own ignorance," Leopold added, a wry smile creasing his lips. "And I am sorry for it. Truly, I am sorry."

Precisely why the son of a lord was apologizing for the vagaries of Society, Kathleen did not know. Still, it had taken a great deal for the gentleman beside her to speak in such a way, and it merited a reward. "You were not jesting, then. When you said that you had been raised to apologize."

He gave a laugh and retrieved his plate, taking a bite of a delicious lemon and blueberry cake before replying. "My parents are good people, proud of their station but not proud of themselves. I was raised to recognize when one makes an error, apologize for it, and improve. I am afraid that apologizing appears to be all that I am good for."

He laughed again, another one which did not ring true, and popped the remainder of the cake in his mouth.

Kathleen did not reply immediately but watched him.

To live such a life...to be nobility and yet to know that no title, no real wealth was coming to you. To always be the second in a family, second in importance, second in attention...

It was hard enough being a second sister, but a second son, and in a family of title and prestige?

Though she knew he was privileged even so, that he would certainly agree on that point, it was difficult not to feel sorry for him. It could not have been an easy life. It almost certainly was not now.

"You are good at many things," she said softly.

Leopold's snort was altogether too practiced. "That is very kind of you, Kathleen, but I cannot think of anything."

"Well, I can."

The words had slipped from her lips before she had thought of the impropriety of the situation.

When Leopold looked at her, his lips clamped together and fighting back a smirk, it was only then that Kathleen realized just how close he was. Had he moved on the sofa—had she been only occupied with the cake?

"Like what?" he challenged softly.

Kathleen's smile was unbidden. "Archery, for one."

Their laughter filled the room and she glowed. This was perhaps the first time in weeks that the room had even known laughter. There was not a great deal to giggle about, when you were two ladies likely to become spinsters without the support of their family.

"Oh, well, we have discovered one thing," Leopold said with another chuckle. "One thing I am good at, and it is not as though I can do much with it. Besides, the London Archery Club being barred for some of the people I most care about, little good it can do me."

And all of a sudden, Kathleen needed a glass of lemonade. Or tea. Something to quench the interminable thirst that had suddenly risen up.

"The people you care about? Like... Like who?"

Leopold's eyes fixed on hers and he did not look away as he said, "Like... Like... Like my mother. My sister, Maude. Naturally."

"Oh, naturally," Kathleen said hastily, looking away and taking an overly large bite of her cake so she would not be required to speak for a good few minutes.

His mother. His sister.

Why she had thought that he would say her name... No, that was ridiculous. Embarrassingly ridiculous, sadly. Leopold may have said that he found it difficult to stay away, but he had said nothing of affection. He may have... He may have liked her, as a friend, as an acquaintance, and may be seeking out that friendship. He couldn't stay away from her because he was undoubtedly lonely.

Nothing more.

Though how many people proclaimed they would die without an acquaintance? Perhaps he had just been exaggerating to get her attention when she'd been determined to get away.

"And it will be difficult for you to return to the club."

Kathleen swallowed her mouthful of cake so quickly, she almost choked. "It will?"

"Naturally, I will attempt to schedule our lessons when there are the least people about to make things less difficult for you," Leopold said hastily. *But really, for your own benefit*, Kathleen wanted to say. "I am ashamed, Kathleen. Ashamed that I am part of a club that would seek to restrict our members merely because it has always been that way."

His words flickered warmth within her. That, or it was indigestion from eating those cakes too fast.

"It is not as though I am shocked," she assured him. "There are a great number of places where I may not go." She almost laughed to see the look of incredulity on his face.

"There are?"

"Consider, Leopold, just how many places you go where there are no ladies. No ladies, that is," Kathleen added, her cheeks flushing, "of good report. Places you would never take your sister."

She could watch the dawning realization flow across his face. His handsome, eminently kissable face.

"There are a great number of things ladies cannot do," Kathleen said quietly, putting down her plate on the sofa beside her. "A great number."

"I suppose there are," mused Leopold. Then he reached out and took her hand. "Let's do one of them."

Her eyes widened. "But—"

"Why not?" Leopold's voice was persuasive, low, like honey dripping off a slab of bread. "We have little to lose in our reputations and I am certain we will not be recognized. Not where I am thinking of going."

Kathleen's mind was reeling and she could barely think as Leopold pulled her to her feet and started moving to the door. "But—Angela!"

He halted. "Is she likely to finish her letter soon?"

The truth warred with what was appropriate to say. Truth won. "She's not writing a letter, she's reading a book. She won't come out until I call for—*Leopold!*"

Her hiss went unheeded as Leopold pulled her to the door, out onto the corridor, and then along it before racing down the stairs. Her pulse was pounding, her lungs heaving. What, precisely, she thought she was doing, she did not know, nor whether or not this was a disastrous idea to even *contemplate*.

And yet she was doing far more than *contemplating* it.

"Leopold, this is madness!" She wasn't wearing her gloves. She didn't have on a bonnet or a cap of any sort. Even Leopold had forgotten his hat at the door.

"Perhaps it is," he shot back over his shoulder as he pulled her, laughing, down the street. "And yet I would rather do it with you than anyone!"

Joy vibrated through her as Kathleen heard his words. It was nonsensical, it was ridiculous—it was a risk, a risk they were both taking when on shaky ground already.

But her hand was in his and she did not wish to let go.

"Here," panted Leopold, drawing up outside a nondescript door she could not have recognized if she saw it tomorrow.

"Here?" Kathleen was similarly winded, their running through the midnight summer streets of London making her feel far more adventurous than she had ever been in her life. Approaching the archery club had not been without risk, her daring bet with Leopold even bolder of her, but this was the sort of thing that Angela did!

That Angela *had* done.

A curl of foreboding tightened around her. And that was precisely how her sister had damaged her reputation. Was this a good idea? Perhaps she should go back.

Leopold knocked on the door. "I've never come here before, but Cousin Samuel always said—ah. In we go."

The door had opened and noise spilled out through its frames. Kathleen had no time to think, no time to dwell on whether or not this was the worst idea she had ever gone along with. All she could do was allow herself to be pulled forward into—

It was quite clearly a gaming hell. Having never been in one before, Kathleen supposed she could not swear to it, but she had eyes. She had read the newspapers.

There was the bar, along which a number of gentlemen were attempting to attract the attention of a pretty woman in a gown so low, it revealed parts of her corset. Precisely what they wanted to attract her attention for, Kathleen decided not to speculate.

There were a number of tables dotted about the dingy room

lit by a plethora of candles and, even in the heat of midsummer, a roaring fire at the other end of the room. The inhabitants of the tables ranged from refined gentlemen and absolute rakes to working-class men with dirt under their fingernails and mended rips in their jackets.

There was laughter, and music from a fiddler in the corner, and the smell of ale, and cigars, and it was so intoxicating that it was a few moments before Kathleen realized what her mind had been shouting since she had stepped inside.

Apart from the woman behind the bar...she was the only lady.

"So," Leopold said with a wink. "Worth coming?"

Flickers of uncertainty mingled with flutters of excitement. Kathleen hardly knew what to say. "This is a gaming hell?"

His grin said it all. "Fancy a game?"

A game of cards, here? With strangers—with unsuitable acquaintances for an Andilet?

"Well...I suppose...why not?" Kathleen said breathlessly, trying to be bold. "After all, there is not going to be anyone here who will recog—"

"Leopold Frederick Matthew Chance, what the hell do you think you're doing here?"

She had expected him to drop her hand, to step away, to immediately dissociate from her entirely.

What Kathleen had not expected was for Leopold to pull her closer to him, to place an arm around her waist and to stare determinedly at the gentleman who was bearing down upon them.

Panic flooded through her, disrupting any semblance of good ideas, and all she could do was look at the stranger and wonder what he—now she came to look at him, he bore a striking resemblance to Leopold.

Certainly not identical, no—but the same jawline, the spark of intelligence in the eyes. While Leopold had a softness in his smile, this man had pressed his lips firmly together and was crossing his arms as he walked.

"What possessed you to come here, cousin?" muttered the gentleman as he halted before them, his eyes darting about the place as though terrified they would be seen together.

"And it is lovely to see you too," Leopold said in an undertone. "This is my cousin, Samuel, and this is Miss—"

"Do not even *think* of saying her name here, you idiot!" hissed presumably Lord Samuel Chance. "What were you thinking?"

Kathleen swallowed. It was more than a little scandalous, now she had time to think about it—but she had been swept away on the excitement of it all. The opportunity to see a part of the world that had always been hidden from her, the rebellious side of her taking over…

Only now did she think of Angela, reading at home, presuming her obedient and respectable younger sister was still in the next room. Eating cake.

"I never thought I would have to berate one of Uncle William's boys," Leopold's cousin was saying under his breath in a flood of words, "but honestly, what made you think this was suitable? Bringing a lady, for she is quite clearly a lady and not a—"

"Careful, man," Leopold warned in a low tone.

Cheeks pinking, pulse flickering, Kathleen tried not to think about it.

"*I*, careful! You are the one who showed up here like this!"

"Miss Andilet and I wished to see a gaming hell, and that is precisely what we have done," Leopold said carefully, his hand on her waist unmoving.

He would not disown her. He would not abandon her, as that odious other man had done her sister.

And the joy of that realization, the understanding that this was a man far different from those she had met, and that she wanted to know him, wanted his hand on her waist, wanted more, in fact, crashed over Kathleen's mind like a torrential wave.

"…and now we will leave," Leopold was saying, his grip

around her unrelenting. "Come, Miss Andilet."

Leopold's cousin Samuel was looking daggers at him but appeared unwilling to argue with their swift departure. "No one in the family shall hear about this."

"They had better not."

The murmur was surely not for Kathleen to hear, but she did, and it twisted her conscience. Had she not learned enough of the risks of losing one's honor? Must she be a viewer, nay, a participant this time in another's downfall?

The air of London had never smelled so fresh as they stepped outside, the door snapping shut behind them.

"I am sorry," Leopold said helplessly.

And Kathleen could not help but smile. She was starting to fall in love with him, which was a complete mistake. She felt things for Leopold that he would surely never return, and she would have to learn to accept that.

Yet he was the one apologizing again.

"Will you not escort me home, Lord Leopold?" she said primly, though with a dazzle in her eye. "I believe my sister is expecting me."

For a moment, it looked as though Leopold was going to say something. Something, that was, other than what he did say. "It would be my honor."

Chapter Ten

July 27, 1840

"I HIT IT! I hit it!"

"Yes, you most certainly did," said Leopold with a smile.

Kathleen had hit the butt. Admittedly, she had hit the edge, not actually reaching any of the rings. It was a bit of a fluke, the wind helping her edge the arrow slightly to the left. And it had fallen out almost immediately.

But still. She had hit it.

"I can't believe it—I finally hit it!" Kathleen's face was shining with delight, her expression full of elation. "And all this time, I never thought I'd be able to do it!"

"All this time, I believed that you were not hitting it on purpose, to win our bet," Leopold said with a wiggling eyebrow, taking the bow from her.

She shot him a rueful look. "If only it were that—it would excuse a great deal of pathetic effort. Are you not proud of me?"

Leopold swallowed hard as he turned away, the dying sun behind him, to replace the bow into the rack.

He was proud of her. *Painfully so.* He had never taught anyone anything before, and despite expecting the whole thing to be a great deal of discomforting work with little reward save the pleasure of proving someone else wrong—always enjoyable—he had actually found himself warmed by the process.

Helping Kathleen, guiding her in the best way to hold her bow, showing her and then adjusting her stance…

It was gratifying.

"I am very proud of you," he told the bow rack before turning on his heels and taking in the sight of a grinning Kathleen. "Not that you don't have improvements to make."

She snorted and his pulse skipped a beat. "Very diplomatic of you. Don't you fret, I am more than aware that I have some improvements to go. Although I will say, the limitations of the bet may reduce our opportunities to practice. Not that your key plan wasn't an excellent idea, of course."

Kathleen gestured around them at the empty field, the club closed up, the dying embers of the sun drifting down below the horizon.

Leopold nodded. It had been a good idea. A few guineas deposited carefully into the pockets of Cooper and Marston, and a key had been procured. He was trusted, naturally, not to take advantage of the fact that he now had access to the London Archery Club, but as he had said to Kathleen, few people wished to practice after eight o'clock in the evening, and the sun had only just started to think about setting when they had arrived.

It was almost gone now. The long shadows cast across the lawn by their forms seemed almost magical, elongated and shimmering across the uncut grass.

"I… I suppose I should go home, then." Kathleen's voice was uncertain, the desire to remain so clear, it could have been written on her forehead. "Angela will be waiting for me."

"Yes," said Leopold quietly.

Neither of them moved. Not to depart, but neither to step toward each other.

There was something most discomforting occurring in his ribcage. His heart was not aflutter, he was no fool, but there was a stiffness, a tautness, an expectation, but he knew not of what.

All he knew was that he yearned for these lessons like a sunflower tilted toward the sun. He could not help it; Leopold's entire week appeared to be structured around the snatched moments he could share with Miss Kathleen Andilet.

He desired her, yes, but there was something more. Something beyond what he had felt before. Only now did Leopold realize that what he wished to do, more than anything, was…

Be with Kathleen.

Not like that! His mind hastily reoriented itself, forcing himself to stand somewhat straighter, reminding him that he was a Chance. He could not just go about bedding women because he had a fancy for them.

More's the pity.

No, it was the time spent with her that he craved.

"Kathleen," Leopold said impulsively.

The smile on her face was too knowing. How long had he stood there, thinking?

"Leopold."

Hearing his name on her lips should not have made him shiver. It just shouldn't have. "I wondered…tomorrow, if you are unengaged"—*Why had he used that word, why, why*—"I wondered if you ate luncheon."

Kathleen blinked. It was starting to become difficult to make her out, the dying light covering London with a gray blanket. "Yes. Yes, I eat luncheon most days."

Blast. "I meant—if you wanted, I mean, there is no expectation, and I cannot guarantee it will be a good luncheon— sometimes Cook does nothing but sandwiches, but they are usually top rate—and I'm not even sure who will be there—not Thomas obviously, he's visiting his mother-in-law, but perhaps Maude and maybe Alexander—and obviously, you may be busy; your afternoon engagement may require you to—"

"Leopold," Kathleen interrupted him, suddenly by his side, her cheeks pink in the darkness. "Are… Are you inviting me to luncheon with your family?"

Leopold swallowed. *Am I?*

"Yes," he said quietly.

It was not necessarily the best idea in the world. Why, he still had no clear idea of precisely what Miss Andilet, the sister, had done to warrant being sent away—though he had half a mind, he could guess—and the scandal was likely as not something his father would despise.

Assuming he knew about it. Would it be possible to keep such a thing from William Chance?

Not that his father would approve of all the time Leopold spent with Kathleen unchaperoned, either. Not that he would approve of him calling her "Kathleen" to begin with.

It was a foolish idea.

Then again, his father had been presented with hints as to Leopold's activities, and he'd walked away, pretending, no doubt, he'd had little opinion on the matter. The dowager duke had not brought up Kathleen to his son since.

Kathleen's cheeks were a darker shade of pink now. "I...I would be honored."

Leopold's shoulders sagged. There was no changing his mind now. "Good. Good."

It was not a good idea. He knew it, deep down, but the temptation to test out the waters with his family was too much.

No amount of testing the waters could wash away the stain of her sister's scandal, but perhaps...perhaps his father could look past it, like he seemed to be doing over the lack of chaperone. Perhaps he never had to know. Perhaps they would fall in love with Kathleen as much as he—*careful now.*

"I admit myself nervous to luncheon with a dowager duke and his family," Kathleen said quietly as they walked in the darkness toward the club, the side gate unlocked thanks to the key in Leopold's pocket, and then onto the street, where the gas lamps illuminated their path. "What does one wear?"

Leopold laughed. Then he realized Kathleen was not.

Ah.

"It's just luncheon," he said hastily. "Just wear whatever you think is best."

Her smile was small, her nerves obvious. "I will. Thank you, Leopold. Lord Leopold, as I suppose you will have to be."

Leopold's stomach lurched, but he refused to give in to the trepidation. "Do not concern yourself," he said, far more lightly than he felt. "It is just a luncheon. There is no need to panic."

The following morning, he found himself saying much the same thing.

"There is no need to panic," Leopold told his excited mother hurriedly as she rushed from room to room. "The house is perfectly acceptable. There is no need to fret so."

"A young lady you are courting is about to come here and meet us all!" his mother said firmly, sweeping back an errant curl into her stylish coiffure and straightening a cushion that she had mere moments ago artistically twisted to be lopsided. "A young lady!"

"Lawks!" teased Alexander, a wicked smile quite at ease with his languid laugh, following their mother around the room and undoing all the changes she was making to the drawing room. "Oh, lawks, my poor old heart!"

Their mother whacked him on the arm. "Alexander!"

"Ouch, that hurt!"

Leopold grinned as his brother rubbed his elbow. "Serves you right. As I was saying, there is no need to—"

"Panic! Everyone, panic! I'm out of rosemary!" Cook had marched into the drawing room, apron stained with flour and a harassed look on her plump face. "And how, precisely, will I manage without it?"

"There's plenty in the garden. Take what you want," Maude said, stepping into the drawing room, her rosebud lips pursed and a brow arched. "Honestly, Leopold, trust you to put the house in such disarray. Who is this woman, anyway?"

"She's no one—she's a friend," Leopold said hastily.

It was the wrong thing to say. Cook had meandered back down to the kitchens, but his mother placed a hand on her heart, Maude rolled her eyes, and Alexander was pretending to be sick in a vase of peonies.

"If only Thomas and Victoria were here," said the dowager

duchess, "then she could meet the whole family."

"Why stop there?" Alexander grinned before throwing himself on the sofa, hands behind his head. "Why not invite the cousins? This Miss Andilet must be inspected, after all!"

His and Maude's laughter was not designed to calm Leopold's frayed nerves, and he was starting to wonder whether the whole escapade had been a bad idea. After all, this was supposed to be a calm, unpressurised opportunity for her to meet his family. If they were going to be this raucous…

"What's all this noise?"

Leopold's brother straightened on the sofa, his sister immediately stopped laughing, and his mother relaxed with a smile as she held out a hand to her husband.

"William," she said fondly, kissing his hand before interlocking her fingers between his. "You have remembered that Leopold invited a friend of his to luncheon?"

"Hard to forget. He only informed us this morning at breakfast," said Leopold's father dryly.

Leopold had intended to maintain his smile, but it was a challenge, seeing his father's disinterest.

Not that he wanted his father to be *too* interested. Peer too closely, and he may discover something about Kathleen Andilet that the Dowager Duke of Cothrom would not like. And there was the matter of Kathleen flitting about town, unchaperoned.

The doorbell jangled. Alexander winked at Leopold, who fought down the instinct to throw a cushion at him, and instead addressed his entire family.

"Please," he said, trying not to plead as the footsteps of Nicholls echoed in the hall. "Please, just… just be nice. Miss Andilet is not accustomed to—"

Precisely what she was not accustomed to, Leopold was never able to explain. In that moment, the door opened and the corpulent and stiff-backed Nicholls showed in a nervous and an exceedingly well-dressed Kathleen Andilet.

Leopold swallowed, pinned to the spot by the sight of her. It was not that she was ever poorly dressed; *simply dressed* was perhaps the better description.

But not this afternoon. No, today, Kathleen was wearing a most elegant lace blouse that buttoned up to her neck in the newer style, her blue skirt high-waisted and elegantly embroidered at the hem. There were what appeared to be diamond earbobs in her ears and there was a bracelet that matched around one wrist. And she was…

She was glowing—there was no other word for it. Her smile was genuine, if not a little nervous, and she appeared to glow from within.

The silence in the room was deafening. Leopold wondered for a moment why no one was saying anything, and only after a meaningful cough from his sister did he realize.

He was supposed to be the one talking.

"Miss Andilet," he said hastily, stepping forward and discovering quite to his astonishment that his legs were still working.

Kathleen dropped into a curtsey and murmured, "Lord Leopold."

It was odd, hearing such formality when they had grown so casual and informal in their address. But he could not think of that now.

"Father, you have met Miss Andilet," Leopold said, gesturing to his father and hoping to goodness he remembered.

It appeared he did. William Chance, Dowager Duke of Cothrom, inclined his head. "Miss Andilet." He made no comment on Kathleen arriving without a chaperone.

Good, then. He is going to pretend it is not an issue.

"And I have the pleasure of introducing you to my mother, Alice Chance, the Dowager Duchess of Cothrom," Leopold said as his mother smiled at her husband's side.

Kathleen's curtsey was far lower now than it had been when she had first addressed Leopold. *As it should be,* Leopold reminded himself quickly.

"I have the pleasure of introducing you to my sister, Lady Maude."

Maude actually rose to curtsey to Kathleen, which made Leopold start—but then, his sister was older than himself and did not know of Miss Andilet's...whatever had occurred with the elder Miss Andilet. Besides, it was rather a nice touch.

Was... Was his family behaving?

"Don't forget me!" Alexander bounded up to stand beside him and was gazing at Kathleen with a look that Leopold did not like.

"And I have the displeasure of introducing you to Lord Alexander Chance, my brother," said Leopold with a tickle in his throat as he nudged his brother in the arm. "Try to behave, Alex."

"Don't know what you're talking about. Delighted to make your acquaintance, Miss Andilet," said Alexander with a smooth smile. "I must say, my brother has an excellent taste in friends. Come, sit by me on the sofa, Miss Andilet, and tell me all the things about my brother that he does not wish me to know."

There was gentle laughter that rippled around the room as Kathleen smiled and accepted the youngest Chance's invitation. Maude returned to her armchair and joined in the conversation with Alexander and Kathleen, and Leopold noticed his parents exchanging meaningful looks as they moved to the window and spoke in low voices.

Which left him...alone.

Leopold swallowed. He knew he should not have minded. His family, it appeared, had decided to be on their best behavior, which was not ever guaranteed. And it was pleasant, was it not, that his siblings were taking an interest? Was that not the point of the luncheon?

Still. He tried not to watch the way that Alexander made Kathleen laugh, the way she looked at him with a broad smile, the closeness of the two of them on the sofa.

His brother was a known rake, a reputation unhidden from Leopold and recently discovered by their disapproving parents. He was so...so charming. So easily able to win over the affections of a lady.

Surely, he wouldn't—

"Luncheon is served," intoned Nicholls, the butler appearing at the door almost silently.

Leopold lurched over to Kathleen. "I'll walk you in, Miss Andilet!"

"Leopold, we don't need to be so formal as all that!" Alexander laughed as the trio rose to their feet. "You must excuse my brother, Miss Andilet. He is a stickler for the formalities."

Neck burning, Leopold tried not to let it show how much his brother's teasing was irking him. He was *not* a stickler for the formalities.

"Though he does not always follow the rules," pestered Alexander with a wink.

Now his whole body was burning. Was that a thinly veiled reference to the gossip about him cheating at cards? Surely, he wouldn't bring *that* up.

"I will take Miss Andilet in, to prevent you boys from arguing over her," said Maude sternly, taking Kathleen's hand and placing it in the crook of her arm. "Honestly, you never grow up. Do you have brothers, Miss Andilet?"

"Only the one, I am glad to say," Kathleen jested as the two ladies walked out into the hall. "Mine is younger too, and quite a troublemaker."

"You are smitten," came a low voice.

Leopold's face flushed. "No, I'm not."

Alexander rolled his eyes. "If you ever need any advice, brother, I have no issue sharing the techniques that I—ouch! Mama!"

"I'll have none of that," their mother said sternly after whacking her son once again. "Miss Andilet is clearly a refined young lady and she is here to eat luncheon, not be predated on. Go on, Leopold. Find a seat next to your friend."

It was galling to be spoken to in such a way, but Leopold could not deny it was an excellent excuse to go after Kathleen and Maude. They had just entered the dining room, and Leopold was swift to ensure that although his sister was seated on Kathleen's right, he was on her left.

Right. That was better.

"Just a normal luncheon," he said brightly, trying not to permit his eyes to bulge at the sheer amount of food that Cook had created. "Just like any other—"

"Dear Lord, did Cook think twenty were coming to luncheon?" Alexander grinned as he stepped into the dining room and sat opposite Kathleen. "I like your bracelet, Miss Andilet. How exquisite."

Leopold glared at his brother, but there was no malice in his words, and the delight in Kathleen's eyes showed she'd quite enjoyed the compliment.

Damn. He should have said something about the bracelet.

"Help yourself, do. We do not stand on ceremony at luncheon," said Leopold's mother with a warm smile. "No formality here. Would you like some cold salmon?"

There was cold salmon, and cold potatoes, peas, mushrooms, a trout in a sauce Leopold did not recognize, a cold chicken with slices of ham beside it, another type of potato that appeared to have been roasted then basted with a sauce that smelled absolutely delicious, some sort of pie that could have been ham but could also be pheasant...

Kathleen helped herself, cheeks flushing, and accepted a glass of wine from the footman with an inclination of her head.

She may not be nobility, Leopold could not help but think, *but she certainly seems comfortable dining at a dowager duke's table.*

With his parents entering and beginning a discussion on precisely when they would leave Town for the country estate, a topic that Alexander and Maude entered into furiously, Leopold was finally able to say in a low voice, "Thank you for coming. And sorry about them."

"I don't know what you mean," said Kathleen quietly, a smile teasing her lips. "Your family has been most welcoming."

Leopold tried not to look at Alexander, who was arguing

vociferously with their parents that they should stay as long as possible in Town. "Yes, he's good at that."

"I meant all of them." There was no censure in Kathleen's words, just mirth. "Your sister is most attentive. She has the true look of your mother, does she not? There is not a hint of your father in her."

It was all Leopold could do not to smile. Well, Kathleen had been relatively open about her own family. Perhaps it was time that she learned about my own.

"That is because," he said in a murmur, choosing his words carefully, "there is not a hint of my father in her. Maude is my half-sister. Our mother was married before she ever met my father."

"Oh!"

As he had expected, pink seared the cheeks of the woman beside him as she glanced over at Maude and then William.

It was not exactly a secret. There had been—not precisely a scandal, but something akin to one when his parents had been married, apparently.

"My mother neglected to inform my father that she was a widow with a child when they married," Leopold said in a low voice and a smile. "Rather a shock for him, the story goes. They laugh about it now, naturally, but I get the impression it tested his heart."

"But—Lady Maude *Chance*?"

Leopold nodded. "My father saw through Society's humiliation in the end and adopted Maude within a few months of their marriage. We've always been one family, even though we come from different places."

Kathleen glanced at Maude again, and he felt the fierce protectiveness that all three Chance brothers felt over their sister rise up.

No one would be foolish enough in Society to say anything disparaging about the eldest Chance sibling—the eldest of all the cousins—in front of her family, but Maude had been spoken to in the past in a most upsetting way. Her birth father of course had been a scoundrel, and their mother had not exactly told Leopold's father of the girl's existence when they had wed... It had all grown rather complicated. But William, then the Duke of Cothrom, had made it clear that anyone who spoke to his daughter like that again could expect to be called out. It had never been repeated, but it had not halted his three sons imbibing a strong sense of protectiveness around their sister.

"She is one of us," he said, perhaps *too* fiercely, for Kathleen turned back to him with wide eyes.

"I can see that," she said softly. "Family is made, not a given. And besides, it is clear your parents have treated all three—no, there's another brother, how could I forget? All four of you, equally."

Leopold tried not to snort as he took a mouthful of the pie—it was pheasant—and swallowed hastily. "Yes, we have been. Equally high standards, equally high expectations, equally low tolerance for mistakes."

He did not look at his father as he spoke.

"You... You speak as though you are worried you will be a disappointment."

Kathleen's voice was low and her insight was profound. Leopold was forced to take a gulp of wine before he replied. It was only as he put his glass down that he realized his father had ordered one of their best from the cellar for the table.

"It is not a case of *if*, but *when*," he said quietly, twisting his fork in his fingertips. "I will never... My father's expectations are high. I will disappoint him."

And instead of replying straight away, Kathleen put her cutlery down and placed a hand on his.

It was not highly sensual. It should not have aroused heat, nor shock that she had done such a thing. Out of the corner of his eye, he could see his mother had noticed but was carefully looking away, only the pink tips of her ears a sign that she had seen the intimate movement.

Friend. Yes, that was how he had described Kathleen to his parents. They had been very circumspect, not mentioning that it was highly unusual for a gentleman and a lady to grow a friendship that did not spark gossip.

Except his cousin Irene and her friend Wilf Zouch, obviously. But that was different. They would rather eat dung than fall in love with each other.

But how he felt for Kathleen, in this moment... Well, friendship was only a part of it.

"Leopold," Kathleen said quietly, "you could never be a disappointment."

He wanted to believe her. Who wouldn't? And yet... And yet...

Leopold gave a strained smile as he pulled his hand from hers and returned to his luncheon. "You don't know me well enough to say that," he said, as the sheer amount of money he had lost wavered in his mind. "One day, the disappointment will well and truly come, and it will be all my fault."

Chapter Eleven

July 29, 1840

PERHAPS THIS WAS *a bad idea.*

Kathleen had thought it was an excellent idea. Turn up early, having borrowed the key from Leopold after what had been a most fascinating luncheon, and get some practice in early.

The sun had come up swiftly enough, she had reasoned as she'd trodden as quietly as she could manage out of the rooms she and her sister shared. There would be no one about at this early hour, much less because they were gentlemen who undoubtedly had been out carousing, or whatever they did late at night.

It had been an excellent plan. It was a shame, however, that she had been entirely wrong.

"What on earth are you doing here?" asked a gentleman bluntly as Kathleen let herself through the gate and halted, startled, at the sight of a trio of gentlemen all holding bows.

Kathleen swallowed. "I...ah..."

"Do not ask such daft questions. The woman has a key," muttered one of the other men, nudging the first with his shoulder. "She is evidently some sort of servant. Come on, it's your turn."

Heat flushed Kathleen's cheeks, but before she had the opportunity to say anything, the trio of gentlemen looked away and resumed their turns at the far-right butt. As though she were no longer of interest. As though she were nothing.

Which, she supposed, she was. True, it was a tad hurtful to

think that her outfit, although not her finest, was the equivalent to servants' wear.

It was a small mercy, however, that she was to be left alone. Kathleen carefully selected the bow that Leopold had decided was the best for her, one that was not too heavy, and picked up three arrows.

Practice, that was what Leopold had said she needed. Practice.

"But you've had years of practice!" she had protested just the other day.

And he had winked. *"Exactly."*

So practice she would. Even if it was a mite disconcerting to line up her arrow to her own butt with the trio of gentlemen staring.

Yes, she was not proficient. Yes, it was unpleasant and decidedly uncomfortable to practice when they were so more talented than she. Yes, they were whispering and may soon inquire precisely why a servant had removed her hat and gloves and was helping herself to the arrows.

But she would never gain the skills required if she did not practice, would she?

Trying to slow her breathing and remember what Leopold had said about her stance, Kathleen took aim at the butt. It appeared to be a great distance away, but she quietened her lungs, glared at it as though it had done her a great injury, and let the arrow fly.

It hit the butt, which was an excellent start—and in the second ring.

Kathleen lowered her bow and tried not to feel too pleased with herself. It was an improvement, yes, but she had a great deal of distance to go.

The trio of gentlemen had not looked around, to her great relief.

Notching her second arrow in the bowstring, Kathleen once again lifted the bow, feeling the tension in her shoulders but acknowledging that she was certainly getting stronger. It would have been impossible to shoot a second arrow so soon after the first when she had begun her archery lessons.

"Excellent! So if I can shoot an arrow to hit one of those things from fifty yards within a month, you've won. If not, then I have won."

The second arrow went flying.

"Oh, I do apologize!" Kathleen winced as the trio of gentlemen gawped. She had hit a butt—not the butt she had been aiming for, sadly, but the butt in between hers and the one the trio of gentlemen were practicing on.

Another few feet, and she would have been in danger of hitting their butt.

She raised a hand in acknowledgement of the mistake and called out again. "I am ever so sorry!"

One of the men, the one who had first spoken to her, was shaking his head, but none of them said a word.

Which is probably all to the good, Kathleen thought darkly as she placed her third arrow in her bow. The last thing she needed was for Leopold to have to defend himself at the London Archery Club for allowing a woman in.

This time, she truly concentrated. Her pulse thudded in her ear, but it was a regular, calm pulse that grounded her rather than distracted. A slight breeze rustled her hair, her curls dancing across her forehead, but then it slowed. The air was still. She was still. The only thing that could move was the bow and she held it taut, motionless, as she fixed her attention on the center of her target.

She knew what she wanted. She knew what she was aiming for.

"Kathleen!"

Leopold?

Without thought, acting on pure instinct, Kathleen turned toward the voice that was so familiar and so delightful. Quite accidentally, however, she did not lower her bow.

"Good God, Kathleen!"

Leopold's explosive words rang out as he dropped to the grass, fear in his eyes as he stared at the—

"Oh," said Kathleen vaguely, looking at the aimed bow and arrow in her hands. "Oh, yes—whoops!"

She had not intended to let the arrow fly. It had been a mistake, an accident, a flicker of movement in her wrist that had sent the arrow onward.

It was a good thing, really, that Leopold had dropped to the floor in terror. The arrow flew right over him.

"Leopold," Kathleen whispered, mortified at what she had just done.

She could have killed him! She could have gravely injured him! She could at the very least have given his valet a great deal of mending to do in the shirt and waistcoat department.

Stomach filled with horror, she met Leopold's face.

It was laughing.

"You are an absolute menace," Leopold said, still chuckling as he pushed himself to his feet. "Dear Lord, Kathleen, what were you thinking?"

"I wasn't," she said honestly, dropping the bow to her side and rushing over to him.

Why she had done so, she was not sure. It was quite plain that no injury had been inflicted on him, and yet her fingers wanted to brush over his jacket, his shirt, his cravat, to ensure he was all in one piece. Quite why her flickering fingertips gained such jolting sparks as she did so was quite beyond Kathleen.

She hadn't been thinking. No, she had been feeling, her instincts prompting her the moment she had heard Leopold's voice to turn to him.

Leopold carefully captured her hand in his as he spoke in a low tone. "I am quite well, Kathleen. You did not hit me."

"But I could have," Kathleen said quietly, her ribcage tightening. "I could have injured you."

And that would have been a disaster. To hurt Leopold, to wound him in any way, to realize she could have damaged a man who meant…who meant so much.

"I appear to have forgotten to teach you the most serious lesson of all."

Kathleen blinked away foolish tears. "Y-You have?"

"Yes," came Leopold's calm and merry voice, his fingers still clasped around her hand. "Do not shoot your tutor."

She laughed, she could not help it, and some of the nervous tension within her exploded, relieving her of the pressure within her ribcage. And he was laughing with her, and he was fine, quite unharmed.

"It appears the only company we had is leaving," Leopold said, glancing over his shoulder.

Kathleen followed his gaze and saw that the trio of gentlemen who had been such uncomfortable spectators of her efforts were making their way back to the London Archery Club. "So it seems."

The door closed behind them, and only then did Leopold say in a low voice, "Which means we are alone."

Alone.

A scandal in Society. Something to be feared, to be avoided. There should always be a chaperone, Kathleen knew. It had been the lack of chaperone that had caused such irreparable damage to her sister's reputation, her prospects, the prospects of all of them.

And yet standing here, the bow somehow on the ground now by her feet, both her hands now inexplicably being clasped by Leopold to his chest, there was no sense within Kathleen that what they were doing was wrong.

Quite to the contrary. It felt right. It felt as though she should have been here all along.

"You… You were wonderful."

Kathleen snorted, the moment seemingly gone. "I have much improvement to make if I am ever going to hit the center of that target."

"No, no—I mean, yes, I am afraid," said Leopold with a wry smile. "But I actually meant the luncheon, with my family. You were wonderful."

She had felt slightly out of place and a mite harried by the obvious interest they had all shown in her, but it seemed impolite to point that out. "Your family are wonderful people."

"Yes. I suppose they are. I do not think of it that often, to tell the truth," Leopold said softly.

He was still holding her hands against his chest. Kathleen had made no move to pull them free, did not want to, was relishing this closeness, this connection. And he surely wanted them there, did he not? Why else would he hold them so close, so flat against him that she could feel his pulse thrum?

"It was pleasant to have you there. It is pleasant to be with you anywhere."

Kathleen swallowed hard. Leopold's voice had somehow changed, altered, become something deeper and darker. The way he was staring…a burning, fiery look that darkened the color of his eyes and made him all the more delectable.

She should not do it. She knew she should not; no elegant lady of any class was encouraged to go around kissing gentlemen merely because one was attracted to them.

But there was more to this than mere attraction. This was Leopold. She… She did not love him. Not yet.

But she could.

"Leopold," Kathleen whispered, looking deep into his eyes.

His smile appeared nervous, though why that should be, she did not know. "Kathleen."

And then she was kissing him.

How it had started, she did not know. Kathleen was almost certain she had leaned up on her tiptoes to reach his mouth, pressing a nervous kiss upon them, and had yelped at the sudden and instant ardor that he returned.

And oh, what ardor. There was something so warm and tingling about the way Leopold kissed her. Eager, and hungry, as though he had been aiming for this all along. Though he still kept one of her hands clasped to him, he had released the other so his hand could encircle her waist, pulling her closer.

Closer—Kathleen did not believe she could get close enough to this man who made fiery tendrils of bliss flicker through her body as his head tilted hers and parted her lips, demanding entrance. The twist of his tongue as it swept her mouth, as though he knew precisely all the parts of her that needed his touch, was electric. His desire was perhaps only just matched by her own, as Kathleen instinctively wove her free hand in his hair and tugged him forward.

He moaned at the evidence of her desire, and it thrummed through Kathleen's whole body, vibrating her with need.

Oh, if only I could continue kissing this man for the rest of my life.

The thought was a passing one, all thinking noticeably a challenge as she clung to Leopold, who kissed her senseless, and she tried not to pay it too much heed.

She was here, with Leopold, kissing him. That had to be enough for now.

Eventually, the pair of them had to surface for air.

Leopold pressed his forehead against her forehead. It was all Kathleen could do not to tilt back his head and kiss him again, but this was clearly a moment he needed.

To catch his breath? To catch up with his thoughts?

Kathleen did not know and was certain that she could do neither herself. What they had just shared—that had been far beyond a stolen kiss that the two of them could pretend to ignore.

That had been passion. That had been a craving they had felt singularly and now found together. That had been a need within them, a need that had burned and could only be sated by a kiss.

Not that she felt particularly sated.

"Don't…" Leopold exhaled slowly and started again. "Don't tell me that kiss was just to distract me from our bet. Please."

Kathleen's pulse leapt as her stomach twisted. Why she had given that ridiculous excuse, she did not know. It had been callous, and foolish, and wrong. Now she had the opportunity to set it right.

"Nothing we have shared has been a purposeful distraction," Kathleen whispered, relieved in a way that the closeness of their embrace meant she could say this without seeing the expression on his face. "I lied. I wanted to kiss you then, and I wanted to kiss you now."

Their breathing had somewhat slowed at the same rate, their chests moving in rhythm, and all she wanted to do was stand here forever.

What this was, she did not know. Oh, she cared about him, that much was clear. Kathleen had never felt theses stirrings, these longings, for another person—she had also never met a man she liked more. She liked him: Leopold's smile, and his laugh, and the way he looked at the world, the character that showed through whenever he had to make a decision, the way he held himself to a higher standard than the world did.

Whether or not there was more in her heart for him…

Kathleen shrank away from examining that too closely. Nothing could be gained by such a thing. He was the son of a lord, a Chance, from one of the noblest families in all of England. There was no possibility that he would—it would not even occur to him.

Besides… Angela.

The thought made Kathleen pull away. Not too far from Leopold—the intoxicating presence continued to have a heady effect on her—but enough to straighten and look at him without touching him.

The absence of him on her skin was painful.

But Angela—even if Leopold did feel any sort of affection for Kathleen, beyond the attraction they clearly shared…she could not abandon her sister. A disgraced woman like Angela would certainly not be welcome in the Chance family, lenient about chaperones as they seemed to be or not. She knew enough about Leopold's father to be certain of that.

Leopold swallowed, his throat bobbing. "Kathleen—"

"Didn't realize there were already people out here!" came a

cheerful cry. "You're up early!"

Both Kathleen and Leopold started. She took another step from him, making the distance far more socially acceptable, even as it pained her.

"Hullo there, Walden!" Leopold lifted a hand in greeting as Kathleen looked at her feet. "Yes, it is early—got to get that practice in!"

Her senses had just about settled when Leopold turned back to her. "Your sister will not be concerned as to your absence, I hope? I mean, I hope… I hope you can stay. For a moment."

Kathleen tried to smile. It appeared his thoughts were meandering along the same lines that hers were.

He could never marry her. He would not even permit himself to consider such a thing, not with the specter of her sister's ruined reputation hanging over them.

Yes, he could flirt with a lady almost always without a chaperone, a lady whose sister had committed an even worse sin than that. It was not *his* reputation that was in danger for such a faux pas. But to marry such a woman?

Angela may have ruined her prospects, but it appeared she had ruined Kathleen's too.

Scandal by association was still scandal.

"She will be fine," Kathleen said bracingly, her voice returning to normal, as though she had not just kissed the face off the man before her. "I frequently go for an early morning walk. It is more pleasant to be out before—before… before the heat of the day."

Before the rest of Society. That was what she had been going to say, and Leopold knew it. She could see it in his expression.

"Good," was all he said.

"Besides, she has an appointment with our father's solicitor at ten o'clock. She will be far more concerned about that," Kathleen added.

Why she had told him, a virtual stranger to Angela, she did not know. Leopold's brow rose. "Indeed. I was not aware your sister was in any sort of legal complication."

It was only now that he pointed that out that Kathleen realized she had absolutely no idea why her sister continued to visit the solicitor. Was she? In any sort of legal complication, that was? Was there something vitally important going on that she was not aware of? Should she have asked more urgently, pressed her sister to explain?

"Well, if you wish to accompany your sister to her appointment, you may be able to," said Leopold, glancing at his pocket watch before returning it to his waistcoat.

Kathleen had not intended her face to fall, but it was difficult for it not to. She had hoped—in fact, she had *expected* that they would have the whole morning together. Was that not what they had agreed?

"It is not that I do not wish to teach you all morning," Leopold explained gently, once again demonstrating that rather disconcerting ability he had of reading her mind. "It is more... There is a competition in a few weeks and I am determined to win it this time."

This time. Kathleen smiled. "You have not been successful in the past?"

"I have come third twice and was second last year," he said ruefully, stepping toward the rack of bows as he shook his head. "It is galling, indeed, to be so beaten. I am determined this year I shall beat them all. I will be practicing every day until then."

"You do not give them a very sporting chance to beat you, then," Kathleen quipped.

The corners of Leopold's mouth turned up, but there was a seriousness behind the smile she had never seen before. "No."

They stood there, by the rack of bows, and Kathleen watched as he picked one up along with one arrow. Just one.

Stepping forward, he casually notched the arrow against the bowstring and drew it back. As he had not removed his jacket, Kathleen bit her lip as his muscles bulged through the thicker material. His concentration was absolute, his center grounded, and she tried not to even think as she watched him should that become a distraction for him.

The arrow loosed. As she had expected, it pierced the center of the target.

"I can give you half an hour," Leopold said casually, as though he did such a thing every day—which, Kathleen reminded herself, he did. "Then I will need to practice, and I am certain you will wish to accompany your sister."

It was not a dismissal, not exactly, but it was not far from one. Kathleen nodded brightly, however, trying to remind herself of four things.

Firstly, that she was learning archery out of curiosity and a furious end to prove herself, whereas Leopold had an actual competition he was aiming for.

Second, that he was teaching her from the goodness of his own heart and risking the censure of Society for doing so.

Thirdly, that he was a Chance. That meant responsibilities, responsibilities he would never be able to truly escape unless he was here. This time was precious to him, and she could not always demand it for herself.

And fourthly, that remaining here would only emphasize just how painfully aware she was of him, and how she felt about him—whatever that was.

"Half an hour," she said briskly. "That is suitable."

"Half an hour with you, the rest of the morning to practice, and then I must accompany my sister to the modiste for a fitting," said Leopold with a groan but a wry smile. "The Seatons' ball is this evening, and it is most important, apparently, that Maude have something new to wear, goodness knows why. So. Take your stance."

Kathleen immediately did so, holding up an imaginary bow. It did something to her, to feel Leopold's eyes flickering over her, though she attempted to ignore it.

When his eyes met hers, there was a satisfaction and approval in them that did not help her concentration. "Perfect."

Chapter Twelve

LEOPOLD TRIED NOT to sigh, he really did. But his shoulders hurt and his eyes were sore, and the last thing he wanted to do was precisely what he was being required to do.

"But, Father, I don't—"

"I did not ask what you did or did not want to do," said the dowager duke curtly as he tugged his jacket to ensure a perfect fit. "I informed you of what you were doing."

Leopold's jaw tightened. "Father."

The hallway was empty save for themselves. Alexander had not arrived home that afternoon and was in trouble with both their parents for absconding from the dreaded Seaton ball, and Maude and their mother were still upstairs letting their lady's maids put the final touches on their hair. Or something.

That left Leopold and his father waiting for them, and they had somehow managed to enter a considerably terse conversation.

"But I don't want—"

"It is expected, and therefore, you will accompany your sister and act as her chaperone," the Dowager Duke of Cothrom said sternly. "I do not ask for much, Leopold. You have a significant income, almost total freedom, and the Chance name. Do you think I ask too much?"

Leopold swallowed the answer.

Yes, he wanted to say. *Yes, you ask for too much. You ask for perfection. You ask for no mistakes, no disagreements, and no discussion.*

But those were words he could not say. Words he would never say.

He loved his father. He respected him.

But sometimes…sometimes he did not like him very much.

"Maude is one and thirty, Father," he tried to point out in a way that was respectful. "Many would argue…"

His voice faded away as William Chance turned from the looking glass to stare, unblinking, at his son.

"Yes?" said his father in clipped tones. "Many would argue what?"

Leopold bit his lip. He was not going to be the first in the family to say it, though he was almost certain his mother had thought it. It was not a pleasant conclusion to reach, it spoke nothing of Maude's value and intelligence, but…

Well. She was over the age of thirty. Most of her peers were married. Many were mothers. Some of those mothers were considering bringing their daughters out in a year or two.

And still Lady Maude Chance attended balls and dinners and card parties and picnics, and she did not receive a single proposal.

Soon—painful though it was to think—soon, she would be openly considered a spinster. An old maid. No doubt most of Society already did think that, as there were women five years her junior already with the label.

Though that was probably not something worth saying to her father.

"Nothing," Leopold said quietly. "I misspoke. I apologize for the interruption."

His father nodded, once, then returned to the looking glass as he attempted to straighten a perfectly straight cravat.

Leopold sighed. It was not the evening he wanted. The sun was still up and the air crisp and clear. It was a perfect evening for practicing his archery at the London Archery Club. If he sent a note to Kathleen, perhaps she could join him.

Yet here he was, preparing for a night of polite conversation, which just meant dull, passive listening to the gossip of Society, while attempting not to become the subject of such gossip at the next tiresome ball.

"You surprise me."

Leopold looked up from his gloves. "I do?"

His father nodded, meeting his gaze in the mirror. "I would have thought a young gentleman like yourself would be eager for a ball. An opportunity to…ahem. Meet a young lady."

The heat searing Leopold's cheeks could not entirely be put down to the fact that his mind had immediately soared to Kathleen. No, it was because his father was attempting to have…the conversation with him.

Thomas had warned him about it. *"A few months after my wedding is over, you'll start to feel the pressure,"* his oldest brother had warned. *"They'll want to marry all of you off."*

Heaven forbid his father attempt to matchmake for him.

"I meet plenty of young ladies," Leopold said aloud, hoping to goodness his mother and Maude would soon appear. "Miss Andilet, for example."

Mentioning Kathleen was a mistake. His father's form became even stiffer, if that were possible, and his voice was rough as he said, "Yes."

That was all. *Yes.* The censure was plain.

"I like her," Leopold said boldly, his pulse increasing in pace as he spoke. "You appeared to like her when she came for luncheon. Both you and Mother—"

"She appeared to be a very well-meaning girl," said his father curtly. "Though not well-meaning enough to make her way across Town properly with a chaperone, I noticed."

The rebuke was excruciating. Leopold took a step backward, the moment unsettling. "But—"

"But what is expected of you is to find a lady of a good, noble family, and to make a match through her father," his own father continued. "That is what is expected."

Expected, expected—there are a great many things expected, thought Leopold darkly, but he did not wish to have to do them all his life. Where was the freedom his position in Society was supposed to offer? Where was the excitement?

"There you are," said his mother, descending the staircase as though it had been Leopold who had been holding them all up. "Maude, you look beautiful."

Leopold's sister was following her mother down the stairs and rolled her eyes expressively as she reached the bottom. "As do you, Mother."

"Oh, but it is much more important that you shine this evening."

"Why?" asked Maude innocently as she pulled on her long gloves.

Leopold stifled a smile as he watched his mother tie herself in silent knots. He stepped forward, taking the pelisse from Nicholls and placing it around his sister's shoulders. "Cleverly done," he whispered in her ear.

"I know," whispered back Maude with a giggle. "Really, Mama and Papa are sometimes the most—"

"The carriage is ready for you, Your Graces," murmured their butler.

"Of course it is," said Maude with a snort. "God forbid it not be. Come on, Leopold."

The carriage ride was much as Leopold had expected.

"And I will expect each of you to dance thrice, although clearly no more than once with the same partner," intoned their father as he always did as they traveled to a ball.

Really, Leopold thought with a sigh as he tried not to catch his sister's eye, lest they collapse into giggles. He could probably give the entire speech himself. He was next going to advise against drinking the wine.

"And do not drink the wine," warned William sharply, looking predominately at Maude as he spoke. "No one ever puts out their best wine at a ball, and should one of you fall ill—"

"No one is going to fall ill," Leopold said quietly.

"No one is going to drink the wine," added Maude, a twinkle in her eye. "Not when there is punch, or brandy, or—"

"*Maude Chance!*"

"She is only jesting, my dear," their mother said quickly, placing a hand on her husband's sleeve and casting a warning glance at Maude.

Maude's sigh was the last thing spoken in the carriage for a few minutes. Leopold had thought the whole thing had blown over, but then…

"We are adults, Father," his sister said quietly. "You can trust us, you know. At least try to trust Leopold and me. It may have escaped your notice, but it is Alexander who is not here, not us."

Leopold's chest tightened. It was unlike Maude to point out the indiscretion of a sibling. In general, they protected each other. Alexander must have upset her before he'd left the house that morning.

Their father sniffed. "It's little comfort to me that three of my four children consider their duty to their parents as important."

"Now, dear, please," started the dowager duchess.

"We are here," said Leopold swiftly, lurching for the carriage door handle as the conveyance came to a stop before a footman even approached them.

It was a relief to half-step, half-fall out of there. The tension had been growing the entire journey, but it was only going to increase.

Thankfully, however, he now stood on the pavement before the Seaton residence, the dying sunlight setting the windowpanes ablaze. It was just a ball. True, he had no hope of enjoyment. There may be a few of his cousins here with whom he could converse, and perhaps dance, but there was no possibility that Kathleen would be invited, not in a million years.

Throw it all to hell. He could not spend this entire evening thinking about Kathleen.

"They are impossible." Maude sniffed as she took the footman's proffered hand and stepped out beside her brother, not bothering to lower her voice.

Leopold gave a quiet smile. "They are doing their best."

"At infuriating me, I quite agree," said his sister with a sigh, slipping her hand into the crook of his arm and marching him forward before either of their parents descended from the carriage. "I don't know how you can stand it."

He stood it because that was the way it would always be. His father was not going to change. There was no point in hoping for different.

"I, for one, will be spending as much time as I can far away from Papa," said Maude as she allowed a Seaton footman to take her pelisse. "You know he's actually started to threaten to pull Miss Ashbrooke out of retirement?"

Leopold's eyes widened at that. "No. Surely not."

His sister gave a slow nod as they walked through the open double doors into the ballroom. "You had better be careful. If I find someone to take me off their hands, they'll use her match-making skills for you instead."

The thought was indeed terrifying. Leopold had met the Countess of Lenskeyn only once. She had given up matchmaking upon her own marriage, yet her maiden name was still spoken with reverence by many of the mamas seeking good matches for their daughters.

"You know our parents only want the best for you," Leopold said quietly as he picked up a glass of champagne from a silver platter being held out by a footman, handing the drink to his sister.

Maude's eyes softened. "I know. If only we agreed on what was best."

She probably said something else. She almost certainly did; Leopold could hear a vague sense of continued chatter in his ear, though it sounded rather like the words were coming through water.

Because there were other words demanding greater attention.

"—there he is, the rogue," someone was muttering nearby them. "Lord Leopold. If he makes a break for the card room, we will have to drag him away, scandal or no."

Muffled laughter.

"—surely won't be foolish enough to attempt it," came another voice. "The man's reputation is in tatters. It's bold of him to even be here."

"—loan sharks, that's what I heard—"

"—card room—"

"—Leopold—"

"Ignore them."

Leopold blinked. Maude was standing before him now, not quite clicking her fingers before his eyes, but not far off. "Wh-What?"

"Ignore them," his sister said firmly. "They don't know you like I do."

"The whole of Society thinks it knows me."

"Well, it's wrong," Maude said with a sniff that was not unlike their father, though wild horses would never have dragged such a remark from Leopold's lips. Not if he wanted to live. "Besides, the people who truly matter know the real you, don't they?"

Leopold was about to nod and thank his sister for her support, he truly was—but his attention had been caught by someone else.

Kathleen.

He was not dreaming. At least, he was almost confident he was not, though there was a weakness to his knees and his hearing had gone most mysteriously vague. The figure was right on the other side of the ballroom and she was walking, his view of her flickering between her, a gentleman in a blue waistcoat, her, a woman with feathers in her hair screeching with laughter—

"Is that not Miss Andilet?" asked Maude, peering forward. "You know, I think it is."

It couldn't have been—it just couldn't have been. This ball

was being hosted by a marquess and certainly not someone who knew the Andilet sisters. If they did, they would also have heard rumors of the scandal, whatever it was.

Either way, Kathleen would not have received an invitation.

"How pleasant for you."

Leopold started and looked at his sister's beaming expression with a lurch in his stomach. "What makes you say that?"

"Well, is not one of the most tiresome factors of a ball the fact that there is often no one of interest with whom to speak?" Maude said lightly, as though she were merely pointing out the obvious. "Now you have a friend."

A friend. Yes, Kathleen Andilet was his friend. The fact that he wanted so much more did not appear to be important.

"I...I..." Leopold swallowed. There were words, words in his mind, words his tongue could say. He was sure there were. None of them appeared to be particularly obliging at the moment, however.

"She looks a little lost. Lost, Leopold."

If he hadn't been convinced that it was not in his sister's nature to matchmake, Leopold would almost wonder whether she were being sly.

"Perhaps you should go over to her."

"You're as bad as Father," muttered Leopold, trying not to smile.

His sister nudged him. "Probably. Off you go."

It felt somewhat like being dismissed from a lecture. Leopold found himself wandering through the crowd—the Seatons had certainly invited a great number of people—attempting not to meet anyone's eye. Not that he was ashamed of his intentions. Far from it. No, quite to the contrary, he did not wish to become entangled in a conversation that would divert him from his ultimate goal.

Kathleen Andilet.

And she was real.

She looked radiant. Leopold was not one to follow ladies'

fashion; he was vaguely aware it existed, and that things changed over time. There was a painting of his parents, taken from life two years after they'd been married, that showed his mother in a gown tight below the bust and flowing thence down, which was most definitely not what the young ladies were wearing now.

But Kathleen did not just wear a gown. It flowed around her, as though the silk were somehow a cloud. Every movement, and she still appeared to be walking away, caused her form to be revealed through the layers and caused his loins to lurch.

Not something he could think about.

Leopold's pulse quickened as he pushed past a few gentlemen, his eagerness to reach her growing with every step he took. If he could just reach out—

His hand moved before his thought could be completed. His gloved hand found hers, hanging by her side as she faced away. He grasped her fingers.

Heat, and power, and shaking ground, as though an earthquake had befallen them. Sparks could have flown between the two gloved hands and Leopold would not have been surprised.

Kathleen halted, the whole room lost its sound again, and as she turned with a flushed expression, her mouth agape, her features then softened to see that it was he who held her hand.

Leopold melted.

How could he not? What gentleman did not wish to be looked at like that?

"Leo—Lord Leopold," she amended hastily.

Her cheeks did not appear to be dimming in temperature, but that was all to the good, for Leopold's were starting to match hers. At least, he thought they probably would. His burned, the presence of her here, in this unexpected place, doing something most unsettling to his pulse.

"Miss Andilet," he said aloud, remembering just in time the proper address.

"I—I did not—hello," Kathleen said with a smile, bobbing a quick curtsey.

Leopold returned her movement with a bow, and as he straightened realized he had absolutely no idea what to say to her.

Which was the best opening gambit for a conversation? *I have missed you? I am sorry I sent you away to practice my archery? When I close my eyes at night the only person I see is—*

"What a splendid ballroom," Kathleen said, vaguely waving an arm around them.

Leopold almost choked as the words that had almost slipped from his mouth needed to be held back. "I—yes."

"And the musicians. Very talented, I must say," she continued, her cheeks still pink. "I...I did not think to speak with you here. At a ball."

Precisely why, he was not sure—had he not mentioned the ball in passing? Mayhap he had not. It was certainly odd that she had not expected to see him here—it was a ball hosted by Mrs. Seaton, after all. The Chances were essentially obliged to attend. He certainly had been.

"And you are here," Leopold said, hardly knowing what words were coming out of his mouth. A pair of gentlemen passed him, knocking into him, pressing him closer toward her. "At this ball. At *any* ball."

It was not well done. Cursing himself for his oblique reference to her loss in social standing, Leopold tried to ignore the way her cheeks blazed even redder.

How was this so difficult? When the two of them were at the butts, conversation was easy. It became like breathing, something that occurred without a single thought required.

And yet here...

"I must let you get back to your friends. Or family, or whoever it was you came with," Kathleen said quietly. "I would not wish to...to injure your reputation with mine."

It was that which settled it. Leopold had considered it for one brief flash but had immediately discounted the idea as preposterous.

He could not dance with Miss Kathleen Andilet. Not in public.

Now he had to.

"Miss Andilet," he said formally, straightening up and finding his ribcage most unaccountably tight. "Would you do me the honor of this next dance?"

Leopold did not know what response he had expected. Effusive thanks were probably off the cards, but just as unlikely was a stern rejection and a storming off. Something in the middle, then.

What he had not expected was for the flush on Kathleen's cheeks to descend, rapidly, to her—

He jerked his focus back up to her eyes and tried not to think about the intensely heaving breasts he had just stared at.

"If... If you are certain," Kathleen said in a low voice as the musicians finished their current piece and gentle applause rang out across the ballroom.

Certain? Leopold had never been more certain of anything in his entire life.

"But a woman with my reputation—my family's reputation, I mean—and again, I am here without a proper chaperone—"

"I do not care about your reputation," said Leopold, far more honestly than perhaps he should have. "I do not care about the chaperone. Society can go hang. I want to dance with you."

Kathleen stared in wonder and only then did Leopold realize he was speaking the utter and complete truth.

He wanted to dance with her. And nothing would stop him.

Offering out his hand, Kathleen took it. The same sensations occurred again, heat and exultation, and Leopold swallowed hard as he led the woman he cared about far too much to the dance floor.

There were a number of couples already there. One of them contained his sister, though Maude looked a lot less happy with her partner than his own. It was poor old Sharnwick, a harmless enough, weak-chinned chap, but not someone most of the ladies could summon up much enthusiasm. There was also—

"Your parents are dancing," said Kathleen with a bright smile, her nerves blatant in her eyes. "How pleasant."

It *was* remarkably pleasant. Another Chance quirk—his fathers and uncles had never liked the idea that married couples were not supposed to dance with one another in public. It was also convenient. Leopold gave a sigh of relief. With their attention on their own dance, they would not be able to fixate on—

"Ah, Miss Andilet, how pleasant to see you again," his mother called out across the ballroom.

Leopold groaned but managed to keep the worst of his irritation at bay. It was not difficult. The music started and Kathleen stepped into his arms and…

It was only a waltz. Only a dance. Only the opportunity to hold her in his arms before the entire world and declare that he enjoyed dancing with Miss Kathleen Andilet.

The flush on her cheeks and her décolletage remained, but there was a defiance in Kathleen's eye that Leopold saw with delight. It was just the sort of look she had given him when they had first met.

"You're the Peeping Tom. How intriguing to make your acquaintance."

"Surely, I am a Peeping Thomasina?"

"You are beautiful," he murmured, unable to prevent the words from slipping out.

Kathleen smiled, dropping her gaze as she replied. "Thank you. I borrowed the gown from my sister. She wanted me to—"

"I did not say that your gown was beautiful. I said that *you* were beautiful," interrupted Leopold, his affections demanding that he speak. "You are beautiful, Kathleen."

It was too forward, he knew. Too intense. Too intimate.

But what could be more intimate than this? Dancing arm in arm, her breasts pushed up against his chest, her pulse in her fingertips pressed against his own, her hips swaying as he moved her around the space…

Leopold could do nothing but look at her and dance. That was all his mind could manage. She was so elegant, so refined, yet so bold. Her desire to learn archery, the self-assurance to issue a bet with a gentleman she had just met, the way she had persevered even through the trying times when a good shot felt impossible.

She was beyond anything he could have ever imagined. And she was dancing in his arms.

"I had hoped to do this."

Leopold blinked. "Dance?"

"With you," murmured Kathleen, still directed toward his chest.

He squeezed her hand. Did she understand what he meant by it—did she understand her presence here was the only thing that made this ball worth attending?

Maybe she did. Kathleen looked up and her smile was nervous, yet it did not dim as she said, "Leopold."

That was all she said. That was all she needed to say. He could quite happily dance the night away with this woman, this puzzle, this intricate and beautiful thing.

Not that he truly could.

"And I will expect each of you to dance thrice, although clearly no more than once with the same partner."

His parents swung by behind Kathleen, still dancing together, as his father's words rang through Leopold's head.

His grip tightened on Kathleen's waist. He did not want to let go—but he was not willing to pay the price. Dancing more than once with the same woman at a ball... It would invite speculation. It could invite scandal. Far more obviously than Kathleen wandering around Town without a chaperone, than him meeting her alone for archery lessons with fewer witnesses than there were here.

And he would not do that. He was a Chance. He would not be a disappointment.

Chapter Thirteen

KATHLEEN HAD NO need for the pelisse being placed carefully around her shoulders, but she was hardly going to argue that, as Lord Leopold Chance was doing the placing.

"Thank you," she said with a smile, a smile that became a laugh as he bowed obsequiously. "You make a very fine footman."

"I thought I would," Leopold said blithely, the two of them ignoring a pair of the Seatons' footmen as they stepped out of the hall and into the dark, fresh air. "Perhaps if I do not excel as an archer, I can always go into service."

Their merriment echoed out into the almost-deserted street. Kathleen could hardly believe it, but there were still people apparently going about their business, even at this time.

A pie seller on the corner of the street was trying to tempt any passersby with their wares. There was a pack of gentlemen, a little worse for wear, truth be told, just about managing to walk as they continued along the street, chattering loudly. A carriage rumbled by in one direction, passing another, their drivers exchanging the understanding nods of those who worked and worked hard for their livings.

And yet the city was in many ways utterly silent. The carriages rumbled by and disappeared, the gentlemen turned a corner and their loud babble quietened then ceased, and the pie seller gave up their attempts as a bad job. To all intents and purposes, she and Leopold were now alone.

It would have been romantic, had Kathleen's feet not hurt so much.

"I never expected to stay so long at the ball," she said aloud, smiling nervously at the man beside her. "Perhaps dancing is an endurance sport."

"Oh, I suppose it is like archery—the muscles it demands are quite unlike those one uses day to day, so one feels it all the more acutely," Leopold said with a shrug.

"I thought I used my feet sufficiently, but evidently not."

They were standing just a few feet from the entrance to the Seatons' home. The ball was still in full swing, the musicians outdoing themselves and the guests clearly enjoying the late supper his wife had put on.

It had been Kathleen's decision that had brought them outside. Well, had brought *her* outside. And he had followed.

"My sister will be waiting up for me, expecting me to return," was what she had said.

She had uttered no words about requiring any assistance in departing, yet here Leopold was...by her side. As he had been since they had first danced.

Kathleen swallowed, her throat suddenly dry. And what a dance. There had never before been a moment when she had been so close to a person, so utterly sure of their intent, so aligned with their desires—until the dance had ended, and Leopold had bowed politely, and escorted her back to the side of the room, and...nothing.

Nothing.

Truth be told, it had not been what she had expected.

Precisely what she had expected, Kathleen did not know. A kiss had been out of the question—in public? In the middle of a ball?

Absolutely not.

The same could be said about a declaration of love. Oh, despite his intense declarations of dying without her, Leopold was not truly in love with her, Kathleen was certain of that. And even if he were, which he wasn't, he would not do anything so riotous as to admit that in a ballroom.

Even if his eyes had lingered on her lips and he had brushed his hand more than once along her arm for no apparent reason…

"Your sister, yes. We should get you back to her."

Kathleen smiled up at Leopold and wished, not for the first time, that her sister had never come to London. That Angela was not a cloud hovering over any interaction she had with Leopold. That, in short, her sister had not been ruined.

But then, if that had been the case, they would not come to London. She never would have met Leopold, there never would have been the chance for these feelings to flourish.

Oh, it was all such a puzzle.

"If you wait a moment," Leopold said in a low voice, "I can find our carriage."

She did not mean to do it. It was pure instinct that made her reach out a hand and grasp his arm. "No!"

"Ouch," said Leopold lightly, looking at her hand clasped on his arm with a slight smirk. "You do not wish to be transported home in our carriage?"

"Absolutely not," Kathleen said firmly.

The very idea of leaving the ball early with a duke's son, entering his family's carriage, traveling through London, just the two of them, in that secret and hidden vehicle…

Kathleen fought the instinct to change her mind. It was tempting, but that was precisely why it could not be allowed to happen. Did she not run enough of a risk, learning archery?

"My feet do hurt," she admitted aloud, "but I will be quite fine walking."

"I could order a hansom cab," Leopold said softly, "if you would prefer."

Meeting his eyes, Kathleen could see he understood her reticence about his family carriage. And yet still, he cared about her. About her feet, at the very least.

Was caring about feet a typical gentleman's approach? Or was this…different? Special?

"Oh, no… No, it's such nice weather." *Nice weather?* What on earth was she talking about? It was pitch black! "I believe I will walk home."

Kathleen's feet immediately protested, and so did Leopold. "But you cannot possibly think to do so. You're are miles from home."

"What is a mile or two to a country girl?" Kathleen started walking along the pavement in the direction to her lodgings.

Probably.

"But—But—it's the dead of night!"

As though to emphasize Leopold's point, a church bell started to peal in the distance. It did not peal for very long.

"One o'clock! Kathleen, please, you cannot consider walking through London at this hour!"

Leopold had rushed forward to walk alongside her and she had to admit the experience was moderately gratifying.

He would act in such a way for any young lady walking home, a part of her reminded the rest of her. And yes, that was certainly true. Though what other woman of her standing would be walking alone in Town without a chaperone, she could not say. But he was not doing it for just anyone. He was concerned about her.

Leopold sighed heavily, took her hand without a single word of request, and placed it through the crook of his arm. "I shall accompany you."

Kathleen glanced up through her eyelashes. "You will?"

She knew she was being a terrible flirt.

Not a mischievous, wicked one. An unskilled one.

Leopold's cheeks appeared to pink in the darkness of the evening as he nodded. "Yes, I will. For three reasons."

However you want to justify this, Kathleen wanted to say, but she did not have the courage to. Besides, having her hand in the crook of his arm was doing wonders for her feet.

"It is far too late at night, and you are a young woman without father or brother in Town to accompany you," Leopold said decidedly.

Kathleen smiled. "And the third reason?"

"Because you are going entirely the wrong way," he quipped cheerfully, wheeling her around to continue in the opposite direction.

Their laughter mingled and rippled out from around them in the otherwise-silent street. Mirth was tickling through Kathleen's ribcage and she could not help but giggle as they crossed a deserted road.

"Serves me right for attempting to be clever and independent," she said ruefully. "I always know where I am in the country, at least around the village where I grew up, but everywhere here looks the same to me."

Leopold glanced about him and Kathleen took the opportunity to examine him.

He was worse for wear after the ball, it was true. His cravat was slightly lopsided and his hair was ruffled, as though he had pulled his hand through it a number of times, which he had. His jacket was unbuttoned and there was a crumpled look to his waistcoat.

In many ways, Leopold looked precisely as he did after an hour of archery. It was how Kathleen liked him best.

"I suppose most streets look the same in the dark," he mused. "I suppose York, Edinburgh, Brighton could all look remarkably similar."

"I suppose so," Kathleen said brightly. "Never having been to any of those places, I would not know."

No, she was hardly a well-traveled young lady—and here she was, promenading down a London street in the dark arm in arm with the son of a lord.

A gentleman she very much wished to kiss again.

Which was nonsense. Kathleen was fully aware that what she was doing right at this moment was wild and radical enough as it was. Should her father hear about such a thing…

Well, he would probably say that Angela's influence had finally rubbed off on her. It was an unpleasant thought.

And a true one. Kathleen swallowed as they turned a corner, the warmth of his presence beside her comforting her as she cooled from the excitement of the ball.

Was this not how the whole trouble had started with her sister? Was this not the very same slippery slope she had encountered? Was she not allowing herself to be just as vulnerable, just as tempted, as Angela had been?

"You are lost in thought."

Kathleen started, proving his point, and smiled weakly up at the man who was occupying far too many of her thoughts lately. "Yes, I am."

"And just what are you thinking about, if I may be so bold?" Leopold spoke with a jesting smile, as though he had absolutely no fear of hearing the answer.

Perhaps he should have been leerier. It was on the tip of her tongue to admit that she…liked him. She had no additional words for such a sensation, this warmth curling around her heart, this eagerness to be with him, to be near him.

Thinking of those fiery kisses.

But of course, she could not say such a thing.

"I am thinking about *you*," Kathleen said before her mind could intervene.

Leopold grinned, seemingly unaware of the terrible faux pas. "Oh, you are? I suppose you are wondering whether your archery has improved. We shall have to practice tomorrow, see how you have been coming along."

Her smile faded. "Yes. Yes, that is a most excellent idea."

Archery. It was the way they had met, she supposed, and it was a brilliant excuse to see each other at least two or three times a week.

But that was not the only thing that connected them, was it? When she had mastered the basics and had improved from there, would Leopold cease to meet with her?

Was their connection only real, only likely to continue, if she was bad at archery?

"For I do enjoy our lessons," he said softly.

Kathleen's spirits immediately brightened.

He enjoyed their lessons.

Of course he did. He'd die without them, remember?

"I enjoy all my time with you. I enjoyed the ball."

Kathleen's elation faded as Leopold's mouth continued to utter complete nonsense.

"Very enjoyable, very enjoyable, indeed—the enjoyment was… was good," he gabbled, a slight tension growing in his arm. "In fact, I—"

"Leopold," Kathleen said quietly, squeezing his arm.

His runaway tongue ceased and he looked at her with almost shy eyes.

And it was this vulnerability that she adored. How could she in any way fail to appreciate it? Here was no rake, no man who would lie to her face and take what he could get. This was not a man who teased the ladies then abandoned them once he had bedded them. At least, Leopold had given no sign of that, despite her initial opinion of all bachelors of his rank.

No, he was caring, and thoughtful, and sometimes he got himself tangled in knots.

"The ball was indeed most entertaining," Kathleen said softly as their footsteps slowed, their pace decreasing as they continued along the pavement.

Leopold's smile was grateful. "I will admit, I have never had so much fun at a ball before."

It was difficult not to feel a little pride. After all, it was surely because of her that he had so thoroughly enjoyed himself, was it not?

"The musicians were good," she agreed.

There was a flicker of something unidentifiable in Leopold's eyes as he said, "The dancers were better."

Tendrils of teasing heat were curling around her and try as

she might, Kathleen could not ignore them.

This man, he could set her aflame with his mere words. Had he any idea just how alluring he was? How much she wanted to—

"Yes, I think I would place tonight's ball in the top three of the summer," Leopold said brightly. "My sister is determined to return to the country, we have stayed far later in London than normal, but my brother and mother insisted we remained for a few more balls. How does tonight's compare to those you have attended?"

She almost laughed aloud.

Compare to others? Just when she thought there was little difference between them, that she and Leopold were not so very different really, he said something like that.

Not that she was going to admit to as much, naturally. "Oh! Oh, yes. Very well."

"Would you say that this has been your favorite?"

There was such earnestness in his expression that Kathleen was forced to tell the truth. "Leopold, this is the only ball that I have attended."

His eyes widened at her confession. "What, truly? All year?"

Ah. Well, she *could* agree with him. It would not precisely be a lie.

Kathleen sagged against him, reveling in the way he immediately bore her weight. "No. Ever, Leopold. I… I have never attended a ball before."

It was a most mortifying confession. Here she was, with a gentleman who had undoubtedly attended more balls in his lifetime than she had had hot dinners since moving to London. Very likely a great deal more.

Leopold halted in his tracks. "What, never?"

Kathleen could not help but laugh at the astonishment on his face. "You speak as though I have not taken a breath in the last six months!"

"But—*never*? No dancing?"

"Oh, I attended the Assembly Rooms twice in our nearby

town," Kathleen said with a wave of her free hand. "And I have danced after large dinners a few times when I lived at home. But a private ball, like that? No, that is a new experience."

One which had dazzled, and delighted, and made her feel small and insignificant. The place had been packed. It had felt as though there'd been more people in that ballroom than had remained in the rest of London.

The ladies had laughed and simpered and smiled, and the gentlemen had admired and stared and chuckled, and it had been a melting pot of beautiful gowns and tall men and the music played better than she'd ever heard before.

"I cannot believe it." Leopold's eyes were wide as he and Kathleen stood on the pavement, his astonishment evidently preventing his feet from operating. "That was truly your first ball—your first private one, I mean?"

Kathleen nodded with a shrug. "Yes."

"But… But I cannot understand it. Your father is a gentleman. He must have some means, some good Society, even though you lived in the country."

And that was when her stomach twisted.

It appeared it was not possible for the two of them to converse for more than ten minutes anymore without returning to the shadow of her sister.

Was this how it was to be for the rest of her life? Never being able to converse with anyone for any great length of time without them referencing in some way the stain of the Andilet name?

Her smile must have faded and something must have shown in her face, for Leopold swore quietly. "I am sorry. I should not have pried."

"It is not prying. It is a very reasonable question," said Kathleen brightly—or as brightly as she could manage. "And yes, your summations are correct. Oh, there are few private balls in the country of the Seatons' scale unless one is acquainted with a very wealthy family, but…but Mother never liked the idea of us going to Town, and ironically, of course, we are now here alone. It was my sister's ruin that put paid to any formal entertainments at home."

Her mouth was dry and her shoulders tight, and she wished to goodness they could change the topic of conversation.

But how could she? No matter what they said, no matter the topics of chatter they shared, there would always be this looming over them. Looming over her.

"I suppose having a sister whose reputation is ruined does put a slight dampener on the invitation rate," Leopold said quietly.

Kathleen looked up sharply, but there was no malice in his face. Her expression lightened. "It does, rather. But then, I had never experienced a proper private ball and so until tonight I did not know what I was missing. It is not difficult to go without that which you have never had."

She saw the confusion, the genuine curiosity in his eyes, and worked hard not to sigh.

He did not understand. How could he? Here was a gentleman who had never gone without anything. Had never had to deprive himself. Had never fallen on hard times or had to sacrifice a favorite pastime or occupation because funds had fallen low.

As far as she could tell from the general chatter about his family, the Chances had always been wealthy, always been respected—save for a few forgivable blips—and always had whatever they wanted.

It must have been pleasant, leading such a charmed life.

"Well, I am glad that you were able to experience it tonight," Leopold said quietly, turning to continue on with their walk.

Kathleen walked by his side, disappointed he had not taken the opportunity to sweep her into his arms and kiss her senseless. Not that he was likely to. But still. There had always been the possibility.

Then Leopold stopped. "Hold on. How did you get an invitation to the Seatons' ball?"

It was all she could do not to panic and blurt out the truth. "What do you mean?"

The innocently asked question was not so innocent, and Leopold's suspicious smile made her toes curl. "Kathleen Andilet, you know precisely what I mean. You are, and please do not take offense at this, hardly running in the Seatons' circles, yet you attended the ball tonight. How did you secure an invitation?"

Lie, whispered a small voice at the back of Kathleen's mind.

She pushed it aside. It would be easy, yes, to pretend a truth that was believable. Leopold trusted her; he would believe whatever answer she gave.

And that was why it was all the more important to tell the truth.

"I did not receive an invitation," she said quietly.

Leopold was staring in complete confusion, for which she did not blame him. After all, she hardly given a sufficient answer.

Sighing and dropping her gaze to her hands, Kathleen told her knees, "I... I am ashamed to admit it, but I cannot lie to you, Leopold. I received no invitation, but you had mentioned the ball was being held on this night and so I...I simply...turned up. I slipped in behind a pair with a couple of preening daughters trailing behind them at the door, disappearing into the crowd before the butler could try to announce two daughters' names only and wonder why there was a third."

There was silence. The silence continued, so heavy and accusatory that she found herself continuing.

"And my sister doesn't know. She thinks I have gone to bed with a toothache," Kathleen added wretchedly. "That is why I am in no hurry to return home."

The silence was maintained, and eventually, she had no option but to look up.

Leopold was silently—laughing?

"You are laughing," Kathleen said, slight accusation in her tones.

He was not just laughing, he was clutching his sides. When he attempted to take a long breath, he burst into peals of giggles. "Kathleen Andilet!"

"What?" she said defensively, unnerved by his reaction.

Was he not supposed to be outraged? Was he not supposed to be disgusted with her, astonished that she would do such a thing? Would he not denounce her as a liar, a charlatan who worked her way into other people's balls?

It was not his censure that she feared, but his rejection. Oh, to have her friendship, or whatever this was, with Lord Leopold Chance ruined before she had decided to march into a ballroom as though she'd belonged there—

"*Leopold!*"

Kathleen had not intended to yelp his name, but she had been greatly provoked. It was natural, after all, to yell when a gentleman suddenly grabbed one's hands, pulled you right into the middle of the street, and then yanked one against his chest.

It was most delightful with this particular gentleman, of course. But still.

Her heart racing, unsure what on earth he was doing, Kathleen found it was only when Leopold placed one hand on her waist and held the other aloft and started to move her in the style of a waltz that she realized what on earth he was doing.

"Leopold, we are—"

"Dancing, yes," he said, swirling her around and making Kathleen feel as though she had left her stomach two paces away. "You have so little opportunity, I thought we should make the most of it."

Kathleen beamed as he swung her around, the silent waltz music dictating their movements as Leopold danced her around the street in the moonlight.

"You are quite wonderful, you know."

The words had slipped out before she could stop them. Kathleen's cheeks burned as she noted the hitch in his chest, the way his mouth dropped open.

Was it truly so unusual for Leopold to hear such a thing?

"One cannot be wonderful alone," he murmured, his eyes fixed on hers.

His speech did not lessen the heat in her cheeks, merely increase it—but Kathleen decided not to think about it. All she wanted to think about, in this moment, was Leopold's hand on her waist, the sway of his hips near her own, and their dancing in the moonlight.

Chapter Fourteen

August 5, 1840

"IF YOU DO not stop fidgeting immediately," came a serene voice, "I will shoot you."

Leopold started. "Wh-What?"

His sister, Maude, was grinning much like he imagined a tiger grinned before it pounced on small, fluffy prey. "Stop it."

"Stop what?" His voice had no business sounding so defensive, but he had no idea what on earth she was talking about.

All he was doing was sitting in the drawing room after their evening meal, their parents out at a dinner with their three Chance uncles—to which none of the cousins had been invited, to their shared relief. Alexander was nowhere to be found, which undoubtedly meant he was somewhere with a paramour, and that left himself and Maude.

He had no idea why she was getting so upset with him. All he was doing was sitting here, minding his own business. Tapping his foot. Tapping his hand on his other knee. Sucking his teeth.

Ah. Leopold thought he had gotten to the bottom of the problem.

"Honestly, what has gotten into you?" asked Maude, throwing down her book from where she lounged on a sofa. "You have been all…all squiggly for days."

"'Squiggly'?" Leopold repeated, a smile creeping across his face. "Really, Maude, if that is your best description, I think it no wonder that I cannot answer your ques—ouch!"

Maude's habit of throwing cushions had been one deplored

by her family, mostly because her aim was so good. Unfortunately, there had not been a cushion to hand.

Leopold picked up the book which had been flung in his direction and hit him. "*The Youthful Impostor*? Is it any good?"

"No," said Maude sweetly.

"Oh? Why not?"

"The edges are clearly not hard enough to bruise."

He could not help but laugh. Five years older than himself, Maude could remember their parents' early days of marriage. She was, in a way, half-sister, half-aunt to him and his brothers. She remembered a time before them, and more, she remembered when their mother had not been the Duchess of Cothrom, nor the dowager duchess, neither.

There was a wit to her, too, that made it rather difficult to dislike her. Not that anyone really tried.

"Touché," he said, gingerly putting down the weapon of mass education onto the console table beside him. "But I have to warn you, throwing books at me is not likely to make me stop fidgeting."

"It might make you stop thinking, though that is hardly difficult," his sister shot back. "I mean it, what has gotten into you? What is playing on your mind so heavily that you do not know what to do but tap feet and make irritating, off-beat rhythms, sighing so heavily?"

Leopold tried not to get defensive. It did not work. "I wasn't sighing."

Maude heaved an overly dramatic sigh that would have been more at home on the stage than in their drawing room. She added a hand to her forehead for good measure.

Tempting as it was to throw the book straight back at her, Leopold had received enough lectures from his father about not hitting girls—and the sacredness of books—to resist. "I was not doing that!"

"You were doing it so often, I was starting to worry you were ailing for something," Maude retorted. "What is it?"

And Leopold hesitated.

They were not a family who talked about the issues of the heart. His father was not Uncle George, who wept at weddings and spoke openly of his adoration of his wife. His father was not even Uncle John, who teased people mercilessly for their affections but was always delighted when one of his children, nephews, or nieces found a love match.

No, his father, William, was far more like Uncle Frederick— another complication in the Chance family. A half-brother of the three elder, it was perhaps surprising that despite not sharing a mother, the oldest and the youngest of the Chance brothers were the reserved ones.

As such, Leopold had not had much experience in confiding in people about… about such things. Thomas had suddenly been given the responsibility of becoming the Duke of Cothrom, and then all of a sudden, he'd been married. Maude had been out in Society for so many seasons, he had lost count and seemed quite content in her spinsterhood. Alexander…

Well. The less said about Alexander and his rakery, the better.

And so he had never… Well. He had never had such an opportunity to talk about feelings and the like. It was all so dashed embarrassing.

"Well…" Leopold said awkwardly.

Maude rolled her eyes and rose from the sofa. "No—no, I don't want to hear it."

His mouth fell open. "You've just spent all this time asking me to explain myself!"

"I know that look. It's about archery, and I don't want to hear about it, I'm sick to death of butts."

Leopold winced. Goodness, he perhaps should not have been so forward with Kathleen. Besides, one hardly liked to hear one's sister talk about butts. "I wasn't thinking about butts!"

"I know that face. I would know that expression anywhere," declared Maude simply. "You love it. Whenever you think about archery, your face does that…that thing."

Lifting a hand to his cheeks, Leopold demanded, "What thing?"

"The thing your eyes do whenever you think of something you love," his sister said. "I'm going upstairs. I know it's early, but I'm tired of you. Goodnight, Leopold."

"Goodnight, Maude," he said automatically.

It was only when the door closed behind her that he truly took in what she had said.

"The thing your eyes do whenever you think of something you love."

No. No, it wasn't possible. Maude must have been mistaken—he surely did not make the same face every time he thought about archery. That would be preposterous.

And yet…

"You are quite wonderful, you know."

Leopold sank back into his armchair and found his mouth twisting in a wistful smile. She was…something. Something different. Something unlike anything he had ever experienced before.

Kathleen Andilet.

The name had meant nothing to him several weeks ago, and now it was all he could do not to think about her from one minute to the next. She crowded his dreams, making it a true challenge to concentrate on anything else.

Even archery. God forbid.

Perhaps that was the solution: archery.

Yes, it was the only rational thing to do. Go and practice a little. Some time at the butts would—oh, hell, now he couldn't stop noticing it. Butts.

Leopold rose and rolled his shoulders. He never felt calmer than when a bow and arrows were in his hands. It would make far more sense to go to the club, late as it was, and get in some additional practice before the competition. That was the sensible thing to do.

He strode out of the otherwise-empty drawing room and saw Nicholls dimming the lamps. "Good evening, Nicholls."

"Good evening, Master Leopold," said the butler with a bow.

Leopold smiled. He had been 'Master Leopold' since birth to this man, and he doubted anything would change that. "I am just going out, Nicholls."

"And I am just going to bed, Master Leopold," the butler said with another bow. "Have a good evening, I am sure."

All too late, Leopold realized he probably should have explained that he was departing at this very late hour to practice his archery, not to bed a lady or three.

He was not, after all, Alexander.

"I'm going to—"

"Very nice, Master Leopold," said the aged butler with another bow as he stepped through the servants' door and disappeared.

Leopold's shoulders slumped. The last thing he wanted was for anyone to think he was bedding ladies. Heaven forbid. Perish the thought.

If that piece of inaccurate gossip reached Kathleen…

The horror of that thought transfixed him for a heartbeat, then Leopold shook his head as though ridding water from his ears. He was no social expert, but he was almost certain that Kathleen and his family's butler did not exchange correspondence.

Probably.

He blew out slowly, trying to center himself as he pulled on his top hat and gloves. He was going to the London Archery Club. He would enjoy himself for an hour or so, then return home and sleep well, with absolutely no thoughts of Kathleen whatsoever.

Leopold opened the door. "Kathleen!"

"Leopold!" gasped Kathleen.

He blinked, hardly able to believe the vision of beauty that was before him. More precisely, the vision of Kathleen's beauty.

Kathleen? Here? How? Why?

Kathleen had frozen with her hand reaching up for the bell

pull. It was clear that she had been mere moments away from ringing it.

Here? Kathleen? Ringing his bell pull?

Something appeared to have broken in Leopold's brain because he did not appear to be able to move. His whole body seemed transfixed on the person before him, and she was similarly frozen, her lips parted—her very kissable lips—and her eyes wide.

"Kathleen," Leopold repeated, unable to say or think anything else.

What was she doing here? Alone, as usual. Though that no longer surprised him.

"Leopold," Kathleen whispered. "May… May I come in?"

Come in?

Leopold could barely think, let alone consider whether or not it was suitable for Kathleen to come in. No one else was at home—that was, there were probably about ten servants currently in residence, and Maude was upstairs, but as the only sister, she had a separate corridor to her brothers. Thomas's bedchamber was empty. Alexander was undoubtedly in someone else's.

Come in?

"Yes," he said, his instincts overriding his mind's ability to wander.

Kathleen gave him a small smile as she slipped inside. He hadn't the presence of mind to step back to permit her entrance, and so she was forced to brush up against him and dear Lord, she shouldn't have been allowed to do that.

Taking a moment to think cold, damp thoughts and brush down his trousers so it was not too obvious that he was aroused beyond belief, Leopold shut the front door.

His mind appeared to have ceased operating. There she stood, his Kathleen—not *his* Kathleen, no, but his Kathleen nonetheless—standing in his hallway, removing her hat and gloves and depositing them on the nearby table. It was all he could do to remember to put his own hat and gloves back beside hers. He thought better of that and put his hat and gloves in front of hers, hiding them from view.

He did not know when his family might pass by and spot the guest's belongings.

She gave a small smile. "I had to see you."

It was a flattering remark and one that put a smile on Leopold's face. "You did?"

"Is… Is there somewhere we can talk?" she asked, her voice low.

Naturally, she would not know that they were, to all intents and purposes, the only ones in the house.

Still, he supposed the hallway was not the place to have illicit conversations.

Not that what would follow would automatically be illicit. Obviously.

Oh, hell, why was his mind now filled with delectable images of Kathleen wearing absolutely nothing writhing on the floor of the hallway and beckoning him down with parted wet lips that promised—

"Leopold?"

"Lips," Leopold blurted out. When he saw Kathleen's eyes widen, he amended hastily, "Let's—Let's go into the drawing room."

Yes, that was safe. They could converse on whatever neutral and absolutely-nothing-to-do-with-amorous-congress topic, she would depart—he would send her in a carriage, there was no possibility of her walking home—and he would have the coldest bath known to mankind.

Right.

Kathleen obviously recalled which door led to the drawing room, for she made for it damned quickly, in Leopold's opinion. Evidently, whatever it was that she wished to speak about was of the utmost urgency.

There had been no fire in the drawing room, as it was far too warm for that, and servants had already dimmed and extinguished the lamps. As the hallway had been barely lit, however, Leopold's eyes swiftly adjusted to the darkness.

Kathleen was sitting in the window seat. Her hands were folded in her lap and her lips were pressed together, as though she were about to say something truly unpleasant.

Leopold swallowed and walked over to her, his instincts telling him that sitting beside her would cause his brain to overload and for absolutely nothing to happen in any case.

He sat next to her. His knee brushed up against hers.

"Arghh," he said confidently.

Kathleen blinked. "I beg your pardon?"

Closing his mouth, swallowing hard, and attempting to speak again simply did not work. *This is the trouble with becoming fixated on a woman you cannot have*, Leopold tried to tell himself.

Besides, she felt nothing of the sort for him. Oh, she accepted his kisses, but she had shown no real interest in him beyond that. Surely, if she had, she would have pressured him for more by now. More than he could give.

"Leopold," Kathleen said seriously. "I need to tell you something."

The gravity of her expression rushed through Leopold, centering him on the conversation right now. His foolish attraction could wait. "You do?"

"Yes," she said quietly. "I need to tell you that I... I have been pretending."

His heart fell.

Pretending? He should have known this was all too good to be true. Should have known his affections were not returned. Should have known—

"I've been pretending not to be good at archery," Kathleen said in a rush.

Leopold blinked. "I... I beg your pardon?"

Her smile was awkward and her lips were—*pay attention, man!* "You are an excellent teacher, and I have been getting much better, but…but I did not wish for you to end our lessons. So I have been pretending to be unable to hit the target."

She… She wanted to keep going with the lessons?

The laugh that escaped his mouth was one of relief. "You were so desperate to win the bet that you would feign poor archery?"

Kathleen looked directly at him. "Partly because of the bet. Partly because I wanted to spend more time with you."

"Oh, you didn't have to pretend for that to happen. I would have—"

"Because I have fallen in love with you."

Leopold stared. Then he blinked, then blinked again for good measure.

He could not have heard… She could not have said…

"You know, I do not believe I have ever seen anyone's face actually flabbergasted," Kathleen said with pinking cheeks, peering at him closely. "You do look a tad gormless."

The rushing in his ears, the pounding of his chest, the quivering—any one of them could have been more than sufficient a distraction to make it impossible for Leopold to think.

As it was, the trio of sensations combined made it absolutely impossible. He was fairly impressed he had not tipped over.

"Leopold?"

Leopold blinked. Kathleen was waving a hand before his face. "Hello?"

He reached out, took her hand in his, and stilled it. "I do apologize. I think I… I am not sure I heard correctly."

It was only then that he noticed the nerves. Not his own. Kathleen's. There was a pulse in her jaw that was set to a determined expression, one that had propelled her to make this confession, this confession that surely could not have been true.

"I'm sorry," he said faintly. "I think I need to hear that again. I must have mistaken—"

"I said that I have fallen in love with you," Kathleen said simply.

How, he did not know. How was it possible for her to speak so calmly, so rationally, about something that would entirely upend their lives? How could she be so tranquil, when all he wanted to do was run about the place shouting with delight at the top of his lungs? How could she just…sit there?

"I…" Leopold swallowed. "I do not know what to do with that information."

His body quite disagreed. His loins and his hands had come to an agreement that it would be most delightful to lean forward, push Kathleen down on the window seat, kiss her senseless until she was begging for his touch, and then soundly give it to her.

Leopold gave a strangled yelp, which was due to the combination of trying to cough and speak at the same time.

"You don't have to say anything." Kathleen had at some point, he knew not when, pulled her hand away. Now he had noticed her absence, it pained him. "I did not inform you because you were obliged to do anything, I just—"

"I am obliged to say something," Leopold said, heart in his mouth.

What, did she think she would merely come in, state she was in love with him—*in love with him!*—and then walk out?

Did she think he would do nothing?

"No, you really don't," she said quietly, her cheeks now very red.

"No, really," Leopold said, certainty forming within him. "I really do."

Leaning forward to close the meager gap between them, he kissed her passionately. His hands had grasped her arms and pulled her close and Kathleen did not fight him, instead pressing herself against him, her legs somehow unrelenting against his own.

Oh, she was like nothing else.

She was Kathleen. Sweet, and tangy, and scalding hot. Elation roared through Leopold's veins as he slid his tongue across her lips, parting them as she whimpered in his arms, the noise doing something stiffening to his manhood.

She loved him. She loved him.

And with that knowledge, the certainty that she wanted this just as much as he did, Leopold grew bolder. One of his hands left her arm and slid down to her waist, tightening his fingers around her before they moved up slowly, slowly.

Kathleen squirmed, but she did not shy away, and she gasped with pleasure in his mouth as Leopold's fingers danced along the hem of her bodice.

"Leopold…"

Never before had he known such passion, never before had he known such need. There was an ache in him, a fire that had never sparked but was now ablaze, and Leopold moaned as Kathleen's sweet kisses became sultry as she pressed her breast into his hand.

Dear God, he could feel her nipple through her gown.

Was she not wearing a corset?

The thought broke his concentration and Kathleen pulled away, her eyes hazed with lust. "I knew you wanted me."

"I had no idea you wanted me," whispered Leopold in a jagged voice, hardly able to think. The fact that his hand was still on her breast probably had something to do with it. "You—You love me?"

"And I am not here for a few kisses," she said firmly, her eyes bright. "I-I mean it, Leopold. I love you very much and I very much wish you to take me to your bed—"

Leopold groaned. Did she know what she was doing to him?

"—but this is not a once-and-never-again situation for me," Kathleen finished.

How could he do anything but say the words on his heart. "And nor is it for me. I… I love you, Kathleen."

It felt odd, saying the words aloud. He had hardly permitted himself to say the words even in the solitude of his own mind, but now?

Now he could see the need in her to hear them—and she

deserved to know. The whole world deserved to know.

"Oh, Leopold," Kathleen whispered.

This time, it was she who kissed him and Leopold reveled in her passion as she pinned him back in the window seat. This time, it was her hand splayed against him and the other wove its way into his hair and Leopold was kissing her like his life depended on it, like he would never breathe again if he did not breathe her in.

Her hand was moving, caressing through his shirt, moving down until—

"Dear God." Leopold broke the kiss as a jolt of unadulterated delight rocked him.

Kathleen looked up, lips quivering but smile broad. "Ah. You appear...um. Eager to please."

Trying not to think about the way her questing fingers had brushed up against his aching manhood, he nodded. "Yes. Very."

"So what...what is next?" she whispered.

It was an excellent question. What, indeed, was next?

Leopold knew precisely what his brother would do. In fact, Alexander was likely as not deflowering someone as they sat here. It was a rather unpleasant thought, but based on previous activities, almost a surety.

And then there was her sister.

Miss Angela Andilet. Her life had been ruined by such an occasion, he had to presume, and Kathleen was therefore hardly likely to permit herself to fall into such circumstances.

Besides, he did not wish to ruin her. He wished to marry her.

The certainty washed over him like the knowledge that the sun rose every morning and the moon followed at night. It rocked him, causing jumping muscles down his arms and across his torso. And a smile appeared on his face, unbidden but most welcome, when he realized precisely what he was about to do.

"What are you thinking?" Kathleen's voice was quiet—not fearful, but uncertain.

What had his expression been, when he'd been considering just how he was going to make this woman so happy?

"No," she whispered as Leopold untangled himself from her embrace. It tightened his senses, just for a moment.

Soon, she would understand exactly why he had done so. Soon, she would be glad he had.

Trembling slightly, Leopold lowered himself down onto both knees before the window seat—that was, before Kathleen. The woman he loved.

"Leopold?" Her murmur was uncertain, but there was hope there now, anticipation.

Leopold smiled as he took her hand in his own. "Kathleen. I… I always knew that one day, I would meet someone who was impossible to ignore. Whom I could not dream of escaping, not because I wanted to, but because there was nowhere to escape to, when I wanted to be with them all the time. Someone who would become the target of all my affections."

Kathleen's eyes were wide and Leopold's loins stirred. Yes, this was right.

"I've never been one to miss my target," he said with a wry smile. "And so this is me drawing my bow back and attempting a bullseye. Kathleen, will you marry—"

His aim was true. So was Kathleen's as she launched herself into his arms and kissed him most furiously, something Leopold gladly welcomed.

How long they knelt there, locked in each other's arms, unaware of the world around them, Leopold could not tell. Not long enough. It could never be long enough.

When they finally broke apart, they were breathless.

"Goodness," Leopold murmured. "I have no idea what to do next."

Was it banns? Or asking permission of her father? Or informing *his* father—or his mother? She would certainly wish to—

"Really?" And there was a wicked glint in Kathleen's eyes he had never seen before. He was quite eager to see more of it. "*I do.*"

Chapter Fifteen

"Goodness. I have no idea what to do next."

Leopold's low mumble still managed to reach Kathleen's ears, though it was not her ears that immediately knew what they wanted.

No, it was the rest of her. Quivering, and aching, and knowing she was now engaged and so could venture further than ever into the depths of pleasure, Kathleen was utterly convinced of what she wanted.

So she would take it.

"Really?" Try as she might, she could not prevent the shake in her voice, but she persevered. "I do."

The sudden widening of Leopold's eyes told her that he had seen the hunger in her, understood the shot she had fired. It was a bold one, yes, but it was also a loving one. She needed him, needed him to quell this fire in her, and at the same time, needed him to blow gently on the flames.

Kathleen squirmed as she knelt. The idea of Leopold blowing on certain parts of her was…intriguing.

In a way, she could not believe what she had said. She had never been so forward before, so utterly forthright in what she wanted. But she wanted him, and she had known that for some time now.

Precisely how long, she could not be sure.

She was aware her foolish behavior had begun after she'd merely lain eyes on him, before she'd even known his name.

Besides…

"I've never been one to miss my target. And so this is me drawing my bow back and attempting a bullseye. Kathleen, will you marry—"

It wasn't like this was some sad, sordid affair that would be best forgotten as daylight reached them. This was the connection between two people who would soon be husband and wife. They were going to be married, to be together forever.

There was not a single doubt in Kathleen's mind.

"I-I beg your pardon?"

Leopold did not look doubtful, precisely, but slightly stunned, as though someone had knocked him on the back of his head with a bow. There was a dazed expression in his eyes that momentarily concerned Kathleen, until she felt the gentle caress of his fingers on her arm, the heat of his passion tangible even in that small gesture.

Joyous tears fell from her eyes, unsolicited. She wanted him. He wanted her. They were engaged.

What could possibly go wrong?

"You know what I mean," Kathleen said playfully, wiping away the tears.

Her smile faded as she looked into his eyes.

At least, she had thought Leopold had known what she'd meant. She had been coy, yes, but was not that the expected routine for a lady who was innocent? There was no possibility of her being more direct, was there?

Had she been too circumspect? Worse, had she believed she had seen the signs of true desire and had in fact been mistaken? Perhaps he merely felt obligated to marry her. They had, after all, been together many a time without a chaperone present.

Kathleen bit her lip as she swallowed, leaning back on her heels. It was tempting to laugh, though that would only be from discomfort. "I… I don't know how to explain it," she said aloud, realizing the truth as she spoke. "I don't know how to ask for… this."

It was mortifying. Just when she had thought she was being

so clever, so enticing, all she had done was confuse Leopold to no end and make it impossible for him to know what she wanted.

And goodness, she wanted it. She wanted him to bed her, to lay her down and show her just how much he wanted her. She wanted him to kiss her all over, to reveal his body, to reveal hers, to worship her until they were gasping and clutching at each other and unable to do anything but cry out their passions for each other.

And she wanted to do all that without actually having to say any of those words. *Heaven forbid!*

How, precisely, did a woman request such things?

"I don't understand," Leopold said quietly, though his eyes suggested he could have a guess but did not wish to.

Was he concerned, perhaps, that if he were mistaken, he would offend?

It would take one of them, Kathleen realized, to be brave. And Leopold was far too much of a gentleman to cross what he considered to be a line of that nature.

That left only one person.

"I do not precisely know the words to explain it," she said, more than a little awkwardly, "but perhaps... perhaps I can show you."

Leopold blinked. "'Show' me?"

Kathleen did not wait for her thoughts to catch up with her actions—that would surely slow her down, and she had no wish to second-guess herself, or think herself into so tight a knot that she would be unable to untangle herself.

No, she had come this far. She was engaged. There was naught to be shocked at now.

What she wanted was mere inches away. All she had to do was be brave, pull back the metaphorical bowstring...and shoot for what she wanted.

Kathleen leaned forward, slowly, and was relieved that Leopold did not move away. He wanted this, then, just as much as she did.

When her lips met his, there was a sizzle in the air, a tension, a sharpness, and yet a softness, a gentleness. The kiss was passionate, yes, but it seared through her in a way Kathleen had never known before.

The bliss rippled through her but also the confirmation that this was precisely what she wanted. What she needed.

Kathleen pressed herself forward, her body aching to be close to his, and Leopold seemed to know now exactly what she wanted. His hands crept around her waist, pulling her close, and air juddered in her lungs as the sweetness and power of his kiss overwhelmed her.

This was—this was—

"Wait a moment."

She could have moaned with disappointment as Leopold not only pulled away from their kiss, their embrace, but her altogether. "*Leopold!*"

"Shush," he said, glancing over his shoulder.

Even in the throes of passion, Kathleen could not help but feel piqued. "I am sorry, did you just shush me?"

"Shush!"

She stared, pulse pounding as Leopold turned back to her with a smile on his face that could almost have been described as wicked. Not quite. But it wasn't far off.

"Kathleen, are you certain?"

Kathleen did not need to ask him to elaborate. There would be no regrets, she was determined. They were to be married. What could be wrong about a husband and wife sharing one of the most precious and intimate things that two people could do?

Still, she did not completely trust her voice. Instead, she nodded, keeping her gaze on him.

Leopold's throat bobbed. Then he was standing, pulling her to his feet with a hand that was warm and that did not quiver with nerves.

The drawing room door creaked and Kathleen winced, suddenly conscious that there were innumerable people within the house who most definitely should not discover them. It would be a disaster in the extreme, yet the hallway was deserted.

"My family is out for the evening," Leopold said in a whisper, answering the question that Kathleen had not yet articulated. "Except for Maude."

Maude—the sister? She was still here?

Perhaps the concerns she fleetingly thought appeared on her face, for Leopold smiled. "Do not be concerned—Maude sleeps the sleep of the dead, and besides, is on quite the opposite side of the house to me. Any noise we make, she will not hear."

Any noise we make.

Kathleen could not help but quiver at the mere suggestion. True, she was hardly an expert in these matters. It had only been by accident that she had discovered precisely it was that a husband and wife had shared. She was well-read, and she supposed her father had forgotten that particular book had been left in the library. She hadn't needed her fallen sister to explain the details of what went on between lovers in the cover of night.

The truth of the matter was in many ways just as strange. Could a man truly give gratification to a woman by putting his— in her—

"Come on," Leopold said in a low voice, squeezing her hand.

There was something astonishingly erotic about slowly ascending a staircase hand in hand with a gentleman to whom one was not married. Of course she would be—Kathleen could still hardly believe it, but Leopold had made a quite clear offer of marriage.

Still, the knowledge that she would within weeks be Lady Leopold Chance, a name that made her stomach lurch, did not detract from the forbidden feeling of it all. As Kathleen followed Leopold down a dark corridor and around a corner, anticipation curled within her, sparking need across her body that only he could satisfy, and it would not be long.

Leopold reached out and grasped a door handle. Then he hesitated.

Kathleen waited for a beat, wondering if he was merely opening the door very slowly to prevent any creaking. When it became quite clear that Leopold had not moved in almost a minute, she whispered, "Is everything quite well?"

A jerk of his head, a look of surprise, as though he had half-forgotten she was there, and then a smile that warmed her right down to the soles of her feet.

He nodded then opened the door.

It was, Kathleen realized as she stepped into what had to have been Leopold's bedchamber, a very personal thing to do, inviting someone into your most intimate space. Why, other than maids and the like, no one ever saw this chamber.

Curiosity was natural. What she had not expected was astonishment.

It was... Well, it was Leopold. Packed to the rafters with archery paraphernalia.

Kathleen dropped his hand and stepped into the room, open mouthed, at the sight of so many beautiful objects she could not have imagined possible to all pack into one room. Bows—several of them, all different sizes. The smallest were the most worn. Had these been the bows with which Leopold had first learned to shoot an arrow?

Speaking of arrows, there were hundreds. Many of them were packed in boxes or quivers, lying about the place, but on one wall was a cabinet of arrows that had been set most artistically. Precisely why those arrows, it was not clear.

There were books, yes, but books about archery. Books about the history of archery, of archery around the world, of the technique of famous archers and the stance that amateurs could ape. There were notes about archery scattered all over a console table—from one glance, Kathleen guessed that Leopold had been noting down his success rates.

And there, on the wall beside the cabinet of arrows, was—

"My word."

It was difficult to have any other reaction. The painting was truly spectacular; clearly, the Chance family had commissioned one of the greats, because the landscape was truly beautiful, rendered so exquisitely that Kathleen rather thought she could step into it, should she so wish.

But it wasn't the landscape that had taken her breath away. No, it was the figure in the foreground, before the Grecian temple.

He was an archer. He was tall and handsome, with hair that appeared to blow in a slight breeze. He was holding a bow and arrow so naturally, so elegantly, it was as though he had born to it.

It was also, most unmistakably, Leopold.

"Ah," said Leopold.

"What a magnificent painting," Kathleen murmured, stepping up to it and placing an almost shaking hand on the frame. "You… You look otherworldly."

"My cousin painted it. She was desperate for a model and I eventually gave in. Well, my mother volunteered me. *Voluntold*, as she put it," said Leopold hastily, speaking at a normal volume. Evidently, no one could hear them from here. "It's daft. I wouldn't allow my mother to hang it downstairs."

"But you look incredible." She could hardly understand why he would not want such evidence of his handsome features and his talent with the bow downstairs. "And you said your cousin painted it? He is very talented."

"She."

She.

And for some reason, that gentle correction whirled a rush of panic in Kathleen.

She. A lady artist, someone who clearly had to paint family members, not strangers or models, because otherwise there would be a scandal—and here she was, standing in the bedchamber of a gentleman to whom she was not married!

True, she would be…but that did not excuse this behavior!

This was the Chance family. Anything that occurred with

them was instant gossip fodder, and she would be that fodder if she was found here.

Was she truly about to make the very same mistake her sister had?

"I should go."

The three words slipped from Kathleen's mouth as she stepped to the door, skirts swishing, dread pouring through her veins, but she was unable to open it.

That was because Leopold had his hand against the door.

"Leopold—"

"Look, I can understand why you would want to leave," he said hurriedly, "but—"

"Are you truly going to keep me prisoner here?"

Just one moment's look in his eyes told her the truth. Leopold swiftly removed his hand from the door. "I didn't mean—I know this invites scandal. But I love you, I want to marry you—I *will* marry you. And waiting to experience the most delectable joy, the most intimate connection, merely because of a piece of paper and twenty minutes inside a church…"

Kathleen swallowed. There was such hunger in Leopold's face, though it was not a possessive hunger, but a fierce one. One that demonstrated he knew precisely what he wanted.

And he wanted her.

Leopold reached out and moved the handle, opening the door a few inches. "You can go. Of course you can go. But I want you to stay. I want to kiss you all over and worship you for the beautiful woman you are. I want to put my hands on you, and pleasure you, and show you the smallest glimpse of what being my wife will be. And if you don't want that now, I will understand. And I will still marry you. The pleasure can wait—I will wait for you."

Kathleen's breath shortened.

It was perhaps the most incredible thing anyone had ever said to her. And he had given her the choice.

Well. It was hardly a choice, was it?

Slamming the door shut with one hand and grasping Leopold's lapel with the other, she gave in to the longing that had been cresting her desires for so long.

And he responded. In truth, it appeared he had only just been able to hold himself back from tugging her into a tight embrace. His kisses were fire pouring down onto her lips, but they did not remain there for long. Kathleen gasped as Leopold's lips trailed to her ear, pressing heat onto a place that made her quiver, before descending. The descent led to an ascent in carnal delight pouring through her, flickers of bliss quivering through her limbs.

Oh, it was hardly possible that she was still standing, yet his strong arm around her waist prevented her from falling as Leopold teased molten kisses almost the hem of her gown. Only when Kathleen whimpered, pulling him closer, did he laugh and carefully place an almost reverential kiss on her décolletage.

His kisses did not remain reverential for long. Kathleen moaned and wove her fingers in his hair as Leopold lavished devotion in the form of teasing kisses and nibbles over the swell of her breast.

"Leopold…"

Kathleen had not intended to moan his name, but that did not seem to matter. It was tugged from her lips because of what his hands were now doing. Cupping her buttocks with one, the other was doing something noticeably odd with her skirts.

Her skirts?

Almost too late did she realize what he intended and Kathleen's eyes widened as Leopold's hand disappeared under her skirts. Her knee, her thigh, her—

"Leopold!"

He halted, lifting his panting head, which appeared muzzy with desire, and grinned. "Did you want me to stop?"

Kathleen opened her mouth, closed it again, then managed, "But—But I didn't think this was how it was done."

"You're going to like this," he said with such confidence, it was difficult to even consider arguing with him. "And if you don't, I'll stop. I promise. Just give it a sporting chance."

It was impossible not to smile at such a request, most ridiculously put. "You are a fool. You do know that, don't you?"

Leopold's lopsided grin caused the ache between her legs to ripple. "Only with you. Ready?"

Kathleen nodded, though precisely what she was supposed to be ready for, she did not know. His right hand was right by her secret place, her warmth surely now tangible to him, yet he did not appear disgusted or dismayed. Indeed, his ribcage was shortening, his pupils dilated, and his lips returning once more to her neck.

When he whispered, low, urgent, desperate, Kathleen closed her eyes and lost herself in the sensation of his breath on her neck and his fingers slowly brushing over her curls.

"You see, my love, when an archer knows precisely the target that he wants to hit, he does not always aim directly for it."

"He… He doesn't?" Kathleen whimpered.

"Sometimes he goes…near it."

It was all she could do not to cry out as Leopold drifted a finger along her crease. The sudden spasm of boiling pleasure was almost as unexpected as it was welcome.

Kathleen gripped his shoulders, her knees weak. "Leopold—"

"And then he examines the target," he murmured, pressing a kiss on her neck. "Just to make sure it's the target he wants."

A finger—a single finger of his had somehow slipped inside her and despite the pain Kathleen had expected, there was nothing but soaring hedonism. His fingertip had brushed past a nub within her that when touched had shot a bolt of unadulterated ecstasy through her.

It was over just as instantly as it had begun, but the stroking within her continued and it felt most delightful.

Kathleen gasped, trying to think of something to say, something to contribute, but it was all she could do to stay upright.

"And when an archer knows precisely where the target is, he…practices," Leopold murmured.

She could not help but whimper with sensual bliss as he slipped a second finger into her, delving deeper, stroking her, caressing her and causing such waves of satisfaction that she was hardly sure how she was still upright.

And still that first finger danced so delicately close to her nub, his target, that she wanted to weep. "Please…please, Leopold—"

"You want me to hit the target?"

"Please—"

"I'll encircle it first," he murmured, lowering his head to her breasts and licking, teasing, kissing through the soon damp fabric of her gown as one finger stroked inside her and the other slowly, slowly, slowly circled the aching nub that demanded relief.

Relief, it appeared, he would not give.

There was a pressure building inside her that Kathleen did not understand but knew only Leopold could release, and she could have sobbed as she clung to him and abandoned herself to the pleasure—and yet it was not enough.

"Leopold, now, now!"

"Here comes the arrow."

It was like blowing apart from the inside out. Somehow, his tongue had meandered below the hem of her gown and had found a nipple, and as he brought it into his mouth and tugged, his fingers within her finally pressed hard and swirled around that precious nub.

Kathleen cried out, not caring who could hear her, not caring if the whole world knew that Leopold Chance was pleasuring her. Her body roared, arching against him, quivering with unanticipated decadence, and as the pieces of her finally slowed and softened and Leopold brought his fingers out of her, she opened her eyes to stare in wonderment at this man. This man who could do anything.

He could certainly do anything he wished to her.

"That… That was…"

Leopold hummed, evidently delighted that he had given her such exquisite ecstasy. "There's more."

Unquestionably, there was more. There had to be more. Kathleen was aware they had not done what she had expected two people to do together, but...more? More pleasure?

Her knees managing to hold her, Kathleen accepted Leopold's kisses as he slowly undid the ties of her gown, allowing the fabric to fall to the floor. She had not worn a corset this evening, having re-dressed herself quickly after initially heading to bed. Stays, stockings, all were slowly and lovingly removed by the man she adored.

What was most impressive, however, was how he managed to do so and remove most of his own clothes as well. When Kathleen blinked, coming to herself, it was to see that Leopold had divested himself of jacket, waistcoat, shirt, and boots.

Naught but his trousers stood between her nude body and his own.

She watched him swallow, his throat bobbing, and felt her body tingling. This may not have been entirely new to him, but this moment was—this sharing of himself. Of themselves, with each other.

Slowly, without taking her eyes from his own, Kathleen lifted her chemise with trembling fingers over her head. Though the eye contact was lost for but a moment, it was a relief to restore it.

It almost helped her to forget that she was now naked.

Leopold's eyes were wide and he almost fell over as he rapidly pulled his trousers off and stood before her.

Kathleen stared.

Well. It wasn't as though she had never known what was beneath a man's trousers. She'd been to the British Museum, after all. They had a whole heap of naked statues, not that Angela had approved of them visiting.

But this was... Well. So much...*more.*

"I love you," he whispered.

And the moment of shock was gone, replaced with nothing but affection. Kathleen reached out and took his hand, surprising herself in her boldness as she led Leopold to his own bed. "And I love you."

They ended up in a tangle of quivering limbs, touching and tasting and kissing to the point where she hardly knew where she ended and Leopold began. Somehow, he twisted her onto her back while he remained nestled between her knees and—

"Oh!"

Kathleen arched her back, expecting pain but feeling nothing but pleasure as Leopold speared into her, his manhood thrusting true into her very core.

It was a reminder of the elation she had felt as his fingers had entered her, but this was deeper, and darker, and all the more delicious.

"Kathleen? I have not hurt you, have I?"

She looked up to see Leopold's concern and could have kissed him—would have done, in fact, if she had been able to reach him.

"You are not injured?"

When she spoke, it was in a strangled voice. "I soon will be, if you do not bring me to ecstasy again!"

And it was laughter and kisses that Leopold rained down as he moved into her arms, leaning on an elbow as he withdrew almost all his manhood then thrust forward, an arrow unleased from a steady bow again and again and again, and Kathleen whimpered as the waves began to build.

His kisses, his touch, the safety of their love, their affection for each other, and the knowledge that such heights of bliss would soon be reached—it was all too much.

Kathleen clung to Leopold's shoulders. "It's happening again, it's—oh—oh, Leopold!"

And her body spasmed, clinging to him, keeping him as tight and as deep as possible, and he swore as his body twitched, the careful and measured movements becoming frantic and faster, until he was pouring himself into her and Kathleen could do nothing but hold on for dear life.

Then Leopold collapsed into her waiting arms.

"Kathleen," he moaned, nuzzling his head on her neck. "Oh... Oh, Kathleen..."

She held him, knowing this moment was just as much a part of becoming one as all the rest. And when she pressed a kiss against his cheek Leopold lifted his head and met her lips, and it was everything. He was everything. This would be every part of their future.

Their future together.

Chapter Sixteen

August 6, 1840

THE SLOW, DAWNING light that crept through the undrawn curtains was enough to wake Leopold, if the aching in his bones had not been sufficient.

Unconsciousness was dragged from him. Protesting at every juncture, his mind slipped from the welcoming grasp of slumber and was drawn inexorably toward the light. Toward waking. Toward dawn.

Leopold groaned.

He was lying face down in his bed, without his nightshirt, tiredness pulling at the corners of his eyes most inexplicably. He had, after all, had a good night's sleep, had he not? He could feel the satisfaction in his limbs, how comfortable the bed was, the way Kathleen had earlier wrapped her legs around his—

He sat up so hastily, his pillow tipped to the floor as he stared at the now-empty bed.

Kathleen.

"It's happening again, it's—oh—oh, Leopold!"

The memories were slipping back now, startling him not only with their power, but at how readily he lost himself within them. Kathleen, naked and writhing beneath him. Kathleen, gasping his name and attempting, quite unsuccessfully, to be quiet. Kathleen, looking at him like…

Like he was the only man in the world.

Leopold smiled in slight awe as the recollections soared into his mind. Dear God, he had—and she had… They had…

"You are not injured?"

"I soon will be, if you do not bring me to ecstasy again!"

It was more than he could have ever hoped for. It was more than he could have imagined, after ruining his reputation with that foolish rumor that he was a cheat.

Well, Kathleen did not believe so. She believed in him, in his word—so much that on the mere verbal agreement between them that no one else had heard, she had been willing to give herself to him.

It was an honor. It was a privilege.

It was certainly more than he had expected from a quiet night at home.

Sinking back into the remaining pillow on his bed, Leopold tried to think, but it was a distinct challenge. The taste of Kathleen was still on his lips. The giddiness she'd given him remained, like a port drunk too late in the evening and not rid from his system by morning.

Not that he wanted to rid Kathleen from his system—far from it. No, she was spectacular—everything he had been missing from life, everything he had not known he had wanted.

And she was his.

Blinking at the astonishing turn of events the evening had taken, Leopold spent a few minutes in bed trying to understand precisely how it had happened. After a while, he decided it did not matter.

It had been done. That was the most important part. He had gained a wife, one who was brave and outspoken and refined and elegant. She was beautiful, and scalding to the touch, and gentle.

His happiness had never been greater.

Leopold spent at least another hour in bed reliving the memories of the night before and then wondered with great pain how Kathleen must have slipped out of the room, the house, even, in the early hours of the morning, without saying goodbye.

Well, she was perhaps wiser than he was. Lord knew what his father would say if he found—

His father.

Leopold swallowed. It was going to be an interesting conversation. He would have to speak to his father immediately, of course, and make the case for marrying her. It would require confessing—or as relating as much as he could—about Kathleen's sister's past, and he would have to be firm in his resolve.

He was going to marry her, ruination of her sister or not. He would make the case for marrying her, make it absolutely clear to his father that he would brook no argument…and then ask for his portion with which to establish his new household.

Oh, that was going to be awkward.

When Leopold descended the staircase, however, it was to discover much to his surprise that neither his father nor mother were at breakfast. In fact, no one was.

"Where is everyone?" he inquired of Nicholls, their butler.

The servant cleared his throat professionally. "I am afraid the rest of the family has already breakfasted, my lord."

"'Already breakfasted'?" Leopold repeated.

That was most unlike them—his siblings most especially. None of the Chances were particularly known for their ability to get going in the mornings—at least, not this branch of the family.

"Yes, breakfasted, my lord," confirmed Nicholls.

It was most odd. "Why so early?"

The butler cleared his throat again and made a dramatic turn to look at the longcase clock in the corner. Leopold followed his gaze.

Ah. That was why.

"I was actually about to serve luncheon, my lord," said the man delicately, with only the most delicate hint of reproach. "Shall I—"

"In fact, Nicholls, you could do me a favor and ask a footman to deliver a note for me," said Leopold, his mind sparking with the idea. "As my parents are undoubtedly out by now?"

The servant inclined his head. "The dowager duke and duchess are out visiting, Master Leopold."

"Yes, yes, right..." *How very like Father to be unavailable for conversation just when I need him*, Leopold could not help but think. It was most irritating, but there it was.

And it would give him the opportunity to speak to a certain someone beforehand.

"Your note, my lord?"

Leopold blinked. "I beg your pardon?"

The long-suffering butler sighed and attempted to smile, but he was clearly out of practice. "Your note, my lord. The one you wished the footman to deliver."

"Oh. Oh, yes."

It did not take long to write. At least, it did not take him long to write the note, which eventually was given to a footman along with strict instructions to place it into the hands of the younger Miss Andilet and no one else. Leopold spent almost ten minutes writing the other notes first, but they were all given up as a bad job and thrown in the fireplace to be burnt when the weather dipped low enough to warrant it.

Rather embarrassingly, the resulting note was painfully short.

Miss Andilet—archery today at 3 P.M.

Leopold had thought of a great deal that he wanted to put in the note. That she was special, and rare, and precious. That if he did not follow through on his offer to her, then he would be a fool, and worse, a coward. That she could have her pick of the gentlemen in Town and he was honored to be hers. That he wanted to—

That was when he had run out of both paper and decisiveness. Having Nicholls breathing over his shoulder did not help.

As it was, the note was hopefully succinct and to the point. Making the arrangement to practice archery with her was one thing. Seeing her, and preventing himself from kissing her, was quite another.

How Leopold managed to endure the following few hours, he did not know. Maude wandered in and attempted to speak with him about something that she said was important, but he could not make his mind focus, and eventually, she snorted and wandered out again muttering about useless brothers, which Leopold thought was a touch harsh.

And then it was time. He stepped out into the crisp, afternoon air and felt the wave of heat, and he wondered how it could no longer compare with the heat he had shared with Kathleen.

Leopold beamed at almost everyone he passed on his way to the London Archery Club. Wasn't life wonderful? Wasn't it easy? After all his desperate attempts to make people believe he was no card sharp, it did not matter. Kathleen believed him. She trusted him, and she was the only person who would ever matter.

The Club was busy when he arrived. Chatter erupted from all sides as he entered, and Leopold heard a few people mutter about a shady dealer.

It took him a moment, in his buoyancy, to realize whom they were talking about.

For a moment, a flickering heartbeat, the elation from his evening with Kathleen wavered. Was he ever to be truly rid of this reputation—one he had done nothing to earn?

And then stability resumed. What did it matter what others thought of him, if Kathleen believed him? What did he need the respect of others for, if Kathleen esteemed him?

"Gentlemen," Leopold said politely, inclining his head as he walked through the London Archery Club and out to the other side.

There they were: the butts that were such a centralized part of his life. Now they had combined with Kathleen, it was hard to think of another firm foundation of his life.

So all he had to do was select the bow she liked and find one of his own, and—

"I thought you would be here early," came a teasing voice.

The recognition of that voice sent heat soaring through Leopold's limbs and made him want to forget about archery completely and instead turn around and kiss the owner of that voice most heartily.

As it was, there were other gentlemen out by the butts, making the instinct impossible to follow through on. Which was a shame.

Kathleen was beaming, her cheeks pink as she met his eye, but her gaze was nonetheless unabashed. "Good afternoon, Lord Leopold."

There was a slight tease in her air, not a mockery but a flirtation, and he reveled in it. After all, it was not as though he spoke this way with anyone else. This was something they shared, something unique to themselves. It was precious, and perfect, and he could not comprehend anything more splendid.

Well. Perhaps not many things.

"Good afternoon, Miss Andilet," Leopold replied, smiling at the mischievous formality she was using. "I hope you slept well?"

Perhaps that was too direct a prod, for her cheeks blossomed then into dark red. She overcame the sudden shock of his directness soon enough, however, and with only the merest glance over at the other gentlemen of the London Archery Club, stepped closer to him.

"I am sorry that I departed so swiftly when…when we were last together," she said softly, her eyes expressive. "I thought it best that I not be discovered."

"You were quite right, even though I admit myself disappointed to find you gone," Leopold replied, keeping his voice nonchalant in tone but low in volume. "It was… It was…"

How could he explain precisely what last evening had meant to him?

It had been perfect. It had been astounding. It had entirely rewritten his expectations of the cosmos and yet they had delivered perfection upon perfection. It had changed him in a way that he was still discovering, the sunlight somehow brighter, colors now more vibrant.

And here she was, standing before him, utterly perfect.

Leopold swallowed, his mouth dry. Kathleen was humming.

"It was?" she repeated with a quizzical brow.

Forcing aside the temptation to kiss her furiously, Leopold smiled softly. "It was precisely what I wanted. Whom I wanted."

The delight in her eyes was unmistakable. Oh, they were going to be so happy. Leopold had never presumed he would find someone who could bring him this depth of contentment, yet here he was. Standing before her with a bow in his hands.

A bow, and no arrows.

Leopold swore.

Kathleen hastily turned around as though something had occurred behind her. The instant panic that they had been seen together tugged at Leopold's conscience. Soon, they would not have to concern themselves with such things. The moment he had spoken to his father and then traveled to the country and formally requested her hand from Mr. Andilet, all could be announced. All would be well—well on their way to their wedding.

Heat flickered within Leopold. *Our wedding. Our marriage.*

"What is the matter?" Kathleen asked, whipping around again to stare.

"Oh, it is nothing—I merely did not bring any arrows from the store," Leopold said hastily, seeking to reassure her. "It was a mistake only."

Her shoulders relaxed and her lips quirked slightly. "Something else must be on your mind."

"I wonder what," Leopold shot back with a laugh. "Or rather, who."

Their laughter was unabashed and unashamed. After all, he could not help but think, why not laugh with the woman he was going to marry? They were not even touching—worse luck—and they were not hiding their assignation. Meeting. Practice time together. There was no chaperone, for the appearance of propriety if not the truth of it, but that didn't bother him.

Soon they would be Lord and Lady Leopold Chance.

The thought caused a ripple of something startling to shoot up his spine. Leopold could hardly understand it. How was it possible to be this happy?

"You know," Kathleen said as Leopold stepped toward the London Archery Club to retrieve some arrows, "I believe I have won our bet. I assured you I was more skilled than I appeared to be these last few practice sessions, but I still can't quite hit the mark from fifty yards."

Leopold halted in his tracks and turned to smile at the woman he loved.

It was impossible not to laugh. "You know, I suppose so. Congratulations, Miss Andilet."

She curtseyed with a chuckling smile. "You are quite welcome, Lord Leopold. I suppose you are going to pay up?"

It was foolish of him to flinch at the phrasing. It was ridiculous to the extreme to think for a moment that she was teasing him about the card-playing nonsense. It was daft of him to connect her gentle teasing with the censure of Society.

It did not help. For a flashing moment, Leopold was hurt.

And then it was gone. She had not intended it, he knew.

Laughing wryly, he said, "Yes. Yes, I suppose so."

He left her beaming, which was precisely how he wanted to leave her, then walked over to the Club. It would not take him long to step inside and retrieve the arrows.

His hand was on the door. He had turned it; the door was ajar. Yet he did not step through.

"—another three shillings then on Lord Leopold bedding the woman," drawled a voice that was painfully familiar. "And two shillings against from Mr. Lister. Are you sure you do not want to up your bet, Mr. Lister? The pot is growing fat."

Murmurs and laughter and chortles. Leopold could barely think.

"Go on, then, another shilling that he isn't tupping her," came a voice he vaguely recognized.

"You're mad, Lister." That was a voice Leopold did not recognize. "He's definitely rolled her in the hay. Have you not seen the way he looks at her?"

"The way they look at each other," retorted Lord Graycott, the first voice Leopold had heard. "God, I had no idea he was such a rake! Just like his brother."

There was murmured laughter again, and voices that spoke over each other so that Leopold could not hear what they were saying. Words like 'cad' and 'brute' and 'deflower' rose to the top and his pulse was thundering so loudly in his ribcage, he could hardly breathe.

He could not breathe. He could not breathe.

"I just hope she wasn't too disappointed," came Lord Graycott's cruel laughter. "I cannot imagine Chance is a great lover."

"Oh, if I were to suggest disappointment, I would say it was all on his side." The sneering voice of Mr. Lister, clearly delighted to be speaking with a lord, came through the gap in the door clearly. "She's never accompanied by a chaperone, like a proper lady ought to be. Runs in the family, I presume. You have heard the story of her sister, have you not?"

And that was when Leopold barged into the room, throwing the door back with such violence that it slammed against the wall.

The room was a tableau. There were perhaps six or seven gentlemen in a group, all laughing—at least, all previously laughing. They were now frozen, looks of shock or horror or embarrassment shading each of their faces.

Almost all their faces.

"Well, well, the man himself." Lord Graycott sneered as he leaned back in his seat and pocketed what appeared to be a great deal of silver. "Are you here to tell us to whom the pot should go?"

It was becoming difficult to keep the anger within. It strained against Leopold's ribcage, demanding vengeance, demanding a slap of a glove across the cheek and pistols at dawn.

The queen did not approve of such things, but surely, as a lady she would understand that it was necessary. He could not, would not, permit such things to be said—and about *Kathleen*.

About his future wife.

"You look a little ruffled, Chance," commented Lord Gray-cott with a smirk that made Leopold's anger darken. "I suppose you're here to put us out of our misery."

"That would be too good for you," snarled Leopold before he could stop himself.

That certainly changed the atmosphere of the room. Where there had been laughter, there was now silence, dropped jaws, pinched eyebrows.

"I told you before to close the pot," Leopold said quietly, a thrum of anger managing to make its way into his voice, despite himself. "I told you all betting about her was off."

"Yes, yes, but once I saw just how many people were willing to bet on that woman of yours, I could not help but keep it open," Lord Graycott shot back.

"I told you to close the pot, and you kept it open."

"Oh, you'll get your share," said Lord Graycott, waving a hand nonchalantly.

Leopold spluttered, unable to form the outrage he felt into words. Did the brute think that was his gripe; that he would not gain a percentage of the proceedings? Did the man have no character, no honor, no—

A sound. A scuffle, no more, but it was enough to gain Leopold's attention.

He turned, as did most of the men within the London Archery Club, but it was surely only his heart that went cold at the sight of what was before them.

Kathleen. She was standing in the doorway, her mouth open, horror in her eyes.

She stumbled backward.

"Kathleen?" Leopold did not understand it—he had not been gone overly long. Precisely why she could not have waited for him, he did not know.

Her eyes met his and he saw such betrayal there, such pain, that it were as though someone had slit his stomach.

Oh, God, had she heard—

"Kathleen," he said hurriedly, stepping forward.

He was not swift enough. She had hurtled backward, retreating from him as though he were a cruel man with no intentions but to harm her.

The laughter of Lord Graycott, of Mr. Lister, of all the cruel and unthinking men behind him faded as Leopold hurried out into the fresh air. The gentlemen who had been practicing their archery had gone and it was only himself and Kathleen, and she was looking at him like he was a monster.

Leopold recoiled. He could not help it. She could not have injured him any greatly unless she had picked up a bow and arrow and shot him.

"You were betting on me?" she said in clipped tones.

"No," Leopold said firmly. She had to understand. "Lord Graycott—"

"I don't want to hear about the friends you've been betting on me with!" Kathleen shot back.

No, no, this is all wrong. "I have had nothing to do with it!"

"I heard you!"

She'd heard him? Leopold did not understand—if she had truly heard him, would she not have heard just how greatly he'd attempted to prevent the damned gambling?

"You said that you had closed the betting," Kathleen said, her eyes filling with tears. "Did you believe you had secured me? That you had wooed me so sufficiently that I would give into your demands, that I would simper and comply?"

"'*Give into*'? It was *your* suggestion. Last night was your idea!" Leopold said before he could help himself.

It was most definitely the wrong thing to say.

Tears were pouring down Kathleen's cheeks now. "I trusted you—I thought you cared about—"

"I *do* care about you—I love you! Please, you have to understand—"

"I *do* understand," she said fiercely. "You think I learned nothing from my sister? You think I did not worry that you would not hold to your word?"

The disaster was upon him and Leopold was still not sure how it had happened. "Graycott wanted to bet on—and I told him to stop, that it was not right—"

"Because you had too much control over the outcome and were concerned you would be called a cheat again, is that it?" Kathleen's words were spoken flatly, as though she could no longer summon any true anger.

It was quite the opposite in Leopold. How could she—how could she accuse him of cheating, when she knew not only what an upstanding man he was, but how he had been accused unfairly before?

Why would she do that? Hurt him, on purpose?

"I suppose I should not be surprised you accepted my bet almost immediately," Kathleen said, sniffing as tears continued to fall down her face. "And now I am ruined."

"You are not ruined!" he all but shouted. How could she think he would not honor his proposal? "This stupid betting pool—"

"I trusted you."

"You had every right to trust me, and to continue to trust me!" Leopold tried to smile, yet it was heartbreaking to see the woman he loved so upset, so convinced of his malice. "Look, I know my reputation as a gambler makes it difficult to believe me, but—"

"What makes it difficult to believe you is that I just heard how you had planned the bet!" she said hotly.

Leopold swore. "That is not what happened!"

She had completely misunderstood, but worse, it appeared he would not be given the opportunity to explain. Kathleen was now marching away, toward the side gate that was unlocked during the day, as it always was—marching out of his life.

Finally able to force his feet forward, Leopold called after her. "Kathleen, wait!"

"I will not," she called over her shoulder, and her tearstained face twisted his gut. "I never want to hear from you again!"

The slam of the gate right in his face made Leopold halt, but it was the grief in her words that had halted his feet.

She did not want to hear it. The explanation, the truth—she did not want to know. She believed him to be a rake, a liar, and a cheat. If it was that easy for her to believe such lies…what was the point in arguing?

Leopold slumped his forehead against the gate and blew out a long exhale. She was gone, then. The woman he loved. And he would never see her again.

Chapter Seventeen

August 8, 1840

S TRANGE. KATHLEEN HAD never noticed a stain in that particular part of the ceiling.

Staring at it, the little black, ragged edges as it crept across her ceiling, she could almost forget about the pain in her ribs. She could almost forget the crusted tears at the corners of her eyes. She could almost forget—

Bang, bang, bang!

"You have to let me in eventually, Kathleen Mary Andilet," came her sister's irate and concerned voice. "You can't stay in there forever!"

Quite to the contrary, Kathleen was almost certain she *would* stay in her little bedchamber forever. She saw no need to ever leave, after all, and she was adequately provided for. A swift stop at a pie seller on her rushed way home from the London Archery Club had given her not one, but four large pies. If she was careful, they could last her an entire week. She would never have to leave before then.

Bang, bang, bang!

"Are you going to tell me what's happened? Because I know something has happened and if you don't tell me about it, I... I..."

Kathleen half-smiled to herself as she lay on her bed, even through her tears. Yes, her sister did not have much of a threatening way about her. That had never been Angela's way.

Her sister's voice faded as Kathleen ceased attending to it, distracted instead by her own very unpleasant thoughts.

Thoughts, and memories.

"Look, I know my reputation as a gambler makes it difficult to believe me, but—"

"What makes it difficult to believe you is that I just heard how you had planned the bet!"

Turning onto her side as though she could turn away from the pain, Kathleen tried not to visualize the look on Leopold—on Lord Leopold's face. Tried not to think about what she had overheard. Tried not to think about how she had been betrayed.

She screwed her eyes tightly, but that could not force the memories from her mind. What had she done? Had she truly been as foolish as her sister?

Difficult as it was to admit, especially to herself, Kathleen had always considered herself... Well, better than her sister. Not better. Cleverer. She had not gotten herself into trouble. She had not been caught out by a gentleman. She had not allowed a scandal to befall the family, even with the way she'd navigated Town without a chaperone.

It had been a priggish sort of pride, and only now could Kathleen see just how foolish and arrogant she had been.

Because here she was, having made almost exactly the same mistake. Despite all the careful instruction their mother had given them, and that which Angela had given her, Kathleen had very carefully and very cleverly made precisely the same mistake.

Bang, bang, bang!

"I will go to Scotland Yard! A bobby will break the door down. He'll make you see reason!"

Kathleen smiled weakly to herself as she stared at the door that was the victim of so much knocking. A peeler would not bother with the likes of her. What had occurred was a tragedy, to be sure, and it would be the end of their meager reputations. They would have to leave London, attempt to get by on their father's allowance in a different city—but it was no crime.

It certainly felt like a crime, what Leopold had done to her. But it was not.

"I should never have allowed you to come to London."

Kathleen sat up. This time, her sister's voice was sorrowful, slow, self-criticizing. The knocking on the door had ceased and instead there was—was that a sniff?

Biting her lip, Kathleen tried to harden her heart. Yes, her sister was crying. There would be a great many tears shed once the truth was out, wouldn't there? Perhaps it was better that Angela was getting the worst of it from her system.

Another sniff. A half-strangled sob.

Guilt twisted in Kathleen's gut as she cried into her handkerchief. This was her fault. She had brought ruin onto the family, perhaps even worse than Angela had, and there was no going back from this.

A shaking hand pressed against her stomach, against the place where they had joined and there could now be... but surely, the odds...

A timid tap on the door. "Please, Kathleen."

Kathleen sighed. Her sister knew she could ignore her until the cows came home when she shouted and raged. It was the quiet that she could never resist.

Tension clutched at her gut. And where had resisting got either of them? Leopold—Lord Leopold was a gambler with a poor reputation who had lost the woman who loved him. She had lost her dignity and her innocence, and perhaps had gained something as well...

"Kathleen?"

Kathleen sighed heavily, rose from the bed, and padded across the bedchamber floor, her handkerchief clutched in one hand. She was going to regret this in about fifteen minutes, she was almost sure of it—but as there was a small chance that Angela would alleviate her worries and lift her spirits, it was worth the risk.

She swallowed a sob and laugh at the same time. *Give my sister a sporting chance.*

The click of the lock seemed to resound loudly around the

room. The instant the key had turned, so too did the door handle, though this time, the movement was coming from the other side.

The door opened, Kathleen needing to step promptly back to ensure her nose wasn't knocked by the swiftly moving wood.

"Kathleen?" said her sister hastily, glancing at her face as though seeking out the truth from her eyes.

Try as she might, Kathleen could not smile. "Angela."

And then the tears came back.

Angela was swift. She pulled Kathleen into an embrace that was tight and reassuring, one hand stroking her hair as Kathleen poured all her frustration and pain into her sobs.

It did not help. But it did help.

When the tears finally abated—and for a while, Kathleen had thought they would never end—Angela stepped back and looked carefully into her sister's eyes.

"Handkerchief," she said quietly.

Kathleen stifled a smile and a sob and passed her sister her handkerchief. It was almost dripping.

"Ah. Right, well. You can borrow mine," said Angela, pulling hers from her sleeve and handing it to her sister. "Come on, tidy yourself up, and then you can tell me what you're moaning about."

It is a special kind of sympathy, that which you receive from your family, Kathleen could not help but think as she used her sister's handkerchief to mop up her weeping eyes and give her nose a good blow. It wasn't always that comforting in and of itself, but it was reassuring in its predictability.

Now she's going to ask me—

"I suppose this is about a gentleman," Angela said quietly as she moved across the room and sat on Kathleen's bed.

What was she supposed to say? The truth would be out there soon—she doubted that the gentlemen of the London Archery Club who had been involved in the betting pool had any honor at all. They would not think twice before bandying her name about the place, ruining her reputation even further, and making it impossible for her to ever go back there.

Go back there? What was she thinking?

"Kathleen?"

"Yes," Kathleen said quietly, turning to her sister and trying to keep her gaze defiant.

"I said, I suppose it—"

"And I said, *yes.*" Kathleen sighed, willing her cheeks not to flush but not holding out much hope. "I… I've made a terrible mistake."

It was painful indeed to see the look of abject horror on Angela's face.

And there it is, Kathleen could not help but think. The fears of her family, her sister in particular, had come true. She had lost her good name, the good name of Andilet, just as her sister had done. Once lost, there was no retrieving one's reputation. It was impossible; no gentleman would ever look at you again. No lady would ever consider conversing with you. Invitations were over, socializing done with, and the best you could hope for was not to be stared at or pointed at.

It was not much of a life to look forward to. Assuming she ever had a chance at a better life, after her sister's fall.

"Oh, no," murmured Angela, dismay palpable in every syllable. "Not…not…a *gentleman.* That man who came here?"

It was challenging indeed to maintain eye contact with her sister as Kathleen nodded, but somehow, she managed it.

The misery that swept into the room was almost tangible. It was like a tidal wave of destruction moving into their lives, making it impossible to think, to see, to breathe.

Everything they had tried to maintain—the veneer of respectability, the joy of being in London, the hope that one day, everyone would forget about how the eldest Miss Andilet had experienced such a shameful rendezvous… All that was over.

Kathleen swallowed, her throat dry and seemingly only made of sandpaper.

What had she done?

Yes, well, obviously *that*—but that was part of the problem. She should never have permitted her desires to overcome her good sense, even if Lord Leopold Chance was the most enticing and intriguing man she had ever met.

But even if that had never occurred, it was his damned gambling obsession that had ruined her. She'd believed him when he'd insisted the rumors weren't true. But now? The archery, that, she could always admire, but the betting pool? He could not leave it alone, could he? He could not allow her to aim to be respectable. He had to drag her name into the mud.

Angela cleared her throat and Kathleen jumped, so lost had she become in her thoughts.

"Come and sit down," her sister said quietly. "I think you had better tell me all about it."

"Oh, there is not much to tell," Kathleen said as airily as she could manage.

Angela was not fooled for a moment. "Yes, there is."

There was. It appeared to take a long time, too, for the sun's shadows moved about the sparsely furnished bedchamber as Kathleen attempted to encapsulate in just a few words precisely how she had fallen into Lord Leopold Chance's orbit. How she had been so attracted to him, so entranced by him. How she had made that foolish bet, a mistake in hindsight but a perceived cleverness at the time. It had bought her time with him.

Angela's eyebrows had risen at that point. Kathleen chose to ignore them.

Her tale continued, explaining how the archery had led to kissing, which had led to—

"I don't actually need that particular detail," said her sister hastily. "I… I get the basics. He bedded you."

We bedded each other, Kathleen wanted to say, *and it was so much more than a bedding. It was a meeting of minds, of hearts, of souls. Our bodies were there, yes, and they sparked a great deal of pleasure—but it was the connection that surpassed anything I could have dreamed of.*

"It all sounds wonderful," her sister said, and if Kathleen was not mistaken, there was a wistfulness in her tone she had never heard there before. "Hang Society and their expectations. But I have to presume that something went wrong, if you are sitting here weeping."

Kathleen's jaw tightened. "It did."

She had not expected such pain in the retelling of the tale, but it grasped at her stomach like a vice as she managed to say the words 'betting pool'.

She had expected the half-stifled sob of shock.

"And I am sorry, I am so sorry," Kathleen said hastily, her regrets pouring out as swiftly as her apologies. "I should never have—and once I had done so, I shouldn't have—but I never expected, I didn't think that he would, but I should have done. I knew a man of his rank couldn't want a woman like me. I knew—"

"Kathleen," her sister said softly.

Kathleen did not heed her. How could she, when she had to purge herself from this unbearable guilt? "You weren't there, Angela. You did not hear him—oh, the way he spoke to that man, they were almost certainly in it together. The whole thing was a trick! Yes, I proposed the bet, but I am sure he originally came over to entice me into something of the sort. I should never have—"

"Kathleen," repeated her sister.

But now her words were flowing and Kathleen did not think she would ever be able to stop. "And I was so foolish, Angela. In time, I learned of his propensity to gamble and I somehow believed him when he insisted it was all lies. I somehow thought he would never—"

"Kathleen!"

Kathleen blinked. "There is no need to shout, you know," she said, almost reproachfully. "I am sitting right beside you."

"Then there should not be anything wrong with your ears," her sister said with a wry look. "Kathleen, take a deep breath."

It was difficult to do. Somehow, a tightness had crept into her lungs and ribcage and stomach. Forcing herself to breathe had never been so difficult in her entire life.

Precisely how she managed it, she did not know. She did know that she felt much better for it.

"What do you think I should do?" Kathleen asked timidly.

It was a prescient question. Their landlady, after all, would soon catch wind of the gossip if it moved fast. It was one thing to have a lady of soiled reputation taking one's rooms if the scandal had happened a great distance away and no one entirely knew the details. It was quite another for the son of a duke to be deflowering one's lodgers.

Especially when the whole of Society would be talking about it tomorrow.

Kathleen's throat tightened. She wouldn't even be able to walk down the street.

Well. Perhaps that was a mite melodramatic. But it had been what had happened to Angela, had it not? The whole village had pointed, and whispered, a few of them hissing as though attempting to drive her out. And it had worked. They were here, weren't they?

"What should you do?" repeated her sister, swallowing. "Well, I... I am hardly the paragon of virtue. But... But I have some news on that score."

Kathleen frowned. "'News'?"

What news could there possibly have been? Had their father written—was he willing to accept them back home? Surely, that opinion would alter once he discovered that he had not one, but two wayward daughters...

But no, it could not have been a letter from their father. Now that Kathleen concentrated on the woman beside her, she found there was a lightness and a joy to her sister's expression which she had not seen in months. The wide eyes, the slackened mouth—it was if she were truly at peace. In fact, now she came to think about it, Kathleen could not recall a time when Angela had looked so...so elated.

Almost euphoric.

He's going to marry me, after all.

The thought, treacherous and nonsensical as it was, flared through Kathleen's mind like a lighthouse in a storm.

Had Leopold sent a note to her sister, perhaps, and reiterated his decision to marry her? Was he going to stand by her, despite the betting pool, despite the suggestion that the whole bedding had been a means to an end?

Oh, she could surely find it in her heart to forgive him if—

"I have had a letter from Paul," said Angela in a rush.

Kathleen blinked. "Paul? Who is Paul?"

For some reason, her sister appeared to deflate. "Paul. The baronet's son from home—you know Paul."

"Oh. Paul," said Kathleen blankly. "Mr. Keystone."

Paul. The boy who had run about with them and the other village children, and who had then disappeared off to school. Then Mr. Keystone, who had returned a man and a most dull one in Kathleen's opinion. Mr. Keystone, who had sat two pews before them at church and gulped whenever he thought someone was looking at him.

"Mr. Keystone," she repeated. "You called him 'Paul.' Sir Paul?"

The man's father had died recently, so she supposed he was the baronet now. But what on earth had he to do with this? With anything?

"You see, he was sent away before he knew the gossip had started and so he had no idea, and then his father died and he had a great deal to manage, and he did not know where I had gone and so his solicitors found me..."

Slow yet dawning comprehension started to creep over Kathleen's mind.

Surely not... Surely not, after all this time wondering who it could have been... Not Mr. Keystone?

"—and though I have almost exclusively made wrong decisions until now, I am certain this is the right one," said her sister with flushed cheeks. "So we are to be married."

Kathleen could hardly take it all in, but she heard the word 'married' and her instincts prevailed. "Congratulations!"

"Thank you," said Angela, her dimpled cheekbones positively shining. "Except…"

The smile was fading and a knot in Kathleen's stomach suggested that somehow, she was the cause. "Except?"

Her sister was looking at her hands now, twisted in her lap. "Except… Well, our engagement was a secret and I could not reveal it, not until I managed to get in contact with Paul again. There is no true scandal, just a misunderstanding—we have not even…"

Kathleen waited for a moment, puzzlement creasing her brow, until she suddenly realized what Angela was suggesting. Her brows shot up. "Never?"

"We did not have much opportunity," her sister said with a laugh. "We simply made the mistake—*once*—of being caught alone in the drawing room when that awful, old gossip Mrs. Trent was visiting Mother for luncheon."

Kathleen frowned. "When was this?" Though not being present for one of Mrs. Trent's visits sounded very much like herself, she had to admit.

"That day you and Father and Johnny went for a walk to see the spring flowers. I'd only stopped into the drawing room to grab Mother's needlework she wanted to show our guest. He'd been waiting for Mother and me to join him, after Mrs. Trent finally left. But just as Mrs. Trent *did* leave, his hand may have… Well. It may have been on my arm at the time she peeked into the room. I'd left the door open."

Kathleen's breath hitched. She couldn't believe everything that had happened because of a brief touch. And a wagging tongue.

"You could have told me," she whispered.

Angela swallowed. "No, I knew I'd made a mistake. And I kept making them. I should never have let Father send us to London without a chaperone. I, of all people, know that just the *appearance* of impropriety is enough to ruin a woman. Yet I've been too depressed to warn you against the same. I let you walk around Town on your own—*I* walked around Town all on my own." She sighed. "I haven't been thinking straight. Father was so unkind to send us here alone, to say those things he did about me, about *you* for being my ally—and I've been too focused on waiting to hear from Paul."

She stared back at Kathleen, her eyelids fluttering. "And now I *have* heard from him. But... Well... When the news gets out about yourself and Lord Leopold..."

Angela's voice trailed off delicately, but not so delicately that Kathleen did not, with a jolt of pain, realize what she was suggesting.

Oh, no. No, no. After all this time, Angela having to wait in the shadows for her swain—it was difficult to think of Sir Paul as a lover or wooer—to be ready to announce their engagement...was her sister's happiness all going to be ruined...because of her?

It was. Kathleen knew it—she could see the shape of it in the air. Once the news got out that Kathleen had not only been bedded by a nobleman, but he had no intention of marrying her and had been involved in a betting pool at the London Archery Club, absolutely no one of repute would ever wish to be associated with her. And that would include Angela. A future baronetess. The sister she had sacrificed her own comfort for.

"Oh, Angela, I am so sorry. I shall go away. You can pretend you are entirely unrelated to me. You can—"

"You think I would abandon you? You stood by my side not even knowing the truth, and you would expect me to disown you?"

Kathleen had never seen her sister so furious. There were sparks flying from her eyes and a great deal of anger in her voice.

She swallowed. "No, it's just... I would never expect you to stand by me. In this situation."

"Well, you should," Angela said firmly. "You are my sister. Your happiness means something to me, and I would not abandon you. I would give up…"

Kathleen did not need to look at her sister to see the pain she was enduring just to say the words.

Because she would do it, too. She would give up her opportunity for true happiness merely because Kathleen had made a fool of herself. Angela would wave goodbye to Sir Paul and accept the life of a spinster and outcast, all because Kathleen had trusted a gambler who enjoyed playing with the lives of others for sport.

"I will find another source of happiness," Angela murmured, still twisting her hands together in her lap. "I will be happy if you are happy. We can be happy together."

Kathleen had never felt less happy in her life. She had seen a spark of her sister's happiness, the anticipation of being reunited with the man she loved, but that joy had been snuffed out before it had truly begun—and because of her own actions.

She wanted that. Not the snuffing. The happiness.

A part of her had dreamed that she could have it with Leopold. For a short time, she had believed it possible.

And now…

"I will not leave you alone," said Angela steadily.

Kathleen smiled through her tears, trying to remind herself that she was not alone. She would never be alone. "And I will not leave you alone. But, Angela, your Sir Paul—"

"Your Lord Leopold," countered her sister almost immediately with a wry smile and sparkling eyes as unshed tears collected in the corners of her eyes.

Just hearing his name was agony. Not trusting her voice, Kathleen tried to smile as she blew out a slow exhale.

They would never see either of them again.

Chapter Eighteen

"Has he already left?"

"He must have gone ahead of us, Maudy."

"Don't call me that!"

Leopold smiled sadly as he sat in the darkness of the library and listened to the chatter of his family on the other side of the door. Despite the fact his sister was over thirty years old, their mother had never really stopped thinking of her as a child. The name Maudy was currently a particular irritant.

Footfalls. They were getting ready to go to the Halifaxes for dinner, something that Leopold had been looking forward to until today. Today, nothing could drag him there.

"I suppose Alexander is meeting us there?"

A snort. A laugh from Maude that demonstrated just how ridiculous she thought their mother was. "Honestly, Mama, you don't truly think that he will be there, do you?"

"But the Halifaxes were most generous in their invitation to all."

"And I am sure if Alexander can pry himself away from his current paramour—"

"*Maude Chance!*"

Leopold lifted his glass to his lips and was surprised to discover it was empty. Empty? Had he not filled it mere minutes ago?

Perhaps it had been longer. It was difficult to tell just how time was passing when one was sitting alone. The sun had been hidden by dark clouds all day, giving an unnatural darkness to the room for the time of year. A maid had come in what felt like hours ago and had drawn the curtains, without saying a word to him, something for which Leopold was grateful.

The last thing he wanted was someone to speak to him.

He had not moved from the armchair for some time, and the pattering of feet in the hall was insufficient to move him.

"So Leopold has gone ahead of us, then?"

Leopold stiffened. He did not want to go to this dratted dinner. What, sit there and politely smile and try to pretend he was not dying on the inside? Suffer the polite smiles and the awkward realization that they had not been able to remove him from their invitation? Hear the mutters of Lady Grasmere as she tried to draw her eligible daughters from him?

How quick would the gossip spread?

The sneer on Lord Graycott's face was indelibly marked in his mind, and no matter how much of his father's brandy he drank, Leopold could not forget it.

Whatever he had done to gain the man's dislike, he would never survive this. His reputation was tarnished forever. It was easy for people like his brother Alexander. Society expected sons of dukes to be rakes.

But cheats?

"I'm sure Leopold has gone ahead of us, Mama," came Maude's calming voice. "Come on. If we do not venture out soon, we shall be late, and you know how the Halifaxes feel about that."

More footsteps, the swish of what could be pelisses. And then—

"Are we all ready?"

That was his father's voice. Hearing it, even through the wall, caused a twinge of guilt to sear through Leopold.

He had let down a great number of people, of course, but his father was the one who would feel the disgrace the most. William Chance, Dowager Duke of Cothrom, had always been so aware of their position in Society, so conscious of their respectability, so desperate to ensure they did not lose that regard.

And now…

Leopold sighed. Now, after one bad gamble and one misunderstanding and one betting pool he'd had nothing to do with, his whole life was over.

"It's frightfully cold out here," said his mother. "Where has the summer gone? Careful with your skirts, Maudy."

"Do not call me that!"

His mother and sister's loving bickering faded in volume. Then there was the creak and snap of the front door closing, and silence.

Leopold blew out heavily. Alone in the house, all because he could not manage to properly court and marry a woman. Thomas, his older brother, had never had that problem. His marriage to Victoria was happy, from what Leopold could see. Why had he not been able to find the same joy, the same contentment?

But he would never be happy now, not with Kathleen Andilet believing the absolute worst of him.

Fire sparked in his belly. And she had been so quick, too, so quick to believe the worst of him.

There was a knock on the door. Leopold started, then slumped back down into the armchair. It was undoubtedly a footman who wished to ensure there was no family in the room before doing something. Lighting a lamp, perhaps. The library had some truly ornate ones in the corners.

The door opened.

"I thought I'd find you here," said Leopold's father quietly.

Leopold tried to do three things in rapid succession. Firstly, he tried to rise to his feet. Secondly, he tried to hide the brandy glass behind his back—he wasn't supposed to be drinking his father's supply, after all. Thirdly, he tried to sober up.

None of these were particularly well achieved.

"Oh, don't worry," said his father awkwardly, his focus lingering on the glass not quite hidden behind Leopold's back. "I knew you and your brother have been dipping into my stash for years."

Leopold smiled weakly, and decided not to tell him that it had been mostly himself and Maude who had done so. There had been enough scandal in this family without that coming to light.

Strange—he had presumed his father had gone to dinner with the Halifaxes. He had certainly been in the hall with Maude and their mother, so why had he not accompanied them?

William Chance closed the library door behind him and then swung his arms slightly without saying a word.

Leopold almost fell back into the chair behind him.

His… His father was not embarrassed, was he?

Oh, God. He had heard the gossip. Leopold had hoped to gain enough bravery tomorrow, once his hangover had dissipated, to tell his father himself. He had hoped to inform the man of the worst before he discovered it from another source, and therefore hopefully protect *himself* from the worst.

But he was too late. *Another blunder.*

"I… Well, Nicholls mentioned a maid reported you were moping in here, his words, not mine," said Leopold's father awkwardly, still swinging his arms and looking all about the room at anything other than his son. "And so I thought. Well. I'd come and see what the moping is all about."

And despite himself, Leopold felt his heart soften.

He had never met his grandfather. The man had died before Leopold had born, before the William Chance had married and inherited a daughter. From all the family stories, Grandfather Chance had been a harsh man who had cheated on his wife and raised his bastard with his sons.

Not the most pleasant of characters.

It was only in moments like this, when Leopold could see his father was doing his absolute best and hating every minute of it, did he remember that William had never had the benefit of a father who had known how to love him.

William Chance had tried to change that. And though Leopold could criticize, and guiltily he certainly did, he knew his father was doing the best he could.

And that could not be criticized.

"I am moping," Leopold said quietly, sinking into the armchair, "because I have made a mistake. I was wrong, and I've hurt someone I care about. They hurt me, too, but I... I should have fought harder. Now it's too late."

Just saying the words aloud were painful. What was even more painful was the silence that followed. His father just...stood there. Silently. Saying nothing. For a quite significant amount of time.

As Leopold silently decided that it was best that he simply rise from his seat and vacate the room, his father said quietly, "I suppose this is about a woman?"

Leopold nodded.

Even in the gloom of the room, it appeared his father could see him, because he sighed heavily. "I thought Alexander was the only one getting himself entangled in those sorts of affairs. I had not excepted it of the both of you."

"It's not like that!" Leopold had not intended ferocity in his words, but he could not help it. Kathleen was not to be lumped together in the category of 'ladies who would willingly part their legs for Alexander.' "It's... It was... It could have been... I love her."

Saying such words in his father's presence should have been mortifying, but Leopold discovered to his surprise that they came totally naturally.

His love for Kathleen, though thwarted, could not disappear. He cared too deeply, knew his affection for her could not melt away merely because a disaster had befallen them.

Because it was more than that. Deeper than that. Intrinsic to who he was now. He could just as easily remove his own heart.

"You love her," said his father slowly, stepping into the room and moving to sit in the sofa opposite Leopold.

Leopold nodded, not quite trusting his voice. "Yes."

"You are sure?"

He gave a laugh at that. "Quite sure, Father. She... She is the best part of the world, and whenever I am with her...I am the bow, and she pulls me back and points me at the world, and I know the power we share only exists when we are together." It was foolish to speak in this way, foolish in the extreme, but he could not help it. He adored her, and he did not care who knew. "Without her, I am nothing."

"You are without her now, I presume, due to a misunderstanding?" asked his father stiffly.

Leopold's jaw tightened. "She would not trust me."

"Ah. Cards."

And it was fury that spilled from Leopold at his father, whom he pinned against the sofa with his ire. "Believe it or not, Father, I am neither a cheat, nor am I a brigand! I played fair in cards and it is slander against my name that I did not, and it is that sort of thinking that has lost me Kathleen Andilet!"

The instant his shout had left his mouth, Leopold regretted it. Pools of twisting anger were still coiling in his stomach, but his father had done nothing wrong, not really. He did not deserve to be shouted at.

"I apologize," he said stiffly. "For shouting. But my point remains. I have done naught wrong, and it is gossip like that which has lost me the woman who ought to have been my future wife."

My future wife.

Leopold had barely been able to utter the words. For a few short hours, he'd had Kathleen's word that she would marry him. And now...

His father sighed heavily. "This is why I have always striven for perfection—for correctness. One false move, one incorrect rumor—"

"I know," Leopold cut across him curtly. "I know, Father. We all know."

It was a challenge to say the words without bitterness. All his siblings knew precisely what expectations their father had for them. Expectations that could not be disobeyed.

Unless your name was Alexander, he supposed.

"I liked her," said the dowager duke softly.

It was all Leopold could do not to point out that he was rather fond of her, too. "I know."

"Miss Andilet had a very pleasing manner, and she was kind, polite, well dressed," listed his father on one hand, as though those were the only requirements for a suitable wife. "Not from a respected family, however. No dowry. Her father has no title. And twice, at least, in my presence, she had no chaperone when she ought to have. Young ladies should not be so bold."

Leopold's pulse jumped. He would not comment on what he knew some of his cousins got up to—what his father's own daughter sometimes got up to. "Well, that will no longer matter, Father."

The dowager duke frowned. "Perhaps… Perhaps I have been too harsh. On the whole, such things should not prevent a man from seeking happiness. If the gentleman takes that step to make it right, no one will comment on the lack of propriety."

"I proposed, Father." It was agony to admit it, but an agony that he had to confess. Perhaps the confession would purge him of the pain. "I proposed, and she accepted, and then we—we argued."

It had been on the tip of his tongue to admit that he had lain with her. That there could be a grandchild planted in Kathleen right in this moment.

The thought made Leopold's head spin.

"You do know of her sister's scandal, obviously."

Leopold's head jerked up. His father had not asked a question, more given a statement, and it was with a serious expression that he looked at his son.

Swallowing, he said quietly, "I know there is one. Precisely what happened…the nature of which I think does not need to be guessed at."

"And yet you invited her here? Knowing that?"

Leopold knew there would be a reprimand in the conversation somewhere, and in a way it was almost a relief to reach it so swiftly. "Yes."

"Knowing her sister's reputation was stained?"

"Yes."

"Knowing that introducing her to Maude—"

"Maude would not have cared, even if she had known," Leopold pointed out sharply.

His father's gaze was just as sharp. "Yet you did not give your sister the opportunity to make that decision for herself. You made it for her, by bringing that woman—"

"*That woman* is the woman I love, and I will not—"

"And yet you are no longer engaged!"

Perhaps his father had not intended to shout. Leopold certainly had not, and he could feel the fire of obstinate embarrassment boiling through him.

They should not have shouted. They were not a family that often did—yet the desperate anger, the self-loathing, the pity: it all had to go somewhere. There was nothing so bad as hating oneself to make one shout.

A flickering pulse jumped in his father's jaw. Then he said, "You know, things weren't always perfect with myself and your mother."

Leopold stared through the darkness. Was this truly the time for some trite family history? Here he was, unburdening his heart to his father in a situation and conversation that was most uncomfortable, and all he could think about was how much he loved his wife?

To be sure, Leopold had always appreciated how his parents were blatant with their affection, but—

"She left me," his father said in a rush.

If Leopold had not been seated, he would have fallen. "What did you say?"

"Your mother left me," said the dowager duke heavily. "When I say that things were not always perfect, I say so advisedly. She kept a secret from me, and when I discovered that secret, I…I shouted at her."

It was hard to believe, hard to imagine. William Chance was a softly spoken, quiet, reserved gentleman. He was a nobleman who believed that the things one did not say were at times just as important as the things one did say.

And now he was asking Leopold to picture him shouting?

"And I shouted at Maude."

Leopold stiffened. "I beg your pardon?"

"It was not my finest moment, particularly when you recall just how small Maudy was," said his father wretchedly, slipping into the family nickname she still hated. "I was angry. I felt betrayed. I felt confused. I felt like a fool."

"But… But she did lie to you," Leopold pointed out, feeling a tad uncomfortable that he was saying such a thing about his own mother, truth or not. "It was about Maudy, I presume. Maude."

His half-sister. The daughter Alice Chance had had from her first marriage. A first marriage that she had, Leopold knew, not told William about before their wedding.

His father exhaled slowly. "She kept the truth from me because she knew what my reaction would be. She didn't believe I would have married her had I known." He grew quiet. "And I'm not sure I would have, though I'd have regretted it my whole life." He swallowed. "She expected harshness from me and then was rewarded with that harshness when she believed that she could finally trust me. I lashed out."

Lashed out?

It was so antithetical to the father he knew that for a moment, Leopold wondered if his father was exaggerating for effect. Attempting to make his son feel better.

And then he looked at the pain etched in the wrinkles around his father's eyes, saw the agony and regret still harbored in his father's brow, and realized that despite the many intervening years, William Chance had not entirely forgiven himself.

"She forgave me. I do not know why, to this day, but she

did," said Leopold's father with a dark smile. "She was always the most forgiving woman, your mother. Still is."

"Still has to be," Leopold could not help but say with a soft nod. "Alexander."

His father muttered something that could have been a curse before saying, "Yes. My point is, I believed the worst of her without all the information. And I lashed out because in my pain, it was easier to direct the hurt at her than at myself."

Leopold stiffened.

It was all too similar. Was it possible his father had heard what had happened at the London Archery Club? Surely, the news would travel swiftly, and though London was full of gossip and nonsense, it was only a matter of time before that particular bit of scandal was whispered into the ear of someone who would whisper it into the ear of the head of the family.

Because was that not precisely what Kathleen had done? Presumed the worst, lashed out, run off rather than face the possibility that someone had made an innocent mistake?

Leopold had been pained by the instant harshness of Kathleen's reaction, but now, speaking with his father…was that not perhaps the most obvious and instinctive response?

"I regretted it," continued the dowager duke. "She probably did, too."

Ah, so it was a pointed reference.

"Perfection in a relationship does not come immediately. In fact, I sometimes wonder whether I will ever reach it," continued Leopold's father with a wry smile.

It was hard to let that go. "But you and Mama, you are perfect."

Leopold hated how the statement made him sound like a child, but he could not help it. They *were* perfect. Their adoration for each other, the kindness they showed every day, the care and attention, the affection. He had never seen it so strong in any other pairing. He had always wanted that for himself one day.

"Besides, I have always tried to be perfect, for you," Leopold could not help but add, feeling piqued. "And now you tell me that all this time, you have not been perfect."

It was not accusatory. Not quite. The tone certainly had not been, and the words had not been completely directed at his father.

That did not make Leopold feel any better when his father flinched. "You truly feel so?"

The tension hanging in the air between them was of a different sort than before. This was, perhaps, one of the first times they had had such a conversation, not just father to son, but man to man. Leopold was not sure how, but he had grown up the last few years and felt a distance with his father, an uncertainty about how he should be around him. No longer a child looking up to a man, no longer a son looking up to a duke, so much had changed and yet they still they did not speak directly.

Not until now.

"I thought I had learned that lesson with my brothers," the dowager duke said.

Leopold blinked. "What lesson?"

"The lesson that being sanctimonious and pretending that perfection is the only requirement of a good life are not very good attributes at all," his father said with a dark laugh. "The lesson that holding the people I love to a ridiculous standard is never going to end well. For them, or for me."

Just about managing to keep his jaw from dropping, Leopold stared.

He had never heard his father speak like this. Never realized that the pressure Leopold had felt, that all his siblings had felt, had been already felt a generation before them.

Did anything ever change? Did progress ever get made? Did the bounds of frustration and difficulty ever truly change, or—

But then Leopold recalled the memories of his grandfather. How harsh he had been. How his own father, despite that upbringing, had never been harsh. Direct, yes. But never harsh.

Some chains could be broken. Some cycles could end. And it

could end with them.

"I will learn that lesson again and again, for as long as I need to," said William Chance softly. "I never intended to pass that pressure onto you, and I will do my utmost to change that. Son."

It was absolutely ridiculous that tears were prickling in the corners of his eyes again, but Leopold did not attempt to hold them back. No, the time for pretending he did not feel what he did was coming to an end. No man should hold back the tide.

"Thank you, Papa," he said quietly.

His father leaned forward, clasped Leopold's arm with his hand, and squeezed it. Just for a moment, they were connected.

Then the clasp was over and his father was leaning back, coughing awkwardly and looking at his boots.

Leopold tried not to smile. They had a little way to go. But they were learning.

"So," William said bracingly. "What are you going to do about your woman?"

The bottom fell out of Leopold's stomach. For a glorious few minutes, he had managed to forget about Kathleen, though the tension around his chest had been an ever-present reminder just on the edge of his thoughts. Now he could not ignore the gnawing ache within him. The knowledge that he was without her. The woman he needed. The woman he loved.

"I have no idea," he said aloud. "But I don't think she's my woman anymore."

Chapter Nineteen

August 11, 1840

KATHLEEN LOOKED DOWN at the piece of paper in her hand and frowned. "I am not sure."

"You do not need to be sure. It is an invitation," muttered her sister, who did not look up from her embroidery. "There is no surety needed."

"I meant, I am not sure if I will attend," Kathleen pointed out with a frown. "What are you doing?"

Angela cleared her throat and looked up. There was guilt, most unaccountable guilt, in the quiver of her chin. "Nothing."

Nothing. It was the frequent rejoinder of her sister since her engagement had been revealed. Kathleen was no fool; she knew it was the response Angela gave her when her sister was happily and busily preparing for the hoped-for new life.

A new life she would only gain if the stain of Kathleen's scandal disappeared.

Kathleen should have known their vow to both stay unwed if one sister did would not last long. Nor should she have expected it to. She did not wish her sister unhappiness.

"Nothing?" Kathleen raised a quizzical brow.

Her sister was unable to resist her query for long. Wrinkling her nose jovially, she lifted up the fabric she had been embroidering. It was a handkerchief. "Just... Just changing my initials."

Kathleen's stomach twisted painfully as she tried to smile. "That's wonderful."

And it was. It was wonderful—or at least, it would be, provided the marriage actually went ahead. Provided Sir Paul would go through with the wedding if the Andilet name managed to survive this latest scandal.

What she would not think were the dark thoughts that intruded whenever she and Angela carefully stepped around the awkwardness of Angela's potential future marriage.

Dark thoughts like…where was Kathleen going to live?

"I thought, daisies and roses because I've never decorated my handkerchiefs before, alongside my new initials," continued her sister with a bright smile that was almost too brittle. "So I decided that today, with the good light…"

Kathleen allowed Angela to talk. It seemed to help, filling the little room with noise and forcing the awkwardness away.

This little room had felt stifling when they had first taken up residence. It was nothing to the drawing room at home.

And now what would become of her?

She could not retain the rooms on her own. She could not live here in London without a single friend. But would Angela expect her to return to their parents? Their father would surely not accept it, not if he heard about Leopold…

The sudden and all-consuming pain that clenched around her was momentary, but it made Kathleen gasp and reach out to clasp the console table.

"Kathleen?"

Kathleen blinked, and when she looked up at her sister, she was both composed and smiling. "I still think this invitation is most suspect."

Yes, that was it, focus on the letter that had arrived that morning, and not the dreaded thoughts about how she would be potentially forced to accept the role of spinsterly aunt to her sister's future children.

Not something she had ever considered.

Her sister shrugged. "So you are invited to go to Hyde Park at two o'clock this afternoon. I do not see how that is suspect."

"Angela, the note is unsigned!"

It was a mark of how much her sister was lost in the prospect of her marriage. Two weeks ago, two days ago, Kathleen was certain Angela would have been most anxious about the idea of anonymous notes demanding Kathleen's attendance in any place, even one so public.

But now…

Angela had returned to her embroidery, her attention evidently lost. "The place will be teeming with people, Kathleen. There can be no impropriety in that. People won't even notice you're without a chaperone—they'll assume one of the older ladies seated on a bench is keeping an eye on you."

Kathleen frowned and looked back down at the note. It was not in Leopold's hand, something which had been at first a comfort and then a detriment. She had hoped… Well, a part of her had hoped it had been from him. A way to make amends, though what a walk in Hyde Park would fix, she did not know.

But no, the hand was quite unlike his own, and it said almost nothing.

Miss Kathleen Andilet,

Your presence is required in Hyde Park today at two o'clock.

A friend.

A friend? She had no friends—not in London, and certainly not after the chatter about this betting pool at the London Archery Club.

It was a strange note. A curious one. And Kathleen could not abide a mystery.

"I am going to have to go, aren't I?" she said despondently to her sister, who was humming a sweet tune.

Angela looked up, eyes blinking rapidly. "Wh-What? Oh, yes, of course. You go."

After that help, which was no help at all, Kathleen had some lunch—leftover pie from the previous evening's dinner, along with a rare treat, some cool lemonade that Angela had retrieved from a street seller but an hour ago—and then decided what to wear.

That was, decided she had nothing to wear. She tried on every single one of her day gowns, all three of them, and even tried on her only evening gown. She had taken one look at herself in the looking glass, realized she looked ridiculous, and taken it off.

She put on the gown she had started the day with.

"You look nice." Angela nodded. She was still humming. "I'm glad you've decided to go."

Kathleen rammed a bonnet on her head and stuck at it furiously with three hat pins. "I'll never be able to live with myself, not knowing."

The walk to Hyde Park was a strange one. Though she was sure she was imagining it, it certainly felt as though there was a great number of people staring. Watching her.

Did that woman point? Were those two children giggling about her?

Getting hot underneath her stays and wishing to goodness she had been a touch rebellious and gone out without stockings—who would have known?—Kathleen tried to remind herself she was undoubtedly being ridiculous.

The news would have spread, yes. There would be a great deal of people laughing at her, considering her ruined and wondering how on earth she had been so foolish. In a way, she was wondering the same thing about herself.

But surely, there could not be laughter about her in the whole of London? Need everyone notice she was without a chaperone? Was it not Angela who had convinced her people glancing her way would assume one of the older ladies about her had her in their charge?

The trouble was, if Kathleen attempted not to look about her as she bustled down the pavement toward Hyde Park, she was forced to contend with her thoughts, which were just as unpleasant.

Thoughts like: why would he have done it? And was there an explanation, but she had not given him the opportunity to share it? And what would she have done if there *had* been a genuine explanation?

Had she, in short, lost the best man she had ever known?

The pain of uncertainty prickled and Kathleen swallowed, desperate to push the thoughts from her mind.

"Moping," she muttered sternly, "will get you nowhere."

"Are you talking to me?" demanded an imperious voice.

Kathleen halted hurriedly. "N-No, madam, I—"

"For it is very odd to be speaking to yourself at all, let alone in public," boomed the woman, bedecked in diamonds and a stern expression. "Who are you, pray?"

It was not the most polite method of introduction, but there appeared to be no way of disagreeing with the woman, for Kathleen found herself saying, "Kathleen Andilet. And you are?"

"Lady Romeril," said the woman with a commanding lift of her chin.

Kathleen swallowed. *Oh, goodness.* Just one of the most important women in the whole of London. Just one of the women who dictated Society.

Just the sort of person who would not wish to be seen conversing with her.

"I see you have heard of me." Lady Romeril grinned.

"I... I have, yes." Well, there was little point in denying it.

"And I have heard of you—at least, I have heard the rumors about a Miss Andilet. Gallivanting with men in the country and being the center of a betting pool here in London," tutted Lady Romeril. "Often spotted without a chaperone. You have been busy."

Kathleen smiled weakly. It would be too much to attempt to explain that there were in fact two Miss Andilets who were sharing the scandals. No point in dragging Angela into this mess.

"Though I do believe it is the gentlemen, if I can call them that, who organized the betting pool who should receive my ire,"

Lady Romeril boomed across the street, causing many people to turn their heads. "I do not consider it blameful on a lady to be the butt of a man's jest, especially if it is so poorly done."

Kathleen almost sagged with relief onto her knees. "You… You do not?"

Lady Romeril fixed her with a sharp look that had clearly seen a great number of scandals ripple through Society, and the lady seemed to think very little of them. "Men, my dear, are usually to blame."

Now that was something Kathleen could agree with.

"But not all of them. There is usually one man attempting to dissuade the others." Lady Romeril sniffed. "One man worth his salt. One man who wishes to give others a true sporting chance."

Now her stomach was attempting to launch itself through her mouth. Kathleen swallowed hard as her pulse thundered.

"One man? A… A sporting chance?"

Lady Romeril's lips tightened as though she knew a secret. She inclined her head and walked away without another word.

Kathleen stared after her. *What on earth?*

It was a relief to reach Marlborough Gate and enter Hyde Park. Here there were a great number of people parading up and down Rotten Row, intending to see and be seen, and she could easily slip into that crowd and—

A smattering of applause. A swish and thunk, a sound she knew well, and more applause.

Kathleen stared.

It was the London Archery Club.

And yet it wasn't—it couldn't have been. She was in the wrong part of London for that, but from what she could see, it was as though the club had been transported.

There were the butts. There were the racks of bows, the arrows. They had all been set up in precisely the same way, fifty-five yards apart, and at one end, there were two men holding bows looking significantly smug with themselves. It surely had something to do with the quivering arrows that had clearly very recently been sent flying into the targets.

The applause died down as one of the archers lifted an arrow up to his bow. The silence was palpable, strange to be found in a place like Hyde Park.

Kathleen discovered she was holding her breath, and she only let it out when the arrow flew through the air and hit the target.

A groan from the crowd. Evidently, it was not nearly so impressive.

"Y'here to see the lady archer?"

Kathleen started. A young woman with gleaming eyes had nudged her, her excitement obvious. "I-I beg your pardon?"

"Miss Annerly, the one who's entered the archery competition," said the woman in a conspiratorial whisper. "I never thought I'd see the day—a lady archer!"

It was all Kathleen could do not to freeze.

Keep breathing. Just remember to breathe.

Miss Annerly. It was surely a coincidence; there could easily be a Miss Annerly who was a passionate archer who had decided to go against all the expectations of Society and enter a public archery competition. Or…

"He wouldn't," she breathed.

"I would."

She knew the owner of that voice long before she turned around. Kathleen's heart had leapt, the tension in her shoulders had lessened, and in that moment, she knew.

It was therefore absolutely no surprise when Kathleen turned on her heels and saw Lord Leopold Chance standing but six feet behind her. He was dressed smartly, his jacket missing but his waistcoat and cravat neatly matching. They were paired with a most painful look on his face, a bob at this throat.

And Kathleen could have melted.

She didn't want to. She wanted to stay angry with him, stay furious, shout at him, make him realize just what he had done to her. Make him see that he could have ruined her, and not in the delectable way they had shared, but in the court of public opinion, a court in which no judgment was fair.

But she couldn't—not with Leopold, her Leopold, so close.

She was still hurt, yes, and the stares of those around them still weighed heavily on her shoulders. But there was nothing she could do to prevent the affection welling up.

He had hurt her. And she loved him. And she could not reconcile those two facts.

"You... You entered me in the archery competition," Kathleen said weakly.

And then she was running, or close to running, and she had no choice because Leopold had taken her hand and was pulling her along with him—and she could not pull away or resist him because a part of her wanted to be touched by him, and the place where his thumb pressed against her wrist just above her glove throbbed like a burn.

"I know I shouldn't have done it," Leopold said, panting as he drew up in a copse of trees just out of sight. It was quieter here too, and Kathleen could hear the pain in his voice—pain she decided she was not going to notice. "But I had to."

"You had to?" Kathleen repeated warily.

She did not see that there was that much 'had to' about it. One did not go around accidentally entering other people into archery competitions. Or betting pools.

The reminder dampened her enthusiasm and when Leopold met her eye, he looked rueful.

"I told you the truth, by the way," he said.

Kathleen swallowed, her mouth dry. "'The truth'?"

"I had nothing to do with that betting pool," said Leopold earnestly. "I mean, I knew it existed, but it was supposed to have been ended—and I originally thought it entirely about your archery skills, not...*that* unpleasantness. I'd thought it all finished. I told them it was shameful, that it had to end. I was very clear."

It was all she could do not to smile, even in the depths of her pain. Yes, she could well imagine Leopold being very clear. He was the sort of man who could be ignored by lesser men.

"But the idea was not mine. I would never—I *could* never—only a brigand would—"

"I heard you," Kathleen said quietly.

There was not much strength to her voice, as she could not summon it—yet Leopold appeared to have found his own.

"You heard me attempt to tell Lord Graycott very sternly that he was wrong. It… It isn't my forte, I'm afraid. Being stern."

She knew that. She had seen it in him, the first moment they had met. The first time she had looked into his eyes and realized that this was a man who was kind. Who was honest.

Perhaps that had been why it had hurt so much, the betrayal. What she had *thought* had been a betrayal.

Because if Leopold could do this, of all the men she had ever met…then what was the point in trusting anyone again?

Maybe something of what she had thought showed in her eyes, for Leopold stepped forward gingerly, then took another step as she did not retreat. "Kathleen, I would never do anything to hurt you. I would never. It is incomprehensible to me to even consider such a thing."

"I know," Kathleen whispered.

And she did know. Where the certainty had come from, she was not sure, but she could feel it, deep within her.

"It still hurts," she muttered, looking down at her hands, the intensity of his gaze too much. "To know that others would happily treat me that way. To know that the scandal is all over London."

"It's not *all over* London."

"If a woman such as Lady Romeril is accosting you in the street, knowing all your history, you know it is all over London," Kathleen said with a dry smile, lifting her eyes.

Leopold winced. "Ah."

"*Ah*, indeed," she said, wishing he would step closer and close the gap between them, then wondering where on earth that thought had come from. "So you see, I am ruined."

His smile did not fade, but there was a nervousness entering his eyes as he said, "You don't have to be. If… If you still want to—"

But she could not let him ask her that question—not here, not now, not with the scandal of her name hanging over them.

No, if Lord Leopold Chance ever wanted to ask her that particular question again, and Kathleen rather hoped that one day he would, she wanted him to ask it because he wanted to, not because propriety demanded it.

"You entered me into the archery competition," she said over him.

Leopold halted, his cheeks pinking, and beamed. "Does this mean you have forgiven me?"

Forgiven him?

Kathleen swallowed. "I… I do not think there was anything to forgive."

Precisely which of them had rushed toward the other, she did not know. Perhaps they both moved. Perhaps it had been as painful for him to be apart as it had been for her.

All she knew was that she was in his arms and she could have shouted to the heavens for joy at the relief she felt at being clasped by his strong hands. His lips were passionate, eager, desperate and she gave him the kiss he wanted, one that parted her lips and welcomed him in.

Arrows of darting delight soared through her, aching along her bones, sparking eagerness for more, and Kathleen clung to him, clung to the man she loved, the man without whom she could not live.

Gentle applause did not interrupt them, but the piercing whistle did.

Leopold stepped back, his eyes bright and his grin wide. "We almost forgot about the competition—you'll be up soon."

"And the crowd. Forget a chaperone, if anyone witnessed *that*." Kathleen laughed—and then halted laughing as she saw he did not join her. "You did not truly enter me in this competition."

"Of course I did! What better test of your skill, and decider of our bet, than to enter you into the competition?" He chuckled.

There was such an innocence about this man, Kathleen decided, even after he had just kissed her senseless. It made it impossible, once she'd truly understood him, to stay angry at him for more than five minutes together—something she thought they would both benefit from.

"Under a fake name," Kathleen said with a wry smile, slipping her hand into his as they started to walk back to the crowd. "It was probably a good idea, considering the numerous scandals my sister and I are managing to create."

Her arm jerked as Leopold halted.

"False name?"

Kathleen nodded, turning back to squeeze his hand. "Yes, Miss Annerley, I heard one of the women saying."

"I entered you under your own name," Leopold admitted with a tilt of his head. "Miss Andilet. I see no reason to hide who you are. It's a perfect name. You shouldn't have to hide it."

She stared, hardly able to believe him. "You did?"

He nodded with a look that clearly told Kathleen he was speaking the truth. Despite all the shame her name could easily bring, despite the fact that being connected with her was surely going to damage his precious Chance reputation, unless Sir Paul made things right with Angela...he had not wavered.

Lord above, this man. This wonderful, wonderful man.

"That's not to say that I would not be adverse to you changing your name," Leopold said, clearing his throat, but his gaze defiant. "If you found someone worth changing it for."

Kathleen could not do anything but giggle. "I'll bear that in mind. In the meantime, I think you'll find I have an archery competition to win."

His snort was not the most encouraging, but then, he was her competitor.

It was all she could do to keep her head high as she marched up to the shooting area. Lord Graycott was there, and he looked remarkably irritated to see her.

"*You.*" He sneered, tapping a foot.

"Me," Kathleen said, far more calmly than she felt. It was most unpleasant having to face him, but there was technically no law against being a cowardly, wicked brute. *Not yet, at any rate.* "I'll take that bow, if you do not mind."

Lord Graycott probably *did* mind, but Kathleen paid his mutterings no heed and marched past him to pick up the bow with which she had practiced. Leopold had slipped from her side into the crowd just to the left—still visible, but not taking up the attention of the crowd.

A flicker of devotion curled within her. He truly was the most remarkable man.

"You'll need three bullseyes to win it," murmured a broad-shouldered man wearing a London Archery Club badge as Kathleen removed her hat and gloves set them aside. "You just do your best, miss. Everyone's a winner if they're having a go."

It was all she could do not to roll her eyes. *Honestly!*

A hush fell onto the crowd as Kathleen moved to the shooting spot, picked up an arrow, and nocked it into the bow.

Then the hush descended into a tidal wave of noise.

"A lady?"

"They can't have a woman. What are they playing at?"

"—hardly strong enough to lift the bow!"

"Does that mean I can learn archery, Papa?"

And it was the final comment that made Kathleen lift her bow with pride, breathing slowly out. One day, little girls wouldn't have to ask if they could do archery. They would just learn.

The air stilled. She was one with the bow. The arrow wanted to soar through the air, clean and true, and so she let it.

The applause erupted.

"A bullseye!"

"Now how does a lady manage that?"

"Did you see that?"

Kathleen looked at no one but Leopold, and he was smiling. He was beaming. He was glorifying in her success and she knew in that moment that she adored this man.

Misunderstandings aside, frustrations aside, he wanted her to excel—even if it meant beating him. That was a man to cling on to for the rest of your life.

The second arrow followed the first. The crowd cheered. Mutterings behind her grew louder and Leopold's smile grew broader, and Kathleen knew, even before she had picked up the third arrow, that she had won.

The third arrow proved it. The crowd erupted. And the man who strode past all others, who was cheering her name and hugging her tightly before he accepted his rosette for another second place, was Lord Leopold Chance.

Chapter Twenty

August 24, 1840

"LOOK, ALL I'M saying is—"

"I know what you're saying—"

"—and I think I have a point," protested Leopold with a lazy smile, absolutely certain he did not.

Kathleen glared, but it was one of her good-natured glares, so he didn't worry. "And I am telling you, I am not going to marry you!"

There was a snort of laughter from the woman also within the carriage. Leopold glanced at Miss Angela Andilet with a wink, gaining him another snort of laughter.

"Oh, you know what I mean," Kathleen said with a smile that was clearly against her will. "I am not going to marry you yet. Not straightaway."

"You would think, wouldn't you," Leopold said conversationally to Kathleen's sister, as though the woman he loved was not in the carriage, "that the woman would be rather pleased to be marrying me at all."

"You would think," said Miss Andilet, entirely ignoring the irritated snort of her sister.

"And yet—"

"Are we almost there?" interrupted Kathleen in a small voice.

And Leopold halted his teasing and immediately took her hand in his. "I am sorry," he said quietly. "I shouldn't be quizzing you. Not today."

Today, of all days, he should have been considering her

needs, her fears. Today, after waiting for so long, he should have been helping her to feel calm and considered and important.

Today was the day.

"What if they don't—"

"They will learn to love you," Leopold said softly, squeezing her hand and wishing he could communicate through that small gesture all the pride he felt for her, the certainty that they would adore her just as he adored her. "They'd be fools not to."

"Plenty of fools in London," Kathleen said in a voice that was far too brave to be genuine.

He had to laugh at that. "I would agree with you there—and there are plenty in my family, but they're not *that* foolish. They know how I feel about you."

How I feel about you.

Leopold was not one for words. He never had been. Doing was always easier than speaking. When you had a bow to your shoulder and an arrow just waiting to take flight, you didn't stop to give a speech.

At least, he didn't.

But with Kathleen seated beside him in the slowing carriage, her nerves jangling through her hand into his own, he wished he could find the words. The words that would calm her, show her just how beautiful and how loved she was.

"You are perfect," he said aloud.

Kathleen snorted.

"You are!"

"You're a hopeless romantic, you know that," she said with a lilting smile. "You do speak nonsense."

"It's not nonsense if I mean it," Leopold pointed out.

He could see in her smile that she wished to be kissed, and he was hardly one to argue with the woman he loved. Unfortunately, just as he leaned forward, his eyes closing, the carriage jolted to a halt and Miss Andilet cleared her throat.

"Damn," he whispered.

Kathleen smiled and kissed his cheek. "Plenty of time for that later."

Leopold groaned. "I told you, I wanted to get married straightaway!"

"And I told you," Kathleen said firmly, pulling her hand away and looking pointedly at the carriage door, "not before my sister. Come on, aren't you going to be a gentleman and open the door?"

He very much wished not to be a gentleman at all and instead throw her sister out of the carriage, order the driver to go to Brighton, and do something very delicious and very inappropriate to Kathleen on the way.

Sadly, he did none of those things.

"I suppose so," Leopold said with a heavy sigh. "Come on, then. Let's meet my family. Officially, I mean."

It was strange. As he stepped onto the pavement and looked up at his parents' home, it was only then that Leopold realized that he no longer considered it his own. His portion of the Cothrom estate had purchased him a pleasant townhouse just two streets away and that was home now. That was where he would be welcoming his bride. That was where he would build this new part of his life. It was the aim, the target of all his thoughts.

The moment when he could bring his bride home.

The family butler smiled as he opened the door. "Master Leopold."

"Hullo, Nicholls," said Leopold cheerfully. "Everyone prepared?"

"As prepared as I believe they can be, my lord," said the butler with a stiff smile.

Which was not helpful. Leopold did not need to look over at Kathleen to know she was stiffening with discomfort.

Hell's bells, but he had hoped for better than this.

"Well, let me be the first to introduce you to Miss Angela Andilet. You have met her sister—my betrothed, Miss Kathleen," he said loudly.

He was not ashamed. There was nothing to be ashamed of.

The trouble was, no one had informed Leopold's stomach of that. As he stepped into the drawing room and saw his mother rise from the sofa, his father standing by the empty fireplace with a somber look, and his brothers—

His brother. *Where the hell is Alexander?*

"Don't look too downcast," quipped his oldest brother, Thomas—who quite inexplicably was lounging on a sofa along with his wife, Victoria, a stunningly beautiful and increasingly rotund woman. "It's only the family."

"Besides, they are far more afraid of you than you are of them," came Maude's voice from the pianoforte.

Leopold tried to smile. "I thought we agreed to at least act as though we were a normal family."

"I actually think that ship has sailed," said Maude, tinkling a few notes on the ivories. "Besides, we've already met Miss Kathleen. This whole thing is rather—"

"It is how it is done," said their father in a slow and formal voice. "And so that it is the way we will do it."

Leopold's spine stiffened. Despite the helpful conversation with his father—not something he ever thought he would be able to say—it was still a tad disconcerting to have the whole family here to formally meet a woman they had already met.

But it wasn't really Kathleen who they were meeting, was it?

Glancing over his shoulder, he saw that Kathleen's sister had lingered by the doorway, hanging back from truly entering the room, and his heart went out to her. He knew just how much Kathleen adored her, how the whole thing between Miss Andilet and Sir Paul Keystone had been a complete misunderstanding.

And now he had to introduce her to the Dowager Duke of Cothrom.

"Miss Andilet," he said formally, extending a hand.

She hesitated, just for a moment, and Leopold saw Kathleen give her sister a smile of encouragement. Miss Andilet took his hand.

"Father," said Leopold, turning and smiling broadly at his

father as though he frequently introduced him to fallen women. Not actually fallen. But still. "May I introduce Miss Angela Andilet? Miss Andilet, my father, the Dowager Duke of Cothrom. Miss Andilet will be marrying Sir Paul Keystone. A misunderstanding during their long engagement led to a…a slight ruffle in Society."

He caught his father's eye and pleaded with him silently to behave.

Not that his father didn't know how to behave. That was the problem; his father knew precisely how to behave, but he was not very good at adjusting his behavior to make another feel welcome.

But Leopold should not have been so concerned. His father smiled warmly and bowed low, as befitting a lady. "Miss Andilet. Congratulations on your forthcoming marriage."

Leopold had not realized just how much tension had built into his shoulders until he'd let it out. *Dear Lord, he was exhausted.*

Miss Andilet curtseyed and smiled nervously. "Thank you, Your Grace. It has all been rather an adventure…"

Carefully, without disturbing the conversation that was ongoing, Leopold stepped away from his father and future sister-in-law and moved to Kathleen's side. "See. I told you."

His words had been spoken in a hush, but he had to fight not to groan loudly as Kathleen's elbow met his side.

"You did not."

"I told you all would be well," Leopold protested in a mutter, "and I was right. See? My father has quite accepted her, now that he knows the full story."

The full story was not exactly what he had told William Chance, but Leopold had… Well, edited it to become a much more palatable tale. He knew his father would frown even at the simple misunderstanding the country gossip had witnessed— though Leopold was certainly guilty of worse.

The tale was that Miss Andilet and Sir Paul, growing up in the same village, had fallen in love. An agreement had been made between them for matrimony, but just when the engagement had been about to be announced, Sir Paul had been called away on family business, and wicked gossips had quite misconstrued the whole thing.

The lovers had managed to make contact and thereafter corresponded secretly through a solicitor, and as Sir Paul's mother had since been reconciled to the match, assured of its propriety all along, it was now going ahead at full speed.

"The point is, with your sister accepted by the former and current Dukes of Cothrom, no drawing room should hold any fear for her," Leopold murmured, smiling as his sister approached Miss Andilet and warmly complimented her on her gown. "Just as long as she manages to stay away from my sister, all shall be well."

Kathleen's smile was warm. "I cannot think what you mean. Lady Maude is the picture of propriety."

Leopold considered the scuffs on his sister's boots, the way Maudy hadn't quite mastered clambering up the apple tree at the back of the house to creep into the house through his bedchamber, and her gambling debts, which he had paid off not once, but thrice.

"Yes," he said carefully. "The picture of propriety."

He watched for a few moments as his family welcomed the woman who had been the scandal of London. There was possibility for change, then. Reputations could be salvaged. Wrongs could be righted.

After all, had not his own been repaired? Had Lady Romeril herself not declared, in that rather direct way of hers, at her dinner just days ago that she thought the whole thing around his betting had been blown out of proportion, that a losing streak one night was hardly evidence of cheating on other nights? That perhaps, anyone with sense would take it as evidence of the opposite—that he usually enjoyed luck and employed skill but had had one terrible evening at the tables?

He'd even received an invitation from her for a card party this afternoon. He wouldn't be going. He had a far more important engagement.

"So, are we all ready?" Leopold's father's voice carried over the chatter of the room as he looked at his son.

Leopold nodded his head. "I believe so."

"Ready?" Kathleen looked confused. "Ready for what?"

Ah, yes. He hadn't told her.

Well, he had not been sure whether he could get the whole family on board. Maude had been easy. Alexander had agreed but clearly had decided not to turn up, the rogue. His mother had been willing, and Thomas had argued his corner, thus convincing his father.

That agreement had only been made that morning.

"Ready for the wedding, of course," Leopold said lightly.

Miss Andilet put her gloved fingers to both cheeks. "I... I really will have to leave soon if I am to make it to the church on time."

"Nonsense," said William Chance sternly.

Silence fell around the room as Leopold's ribcage tightened.

Oh, please. Please, Father, he silently begged him. *Please do not do anything to shame me. Please do not bring judgment on a bride's happy day.*

"You can't be on time," continued his father, his face breaking into a slow smile. "A bride is always late. It is her right to keep the man waiting. You will take our carriage, needless to say."

Leopold's jaw fell open.

Kathleen was tugging his sleeve. "Leopold, what is going on—take your carriage? But that would be tantamount to approval! That would be almost marrying Angela from this house!"

"So it would," Leopold said with a croak.

He had not taken his gaze from his father, who smiled faintly and inclined his head with a shrug, as if to say, *'Who says I cannot be beneficent if I wish?'*

"Leopold Chance, I want you to explain what is going on right now!"

Pulling Kathleen to the window as his family started moving to the hall, chattering excitedly, Leopold said in a low voice, "Look, I knew that there would not be many people at your sister's wedding."

Pink tinges appeared in Kathleen's cheeks. "The scandal was just a misunderstanding, yet my parents still refuse to approve of the nuptials."

"I know—I know your friends cannot travel from the country, and that you and your sister have made few friends here so far," Leopold said in a rush, taking her hand. "You want your family with you on a momentous occasion such as this, and I knew you would not have all your family, but...but *we* are to become family."

Her eyes were shining and Leopold did not know whether he was doing a particularly good job at explaining this—but he had to try.

"We will be family, and that means my family will be yours. I wanted to support you. I wanted your sister to get married before a full church, a church of people who admire her and respect her. She and her betrothed agreed—and agreed to keep it a surprise from you. Father procured a special license for the couple. And I invited my family. All of them."

Kathleen's eyes widened. "All your siblings?"

"Rather more that."

"Not... Not *all* of the Chances?"

"What is the point of having twelve cousins if you cannot get a crowd together?" Leopold said with a smile.

For a moment, she just stood there, frozen to the spot, as though he had spoken Dutch instead of English. Then Kathleen threw her arms around his neck and hugged him tightly.

"You didn't have to do that," she said in a muffled voice into his neck.

Leopold returned her tight embrace. "I wanted to support you."

"We all do," came a stiff and slightly awkward voice.

Breaking apart, Leopold turned to stare at his father, who was now wearing his top hat and carrying a cane.

William Chance smiled. "Come on, then. Let's get the two of you to the church."

In the carriage, Kathleen was doing her best not to cry with happiness, and Leopold was doing his best not to notice.

This was what he'd wanted. It wasn't just a connection, though that was certainly the bedrock of what they shared—it was a determination to share life together, to love each other, to care about each other beyond what was needed or expected.

To go beyond, to give everything one could with no expectation of return.

When the carriage pulled up outside the church, there was a bit of a crush to get inside.

"Careful now!" Maude grinned as she stepped down from the carriage. "Lilianna, you rogue, what are you wearing!"

"Has anyone seen Alexander?" asked Leopold's mother, looking around outside the church with a worried expression. "He most definitely promised me he'd be here."

"Lord, what a crush," Thomas said with a laugh, punching Leopold on the shoulder. "Goodness, they managed to force Frank into a dress—you *do* mean business! And there's Lucy, and Gwen, and Benjamin. You really know how to organize, little brother!"

Leopold hit his brother back, only a mite harder. "Do you think you can organize this rabble into the church and turn them into a congregation?"

Thomas winked. "I'll see what I can do. Come on, Victoria. Time to put this family in order."

It took a startling amount of time to shepherd the Chance cousins into the church, his Uncle George sobbing into a lace handkerchief as he always did at weddings, even when he'd never met the bride or bridegroom before, apparently. It was only when a hand slipped into his that Leopold realized he had been most remiss.

"I do apologize," he said quietly as he and Kathleen slipped into the pew right behind where Sir Paul, a rather lanky and tall man, was standing. "I have been ignoring you."

"You have been doing so to give my sister a wedding she can be proud of," she returned with sparkling eyes. "Thank you. Thank you, Leopold."

And although he knew that one should absolutely not do things merely for the thanks one received, he could not help but smile in delight at the way she looked at him.

She was so beautiful—so kind, so unexpecting of kindness. And that was why he was going to spend the rest of his life making sure that she was adored, and quite rightly so.

"I only wish our mother and brother could have been here," Kathleen said, biting her lip as she arranged her skirts. "And our father. To give her away. She will have to walk in alone now."

Organ music sounded, filling the church with a cacophony of sound, and Leopold smiled as they rose with the rest of the congregation. "I thought of that, too."

Kathleen opened her mouth to say something—presumably to ask him what on earth he meant—but she was saved the trouble of doing so when the doors opened and Miss Angela Andilet appeared in the doorway, arm in arm with William Chance, the Dowager Duke of Cothrom.

She gasped. "Oh, Leopold."

It was rather a challenge to keep from tearing up himself. The bride was beautiful, the groom looked ecstatic, the whole Chance family—all his uncles, aunts, and cousins—had turned up as a show of force. Alexander, the rascal, was the only one missing.

And as Miss Andilet finished giving her vows, and the vicar had declared them husband and wife, and the crowd started clapping—

"Leopold!"

The low hiss was just behind him. Leopold rolled his eyes. "We're just finishing up a wedding, Maudy."

"You know I hate that nickname," came the hiss from behind

him. "I've got to tell you something or I'll burst."

He shouldn't have been surprised, really. "And that is?"

"I'm getting married."

Leopold's ability to breathe and speak and cough at the same time was sadly lacking, so he spluttered for a moment, gaining dark looks from those around him.

Maude—married?

"I don't want to tell the rest of the family yet. I'm keeping it quiet," came the entirely calm whisper of his sister from behind him as she clapped her hands. "But I had to tell someone. Keep it to yourself, won't you?"

Leopold's eyes were bulging and he was in half a mind to get up, turn around, and demand answers, but Kathleen grabbed his arm then, squealing and drawing her attention back to the baronet and his new baronetess.

The rest of the day was a blur. The Chances had invited half the neighborhood for the wedding luncheon. Oh, Leopold shook a great many hands, and directed the footmen as they passed around a good number of silver platters covered with delicious things that Cook had concocted, and made sure not to drink more than a single glass of wine. Maude, who would not stop for even a second to explain more about her shocking, secret news, was having a ball of a time, constantly followed by their mother trying to keep her in check, and Alexander appeared at one point, most distressingly leaving with a young lady whose name Leopold could not quite remember...though her father was shouting it most profusely as he looked for her an hour later.

It was going to be another awkward day for the Chance family when that caught up with them.

By the time the bride and groom had left, Leopold had hidden himself away in the library and was lolling on an armchair, wondering how on earth he was going to survive his own nuptials.

"You look exhausted."

He looked up and felt his heart flutter. "I am."

Kathleen closed the door behind her. "Weddings are a great deal of fuss, aren't they?"

"I'm not an expert, though I have been to a few family weddings recently, and they were all very much a to-do," admitted Leopold with a chuckle as he held out a hand.

His beautiful future bride stepped across the room and took his hand, slipping elegantly onto his lap and making parts of him sit up and take notice. "I don't suppose we could elope."

"We certainly could," said Leopold, kissing her shoulder and reveling in the way she shuddered with delight in his arms. "We haven't had the banns read yet. We don't have a special license. That might mean Gretna Green—Father has some property in Scotland. But it would be an awful scandal."

"Scandal?"

"My mother would be upset, is what I mean," he clarified with a chuckle as he trailed kisses up Kathleen's shoulder toward her décolletage. Dear God, but she was delectable.

Kathleen leaned back to allow him to bury his face between her breasts and moaned, which did absolutely nothing to help him calm his manhood. "Leopold…"

"If you're not careful," he muttered in a low voice, his hand trailing along her leg and caressing her thigh, "I shall be tempted to do something absolutely terrible."

"Why do you think I locked the door?" Kathleen replied, her teasing smile so seductive, Leopold was tempted to slip his hand under her skirts immediately. "I had to give you a sporting chance to seduce me."

He groaned and twisted her round to straddle across his hips, fingers fumbling at the buttons of his trousers. "God, I love you."

"Good," she said quietly, lowering her lips to his and kissing him firmly, her fingers running through his hair. "Because you're about to make me love you even more…"

Epilogue

September 1, 1840

THIS WAS ALL too much, and it was ridiculous that she was nervous.

"Just think of it like archery," said Leopold with a grin as they walked down the stairs and into the hall of the impressive Stamphrey Lacey, the country estate of the Chance family.

Kathleen snorted. "You always say that!"

"And I'm always right," pointed out her husband with a wide smile. "Just breathe deeply and allow it to wash over you. Everything will be fine."

Fine. Yes, Kathleen was certain it would be fine, but she didn't want this visit to be fine. She wanted it to be wonderful. She wanted to feel comfortable, for the rest of the Chance family to welcome her as they had already done her sister, and she had gotten precisely what she had asked for.

In a way.

"There you are! I thought you would be down for breakfast quickly, but you've been an absolute age," said one of Leopold's cousins, who beamed and revealed a pair of dimples.

Kathleen tried to smile. She had absolutely no idea what the woman's name was, or which part of the Chance family she belonged to...which was starting to become a habit.

"Oh, don't hassle her, Frank," said Maude with a laugh, coming out of the breakfast room too. "There are far more of us than there are of her!"

"We're not frightening, though. Are we? Are we frightening?"

Frank, who had to be Lady Francesca, turned to Kathleen and raised a quizzical eyebrow.

Kathleen could not help but laugh. "Only when you're all together."

"But we're always all together when we come to Stamphrey Lacey," said Francesca with a frown. "And so many family weddings this year! Do you think we've finished for the season?"

"Oh, I would imagine so," said Maude airily, though she gave Leopold a look that was most odd. A sort of knowing look.

Kathleen looked at her husband, but Leopold appeared to have found a corner of the ceiling most interesting.

She would have to ask him about that.

"Anyway, the breakfast things have been tidied away, I'm afraid," said Francesca with a sigh. "I don't suppose you were that hungry, or you would have come down earlier."

Leopold coughed and Kathleen colored, heat scalding her cheeks.

Well! What on earth was she supposed to say to that?

Evidently, Lady Francesca was ignorant of… Well, of marital relations. That or she had absolutely no shame, for she was fixing the pair of them with an open, curious stare.

Maude coughed. "Right, well, that's enough of that. Come on, Frank."

The two cousins left, arm in arm.

"She—She didn't really say—"

"Frank is very caught up in her passion of engineering," Leopold said with a grin as he gestured toward the front door. "Walk?"

Yes, a walk. That would help ease a few of the aches Kathleen was feeling. Honestly, bedsport was most enjoyable, but it did leave one a little sore in the hips department.

As they stepped out of the majestic manor that was the Chance family seat, Kathleen smiled at another Chance cousin with a long plait curled about her head like a coronet, walking across the drive. "Good morning!"

The greeting had been gentle enough, polite enough, simple enough—and yet the woman started, glaring at Kathleen as though she had suggested daggers at dawn. "What?"

"I—I said, *good morning,*" said Kathleen, chastised by the unexpected response. She glanced at Leopold. "It is still morning, isn't it?"

That is another trouble with bedsport, she could not help but think with a wry smile. *One rather loses track of time.*

"Yes," said Leopold with a wink. Perhaps he was thinking along the same lines as her.

Kathleen turned back to the cousin, whose name had completely escaped her—there were so many!—and tried again. "Such a pleasant day."

"No it isn't. No, I'm not—no!" The woman did not exactly shout, but it was hardly a whisper emitting from her mouth.

Quite to the contrary, it was a panicked noise that was accompanied by a sudden flush of dark red across her cheeks.

Before any of them could say another word, the Chance cousin had turned around and started marching away from them.

"I..." Kathleen stared as the woman half walked, half ran across the lawn. "Was it something I said?"

"Absolutely not," said Leopold firmly.

For a moment, she thought he was humoring her. It was far more pleasant, after all, not to think that one had terrified one's new family member. Hardly the sort of start to a relationship she had hoped for.

"That's just Jess," said her husband with a shrug. "Miss Jessica Chance, daughter of my Uncle Frederick, is perhaps the greatest wallflower who ever lived. Oh, no, I do not mean it in a bad way," he added hastily with a wry smile. "She's always been shy, always been quiet, but the last few years—it was coming out into Society that did it."

"Did what?" Kathleen asked, looking at the woman who was slowly disappearing. "She seemed pleasant enough."

"She just hates attention, and being out on Society means

people constantly looking at her," said Leopold, his arm snaking around her waist to pull her close as they started to walk slowly through the gardens. "But once she gets to know you, I promise, she is the most delightful, pleasant woman. One of my favorite cousins, after Evelyn. You'll get to know her in time."

Kathleen nodded. *Time.* That was something that they had: time, to love each other and get to know each other and their families over the following months and years. Surely, her own family would accept her and Angela back soon enough. Angela now being Lady Keystone, Kathleen Lady Leopold Chase especially.

Time. Time together. Time to share everything…

"Well, time is something that I have," she said with a smile. "And though there are rather a lot of you, I am hopeful that I will get to befriend all you Chances."

"There are a great deal of us, yes," Leopold said with a laugh, his hand tightening at her waist. "But I do hope to keep you to myself mostly. There is so much I love about you, Kathleen Chance, and I want to be a little possessive of you."

Affection flamed through Kathleen at his words. It was strange, being so adored. She could very much get used to it.

"And we'll have ages, just the two of us, after the house party," Leopold continued.

Her breath caught in Kathleen's throat.

"And we'll have ages, just the two of us…"

Well, yes. But also, no.

Kathleen looked up at her handsome husband and wondered whether this was the right time to mention it. She could not be sure, of course. There were signs, yes, but she was not certain. Her sister appeared certain, however.

Still, it would be perhaps unfair to raise hopes before certain knowledge, would it not?

"What are you thinking?"

Kathleen blinked. Leopold was gazing at her with that knowing look of his, which meant he had been studying her face for some time.

She shrugged. "Nothing of import."

"Don't give me that. I know that expression. What did I say?" he asked as they turned a corner into the sunken garden, a delightful dip of mossy trees and lilies.

Kathleen swallowed. "I… I cannot be certain."

"You cannot be certain what you were thinking?" Leopold's brow was furrowed, and it was all she could do not to laugh.

"You pride yourself on your archery, don't you?" she asked quietly, pulling away from Leopold's side and sitting upon a stone seat that was covered in lichen.

Her husband's face was mystified—and a little rueful. "I would have said so, except a certain someone happened to beat me in the latest London Archery Club competition, and in front of a crowd, no less. Why?"

Perhaps this was the perfect time. It was just the two of them, and if she was wrong… Well, it would not be the end of the world. They would try again—if she were any judge, it was going to be difficult *not* trying.

"You… You consider yourself a good shot, is that true?" Kathleen asked, her pulse quickening as she grew closer to the topic at hand.

Leopold's brow furrowed now as he sat beside her, angled toward her as his gaze captured her own. "What is all this about, Kathleen? Do you wish to cease learning archery?"

"Oh, no! No, it's not that," she said hastily, placing her hands on his and trying to control her breathing. "It's just… Well. One of your shots in particular has most definitely…hit its mark."

Her husband stared, evidently absolutely lost.

Kathleen stifled a smile. "I mean to say that the target of your, well, natural arrows has been well and truly hit."

Leopold was still clearly none the wiser.

She swallowed. Once this was said, it could not be unsaid. "I mean that when you and I… When we first lay as one… Well."

Silence hung in the air for several heartbeats.

Then Leopold's eyes widened. "You mean—you mean we—"

"You," Kathleen shot back with a laugh. "You, and your incredibly potent arrows."

She looked down meaningfully at his trousers and tried not to laugh again as she watched the realization of what she was hinting at crease across her husband's face.

"You're with child?" Leopold whispered.

And it was reverential, and it was potent, and it was a moment she never would have imagined could ever happen.

"I am not definitively sure, but all the signs—"

"Oh, Kathleen!"

Leopold's kiss was devoted and passionate, a heady mixture of need and desperation paired with adoration. Kathleen leaned into it, clutching his lapels to bring him closer, reveling in the abandon within which they lost themselves.

He was everything. They were everything, together, the two of them.

When they broke apart, Leopold's eyes were glistening. "I can't believe it—a child!"

"Almost certainly," Kathleen hastened to add. The last thing she needed was disappointed hopes. "But if not now, then in the future."

"And we haven't even had a sporting chance at being husband and wife yet," declared her husband, full of enthusiasm and with joy sparkling in his eyes.

Kathleen beamed and knew that no matter what lay ahead, they would face the target of their hopes together, side by side. "All the more reason to enjoy our time together now, then. Shall we retire?"

"It's only half past ten in the morn—"

"Leopold," she said with a laugh, rising and offering her hand. "Do not miss this target. I'm going to our bedchamber. Will you accompany me?"

Understanding, and desire, bloomed in her husband's eyes as he rose and pulled her into a tight embrace. "You know, I think I will."

A Short Letter From the Author

Hello! Thank you so much for reading *A Sporting Chance*, the eighth novel in my The Chances series. I truly hoped you enjoyed it and fell in love with Leopold and Kathleen just as much as I did.

If you've read the first seven books of this series (which I strongly recommend!), then you'll have seen the four uncles fall in love, and three of the cousins. I had always wanted to write a series of brothers, but I could never 'meet' the characters who were quite right. After waiting years to meet them myself, I have had a lot of fun writing the four Chance brothers—and now we're diving into their children. Make sure you go back and read them!

If you're desperate to read the happily ever afters of Leopold's siblings, then you'll want to look out for Book 5, *A Chance in a Million* (Thomas's story); Book 12, *Don't Fancy Your Chance* (Alexander's story); and Book 17, *Let the Chance Slip By* (Maude's story). Our next Chance adventure is going to jump to a different branch of the Chance family, and you'll meet Jessica's happily ever after…

Being an author can be a lonely business, but knowing that there are readers from all over the world who are going to adore my stories makes it all worthwhile. Thank you for support, and I hope you love reading more of my books!

Happy reading,
Emily

About Emily E K Murdoch

If you love falling in love, then you've come to the right place.

I am a historian and writer and have a varied career to date: from examining medieval manuscripts to designing museum exhibitions, to working as a researcher for the BBC to working for the National Trust.

My books range from England 1050 to Texas 1848, and I can't wait for you to fall in love with my heroes and heroines!

Follow me on twitter and instagram @emilyekmurdoch, find me on facebook at facebook.com/theemilyekmurdoch, and read my blog at www.emilyekmurdoch.com.

www.ingramcontent.com/pod-product-compliance
Lightning Source LLC
Chambersburg PA
CBHW060341310726
48976CB00003B/674